MW01106942

THE MONSTER OF SELKIRK

# Book II

# The Heart Of The Forest

## A novel by C.E. Clayton

## DEDICATION

*For Megan, who is still the best big sister a girl could ask for.*

# ACKNOWLEDGMENTS

*My village of book-loving warriors has done it once again. Through the help and support I have received along the way, Tallis's story lives on!*

*Thank you to my parents, brothers Joe and Cameron, brother-in-law Brad, lovely sister-in-laws Aimee and Murti for their support, and thank you to Doug and Deb, for being such fantastic cheerleaders. Thank you to my husband for putting up with my rants and philosophical debates on what I should torment my characters with. My incredible friends Colleen, Sophie, Andy, Frank, Sydney, Jessica, Sammi, John, Karla, Brie, Erin, Mandy, Kendal, and Toni, whose friendship and support means more than the world and helps keep my creative fires burning.*

*Thank you to my great editor Rob, and all the people who read, gave feedback, and touched this book. Your work is, as always, invaluable to this process.*

*And thanks to my dog, Dobby, who can't read, but is excellent at always remaining by my side as I type away. Writing can be a very solitary experience, so I'm thankful that Dobby would take me on walks when my eyes began to burn from staring at my computer too long. I highly recommend getting a little furry friend that will be there for you the way Dobby was for me, and there are many such companions waiting for you at your local shelter.*

*Adopt, don't shop!*

*Also, thank YOU, dear reader, for following Tallis along as she grows and battles literal and figurative monsters along the way. If you want a soundtrack to go along with your experience, I've got you covered. Check out the "Selkirk" playlist I created on Spotify: http://spoti.fi/2pijlOG. Music was instrumental in capturing the mood, the spirit, and the essence of what it was like for Tallis growing up as she did in a place like Selkirk.*

# OLD SCARS AND NEW WOUNDS

## ONE

Ⱨᴇ SKULKED BEHIND the injured knight as the man nursed his damaged arm and stomped through the streets with a purpose. He followed from a safe distance, hugging the shadows as if they were friends. His gnarled fingers brushed the dirty facades of the buildings, the slickness felt beneath his fingers having little to do with the muck on the walls and more with his own anticipation.

*We've got you now, Tallis.*

The words rang in Jon's head like a monastery bell as he stumbled after the knight he recognized as one who could always be found in close proximity to Baron Maric and his family, specifically that blighter Henrik. The knight had not been on active duty when the tremps attacked, that much Jon remembered. Due to the injury the knight had suffered, the man could barely swing his blade. It had probably saved his life, keeping him at Henrik's side rather than out with the other knights as they attempted to make sense of what was happening, and all while trying to save as many people as they could.

Jon had wondered if Tallis survived in those first few hours after the initial onslaught, or if she had somehow managed to get out of Kincardine. When he had not seen her with the other townsfolk who had hoped to take ship, he believed she had died. The thought was not all that upsetting; with her to blame for the loss of his wife, Wodan's Pits could take the girl for all he cared. Instead, the loss of the girl was just another wash of disappointment, especially when he considered the coin forever lost from not being able to sell her to the highest bidder on the Bride Block.

No, instead of finding Tallis, he had come across Baird with Donovan's sweetheart, Nessa, waiting impatiently to board one of the crowded vessels.

His heart sank, thinking his nephew had been one of the dozens of unlucky people to find themselves cornered by the tremps as they burned the little village to the ground. But Baird had only grinned, assuring him that Donovan was safe.

That he was with Tallis.

It boiled his blood even now to think that Tallis yet lived while his Lana lay cold and buried at the hovel he had fled. A tear rolled down his cheek just thinking of his poor wife, alone in her grave in a home that he doubted he would ever return to.

*And it's all Tallis's fault. Wretched creature has taken my wife and my home ... taken everything! Let the tremps have her.*

Jon ground his teeth on the thought, savoring its

bitterness as he trotted behind the knight, still oblivious to the old man following behind. Jon had always been easy to miss, amusing to ignore. It had annoyed him when members of the carpenter's guildhall lifted their noses at his talent, but now he was glad that so few paid any mind to the feeble old man never good enough for their company.

He had to see her for himself, the girl he had raised, but never considered a daughter. He had to see for himself if it was truly her, and if so, if his nephew was, indeed, with her. Tallis may have had an unnatural talent for wrapping Donovan around her finger, but Jon was sure that if Donovan were there, knowing his father and would-be-bride were waiting for him would convince his nephew to abandon Tallis once and for all.

Tallis was not worth the trouble that Donovan would find in her wake. This, Jon knew from experience. She had always been odd, that adopted daughter of his. There was always something a bit strange about her. It was just an itching in the back of one's mind when they looked at her, when she spoke to them. Jon had felt it and had noticed when others squinted at her as well; they had the same feelings he did. But unlike Jon, most shrugged it off and either waved Tallis away or teased her.

Until she had grown, that was.

Once she matured, most felt uncomfortable around her because she looked like she belonged in places like this, like Fordoun, not Kincardine.

*Now they'll know better.*

Jon grinned as he skirted around another building, keeping the knight in his line of sight. After the monstrous tremps flooded through Kincardine, ravaging their homes and slaying their people while hissing her name, none would look at her and see an enchanting young woman. Not anymore. No, now they would see what Jon saw.

A monster.

Jon could not guess at how Tallis had managed to get out of Kincardine, not unless she were somehow responsible for the elves suddenly rising up after three centuries of madness, and the Clearing that followed to eradicate them from their borders. Perhaps she had done something when Lana died, or the elves had done something to *her* before Lana found her in the Brethil Forest, Jon did not know. All he *did* know was that she could be involved in nothing good, especially if she were in Fordoun.

It brought up the memory of the last time Jon had seen her. She was declaring she would not stand on the Block. That she was leaving and he would never see her again. At the time, Jon just believed it was a teenager's last act of rebellion before succumbing to her familial duty. But no sooner had she made such a declaration, than the tremps stormed their village in force. It made Jon wonder if Tallis had somehow planned for the coming of the elves.

As the tremps ransacked the villages, everyone fled to the cities for shelter. If Tallis were here, Jon doubted Fordoun would be safe for very long.

*I should see about getting to Isildor with Baird and Nessa.*

He watched as the knight approached the pens where they kept all the drunken sods that did not have the grace to drown their sorrows in silence. A young woman with wavy, diamond-bright blonde hair sat upright at his approach, and Jon could not hide his sneer.

*Tallis.*

At her side was a dark-skinned woman Jon recognized as one of Tallis's no-good friends. He had seen the two racing through the market of Kincardine on occasion, getting into trouble. The lass was not the only one Tallis had managed to bewitch on whatever doomed journey she was on. For Donovan *was* there, too, pressed against the side of the other cage with a rapidly swelling eye, but Jon dare not approach, not with Tallis so close. No, much better if she did not know he was there.

Jon had often wondered if the rumors floating out of Dumfry by the few older folks who had managed to escape were true: That a woman, as beautiful as she was deadly, had followed after the tremps as they burnt the monastery to the ground. The rumors said that as soon as the tremps poured into the nearly deserted town, that the woman they had been hissing the name of appeared, as if they were heralding her arrival. Some said she had saved them, but no one really believed that. Her appearance had been too well timed. Some said she had killed a few tremps, but how could she have? How could such a tiny woman kill such foul beasts?

*Unless they let her. Unless it was all for show.*

Like many others, Jon believed Tallis's supposed act of bravery, had only been a farce. Tallis had not been able to save Lana; he doubted she was capable of saving anyone other than herself.

He watched as she regarded the knight and noted

her haggard appearance, as if she had been recently ill. Part of him wondered what she had been doing all this time, if perhaps she had been hiding due to a crippling illness, or if she were looking for someone instead of…. Jon shook his head, it did not matter if Tallis was sick, or if she were trying to find something. He knew what his heart told him to be true: Tallis was cavorting with the same bloody creatures who had killed his wife. She deserved no pity, no mercy. Jon vowed to tell Baron Maric exactly that, in case they needed any further convincing to hand Tallis over to those monsters.

Jon melted against the shadows as the guards began moving, opening cell doors, and shoving Tallis and those accompanying her away. He frowned as Donovan and another young man were roughly pushed after Tallis and her dark-skinned friend. Jon growled in the night, knowing that if Baird found out he had let Donovan be arrested, that his little brother would never forgive him.

Peering from around the darkened building, Jon followed after Baron Maric's knight once again.

# *TWO*

ᚷALLIS BOLTED UPRIGHT the moment she saw Raghnall. Then her heart sank to the pit of her stomach and she felt her face go ghostly white as she watched him hand a notice to the guard in charge of her cage. Taking Rosslyn's arm in a vice-like grip, causing her to growl in pain, Rosslyn turned to look at what caused Tallis such a fright. When she saw Raghnall, her dark features paled and she gripped Tallis's hand in return. They were fools to think that no one from Kincardine would have heard of the fight, and even bigger fools to think none would try and take advantage of their incarceration.

The guard called over his partner, who stood watch over the men. Whispering and showing him the notice, the guard nodded and went back to the other cage. By then, even Donovan had spotted Raghnall, a sneer of contempt tugging at his face. Without a word, the guards walked into the cages and grabbed Tallis, Rosslyn, Donovan, and Tomas by their collars and dragged them out of their cells.

She could hear Tomas demanding to know where they were being taken, and arguing they had caused no permanent harm in the inn. Trust Tomas to not recognize the man he had shot in the shoulder with his crossbow the first time he had come to Tallis's aid. The guards led them silently through the streets to a large dark stone and brick building with a ragged black flag hanging over its steel-reinforced doors.

Tallis didn't recognize what the building was, but Donovan did, and he began to struggle. "What have we done to be tossed into prison this way? I demand an answer!"

The guard shoved him forward. "Baron Maric's orders on behalf of his son Henrik. You are to be imprisoned for crimes committed in your hometown, and here you shall remain, until your lord sees it fit to release you."

Tallis's eyes widened with the faintest glimmer of hope; Henrik had not told them she was the girl that the elves were using as a battle cry. Whatever game he was playing, Tallis and her true identity was one of the cards he was holding close to the chest. She was not sure what it meant, but for the moment she hoped it was a blessing from Wodan.

Stopping at one of the first cell blocks, the guards pushed Donovan and Tomas inside. Both men sprang at the steel bars as the door clanged shut. Pressing their faces against the bars, they watched as the guards pushed Tallis and Rosslyn away. For the first time in her life, Tallis was too frightened to speak as she frantically looked over her shoulder at the fearful and concerned stares of her cousin and Tomas.

She watched Tomas press his face against the bars as he yelled after the disappearing guards, "Where are you taking her? Where are you going?" Then he addressed her, "Don't be afraid, I will find you." Donovan kept silent, but she could see his mind furiously trying to work a way to get them out of the mess that Rosslyn had accidently placed them in.

The guards stopped Tallis and Rosslyn in a dank hallway lit only by a single brazier. They were too far underground for any windows to allow natural light at this point. It was an oppressive feeling, one that made Tallis break out in a cold sweat. The guards checked them for weapons and easily found Tallis's two knives concealed in her boots, the only article of her armor she had not parted with after her bath. She knew if she tried to take them back now, they would only beat her, or worse. She felt exposed in her simple blouse and trousers, her leather and chainmail armor tucked safely under their rented bed at the inn. Part of Tallis wished she had put her custom-made armor back on, but another part did not want to see what the guards would have done had they apprehended her while completely armed.

Just as Tallis thought they were done inspecting her, one of the guards spied her mother's ring and snatched it off her thumb. Tallis moved like a raging river to take her ring back, causing the guard to bring his fist down hard on her back, driving her to the floor.

"None of that now," he growled down at her. "Can't leave you with anything you could use to escape."

Coughing, Tallis glared up at him. "It's a ring, not a lock pick, you plonker. Give it back!"

The guard picked Tallis up by the hair and shook her. "Scum like you isn't allowed to talk to us like that. You're lucky we got orders not to harm you, otherwise

I'd have you ask for it back in the sweet way only a woman can. You understand me, girl?"

Tallis stared at him, but said nothing even as her hatred for this man burned in her heart like the heat of a summer sun. She couldn't lose her mother's ring, not now, not to a man like this.

Tallis and Rosslyn were pushed into a cold, damp, windowless cell at the very bottom of the prison. Stumbling forward, Tallis caught herself before she could fall, unlike Rosslyn. Standing, she looked around, frightened of the confined space. After being used to so much openness, after climbing the oldest trees in Selkirk and feeling their hopes and fears, this seemed like she was being buried alive. For the moment, her boiling ire at the man who took her mother's ring was momentarily forgotten, replaced by a suffocating fear.

Being confined under the ground, entrapped in cold stone, Tallis felt her chest tighten and her breathing become labored as she imagined the walls closing in around her. She turned rapidly, throwing herself at the stone walls and running her hands over them, trying to find a crevice where she could taste fresh air, only to find nothing. She felt Rosslyn pull her into a tight hug, and in return, she inhaled the familiar scent of her friend in order to calm her own nerves.

She felt Rosslyn soothe her hair like her mother used to when Tallis was afraid, and then she heard her friend coo, "It's all right, everything is fine. Calm down, Tallis. We'll get out of this."

Slowing her breathing and calming her frantic heart rate, Tallis shut her eyes and kept them closed until they adjusted to the utter blackness of their cell.

—

Disentangling herself from Rosslyn, she slid down the clammy stone wall and sat on the cold floor and stared at the thick, bound door where she could barely see the brazier in the hallway illuminating through the portal's cracks.

Losing herself in a moment of despair, she whispered, "We've come all this way just to be stopped now by some stupid tavern brawl." She couldn't keep the anger and bitterness from her voice. As much as she loved Rosslyn and her carefree spirit, it was the reason they had been arrested.

Crossing her arms, Rosslyn turned away from Tallis, her shoulders sagging in defeat. "I know. I'm sorry. This is all my fault, and I know it changes nothing, but I am sorry, all right?"

Tallis wanted to say that it wasn't her fault, but she could not lie like that, not yet, anyway. Instead, she said, "It just doesn't seem fair. You'd think that the barons, the dukes, even the king himself would give us an army or something for our journey, rather than arrest us. If the elves want me so badly, you'd think they would do whatever they could to keep me from them. If the tremps want something this desperately, it can't be a good thing. Instead … instead, one little man's jealousy will now be our doom. And on top of all that, now I'll die without the one thing I had to remind me of my mother. Sometimes Wodan sure does have a twisted sense of humor."

Rosslyn kicked at a loose stone on the ground, then attempted to laugh, but it came out more like a sputtering gasp. Leaning her head back and focusing on the cold stone around her, Tallis said, "I wish I understood any of this, you know? Why this, why me, why now? All my life I just wanted to be normal, to fit in like everyone else. I've been fighting against … something that I don't understand.

"I didn't want the death and destruction that's come along with trying to find out why the tremps are hissing my name, but I can't seem to keep any of the devastation from happening, either. Maybe if I hadn't tried so hard to just be a normal girl I could have seen this coming. I could have done something. I could have done more to protect all those innocent people who've lost their lives and everything they hold dear."

Sighing, she continued in a dejected whisper, "It's not your fault Rosslyn, it's mine. There must have been something I missed, something that would have prevented all this from happening in the first place."

Rosslyn was silent for a moment, absorbing Tallis's words. It was the first time Tallis ever seemed to really complain about the situation they were in, and it was the first time Rosslyn truly grasped just how much weight and pressure Tallis had placed upon herself.

Rosslyn shook her head. "Oi, and what would you have done differently? There was no way you could've known any of this would happen. There was nothing more you could've done besides get yourself out of Kincardine safely. The people you saved along the way, that's all just a bonus."

Shrugging, Tallis said, "I don't know. I just … I should have known. There was more I could have done, more people I could have saved."

"Aye, and you'd be dead in the process of doing it," Rosslyn said, planting her hands on her wide hips. "Thinking you could have stopped any of this from happening, like you should've just known the elves would all go mad at the same time, that's just stupid, Tallis. Even for you."

Tallis couldn't help but chuckle at Rosslyn. She wasn't sure she completely believed her, but her confidence that this chaos was not Tallis's doing was refreshing, nonetheless. "Be that as it may, it won't matter for long if we can't find a way out of this mess." Tallis rose to her feet, gingerly touched the barred door, and desperately tried to think of a plan.

Tomas AND DONOVAN paced their cell racking their brains for anything they could do to get out of imprisonment. They were in a regular cell with a window that looked out to the empty side alley and a door they could easily pick if they had the tools. But the guards had taken their meager possessions, including their belts, when they locked them in, leaving them nothing but their chewed fingernails at their disposal.

However, Raghnall had not been the only one to take an interest in their confinement. A rail thin man draped in a dark gray coat two sizes too big for him, an old bronze-colored jerkin, and stained trousers approached their window. Donovan had seen the man earlier from the corner of his eye, shadowing the guards as they brought them to the prison. Donovan had thought the man looked familiar, but before he could get a good look through his bruised eye, the old man had vanished. It was seeing him again that made Donovan suspicious as to who he was, and those suspicions only grew as the man stopped beneath their cell window, his face concealed in the shadows of the prison.

Standing on the tips of his toes, the man hissed up at them. Donovan looked down warily and was greeted by the graying soft brown hair and dim blue eyes of none other than his Uncle Jon. "Uncle, what are you doing here? I thought you'd died in the elf attack…."

Jon gave a mirthless smile. "Wasn't at home when the bloody tremps hit. Managed to get out with a few of Baron Maric's guards, no thanks to you, nephew. And that fool of a knight, what was his name? Raghnall? Yes, well, that barmpot isn't all that good at hiding his excitement when he thinks he's got the world bent over a barrel. I heard him mumbling about Tallis as he walked through the streets, and figured that if she was here, you wouldn't be far behind. Looks like I was right."

"I'm sorry, I just assumed…," Donovan said with a deep frown lining his face. Then he pressed on: "Where is my da? Is he here?"

Jon shook his head. "No, he's gone to Isildor to be with that Nessa lass you seem to be so sweet on. Gone to keep an eye on her, something you should be doing, rather than getting yourself in trouble like this."

There was a sharpness to his uncle's tone that Donovan did not like. Lowering his voice even further, he asked, "What are you doing here, Uncle Jon?"

Jon glanced around quickly before sliding a key through the bars for Donovan to catch. "It's a gift from the other knights. They aren't too keen on locking up one of their own order just because some fool of a baron's son has it in mind to arrest you for some slight done in a town that no longer exists. Use it and get yourself to Isildor, nephew. Go and take care of your father and marry that nice girl. Baird's been worried sick about you, afraid he's lost his only son on some nutter's quest."

Donovan narrowed his eyes at his uncle. "And by nutter's quest, you mean helping your daughter stop whatever caused the tremps to rise up and cry her name?"

"Wodan's Pits, boy, she's not my child!" Jon said with such hatred that Donovan was taken aback. He was not sure what happened to his uncle between that final day at Kincardine, when he had last seen Tallis, and now, but he assumed it had to do with his departed wife. The elves warring like this and destroying people's homes and families must have brought up old wounds that had never healed.

"How can you even say that?" Donovan glowered through the bars. "Why did you even come here?"

"Because it would kill my brother if I didn't try and talk some sense into you," Jon said, coldness flashing in his dim blue eyes. "If I didn't try and get you to give up on this and go and protect him and Nessa like a proper son and knight should do. You owe it to them, boy. Don't disappoint them again."

Donovan pushed away from the cell bars, key in hand. "I would be more of a disappointment to them if I let my little cousin go off on her own just to be slaughtered."

"She isn't your kin," Jon growled. "Your father *is*, and you would choose her over him?"

Donovan hesitated as he looked down at the key. Part of him longed to go to his father and hold Nessa in his arms once again. Just thinking about her brought to his mind the clean scent of her unruly red hair and the cute way her brown eyes twinkled whenever he kissed her. It was only the uncomfortable shuffling of Tomas as he skulked behind him that snapped Donovan out of his daydream.

As much as he wanted to go to Nessa and protect her, he knew she was safest in Isildor. Tallis, however, was in constant peril from people and elves alike, and had no one to protect her. If he failed to do that now and left her on her own, he could never live with himself again.

Shaking his head and closing his hand firmly over the key, he said, "Thank you for your help, Uncle Jon. Please tell my da I'm alive and well, and tell Nessa that I'll see her as soon as I'm able. But I can't abandon Tallis, your daughter, whether by blood or no—not with so much at stake."

Snarling, Jon threw his hands in the air in frustration. "She got Lana killed, and she'll get you killed, too, nephew. Never doubt that. Aye, I'll deliver your blighted message, but I'll tell Baird and your Nessa how you chose that evil orphan over your own family. And heed my words, if I hear the alarm, that that evil wench of a girl who you claim as a cousin has gotten out, I'm pointing them in your direction. She can't be allowed to roam free. She's a monster in league with those evil creatures, and you'd be the wiser to let her rot in whatever hole they tossed her in." Turning on his heel, Jon once again disappeared into the darkness, as if he had never been there at all.

—

Tomas scratched the back of his head as Donovan turned to look at him. He knew he just heard something he should not have and it made him terribly uncomfortable. "So, um, Tallis … Tallis isn't actually your cousin?"

Donovan shook his head, dazed by his uncle's bitterness. "No. My Aunt Lana found her in the forest when she was just a week old." Shaking his head, he frowned. "I shouldn't have told you that."

Tomas looked down and pressed on before the moment was gone and they were running for their lives once again. "You two are awfully close for not … not really being related. Have you, I mean to say, do you … I don't know, do you love Tallis? More than just as a cousin, I mean."

Donovan's head snapped up. "Absolutely not. Tallis is my family no matter what her father says. I've never thought of her as, well, as anything else. That's just—" Donovan made a face of distaste before he shrugged. "Tallis is more of a little sister to me than a cousin, and she will always be that way."

"Does she know? I mean, she must know about being found and all that?"

They had come too far and seen too much together already for Donovan to lie to Tomas now. He believed Tomas needed to know the truth about Tallis as it very well may have something to do with their current situation. Tomas might very well care for Tallis, but he also didn't know some very important details about her life. The ex-initiate still had a chance to decide he did not want to be a part of their journey now that they entered Fordoun, and Donovan did not want to deny Tomas that opportunity by further withholding the truth.

Donovan nodded, and said almost sadly, "Aye, she knows."

Continuing, Donovan said, "You deserved to know the truth about such things, Tomas. You still have a chance to go about what you'd consider a normal life to be, whether you go back to the monastery or not. If you wish to follow us, or Tallis, really, you need to understand that her being found in the forest may be the reason all of this madness with the tremps got started in the first place. It may even explain why those foul beasts hissed her name and why she was able to kill so many all on her own in Dumfry. If you decide to stay, make sure you accept that fact. And, if you decide not to leave, it may be best if you didn't tell Tallis that I told you any of this."

As Tomas nodded along with Donovan's words, the knight pressed on, "You know I give you a hard time over Tallis because you need to be strong for her. Tallis doesn't need someone to follow her around like a doe-eyed puppy. She needs a man who will rush into battle alongside her, and think of nothing but protecting her above all else. Do you understand me, Tomas? If you stay, she has to come first. Always."

Tomas nodded and said without a hint of hesitation, "Yes, I understand. She will always come first."

Donovan gave him a deft nod before moving to the cell door.

Their portion of the prison was momentarily unguarded, giving credence to what Jon had said about the other knights feeling it wrong to have him incarcerated. Carefully, Donovan turned the key in the door and pushed it open, wincing as its light squeaking sounded like it could be heard all over Fordoun in the silence. Waving Tomas forward, he whispered, "Come on, we need to get them out before Rosslyn gets us into even more trouble."

Tomas followed Donovan as he quietly led him through the torch-lit hallways. "Which way did they take her?"

Donovan hesitated momentarily. "I don't know. They took her down further than I could see. My guess, though, is if they really wanted to keep her safe and away from everything else, she'll be towards the bottom."

Donovan looked down the corridors for a moment before coming to a decision and grabbing one of the torches. Pressing it into Tomas's hands, he said, "Hold this, I may need you to hit someone with it if we get in trouble."

The prison was surprisingly deserted. Most of the cells were empty, as if the dungeons now were only used for the most grievous of offenses. Most of the guards were out patrolling the streets and trying to keep crime to a minimum, preferring to toss those responsible for disturbances into the outdoor cages where they could better watch them and the influx of refugees at the same time rather than actually locking any within such an ominous building.

With the guards out on patrol, the prison was eerily silent, sending a shiver of foreboding cascading down Donovan's spine. Stopping at the last of the windows before he plunged further into the pitch-black dungeon after his cousin, he looked out onto the sky. The sun was just starting to lighten the horizon, meaning whoever was out patrolling the streets would soon be back as morning fell upon Fordoun.

As they crept farther down, they could hear the voices of the few guards left. Pushing Tomas against the wall, they crept sideways down the staircase, listening to the guards as they spoke:

"Don't think I'll get much for it, ain't much of a ring."

"You can always see if that pretty blonde will ask you nicely for it back, she seemed to be partial to it," another said over the sound of shuffling cards.

"Nah, Lord Henrik won't let anyone touch her, in *any* way. Rather not get strung up over some tavern scrubber just because she wants some trinket back. Better sell it and buy me a pitcher of the good ale, none of this piss water they serve near the walls." The two guards laughed as Donovan and Tomas exchanged knowing looks.

Donovan glanced at the walls around him, the only thing he had at his disposal was Tomas's torch, and that would do little good against two fully-armed knights. Just as he was about to toss it at them and hope for the best, they heard a distant bell clang, the guards pushed away from their table, and walked up an unseen staircase. Tomas raised a questioning glance at Donovan, whose brow crinkled in confusion. His eyes lit up as he realized that the guards were changing the watch, which gave them mere moments to break Tallis and Rosslyn out of their cell.

RUSHING DOWN THE hall, Tomas called out as

loudly as he dared, "Tallis? Tallis, where are you?"

Donovan and Tomas stopped as they strained their hearing, hoping they had come to the right part of the dungeon. Tomas's heart caught in his throat as he finally heard the muted pounding on a door and Tallis's muffled voice, "Tomas? Tomas! We're in here!"

Tomas rushed to the thick, bound door and pressed his ear against it. "Are you all right?" he asked, the relief in his voice palpable.

"Yes, we are just fantastic, but would like to be out of here, if that's not too much trouble," Rosslyn said, voice sounding sarcastic, even through the thick door.

Tomas could hear Donovan growl behind him, his anger over Rosslyn's antics reaching a boiling point. "Right, then, just … just give me a minute," Tomas said as he knelt in front of the door.

He examined the door as he fiddled with the heavy metal lock. Furrowing his brow, he mumbled, "I'm guessing it would be too much to ask that the guards left behind keys to the door?"

Donovan gave him a flat look. "You decide now to be funny?"

Turning his attention back to the door, Tomas examined the lock more closely, frantically trying to remember if he'd ever read anything about picking a lock.

"Hurry up, Tomas, we haven't much time before the change of guards notices we're gone and makes their way down here."

Tomas shushed him. "I need pins or-or pliers, anything I can try and pick this with."

Without questioning him further, Donovan scoured

the little room, found nothing, then called through the door, "Rosslyn, you have any more pins in your skirts?" There was silence for a moment before Rosslyn pressed a pair of pins underneath the door.

Without wasting time thanking her, Tomas went to work fiddling with the latch. He began to sweat, as he felt like hours were passing as he carefully tried to free the clasp. If it had been Rosslyn on the other side of the door, she would have been able to pick the lock in a matter of moments. Tomas, however, was too honest of a person to know how to properly pick a lock. Inhaling deeply, he cleared his mind and focused on just getting Tallis out of the prison before the guards returned.

Wodan must have been smiling on them, as it was by sheer luck that Tomas finally managed to free the latch. As the door creaked open, he got to his feet and wrapped his arms around Tallis the moment the firelight from the brazier hit her gentle face. He held her in his arms and was awarded with the gentle pressure of Tallis returning his hug. When he realized what he had done, he released her, but perhaps a little too quickly to be natural.

Tallis gave him a confused look before smiling gently. "We're fine, Tomas. Thanks for getting us out of there."

Donovan gave them a hard stare before turning his ire on Rosslyn, who was doing her best to avoid the knight's cold gaze. Pushing himself from the wall he was reclining on, he growled, "As much as I hate to break up this touching moment, the guards will be back any moment. We'll talk when we get out of here."

Donovan was about to lead them back up the stairs,

when Tallis gripped his arm. "They took my mother's ring. Have you seen it?"

The pain and fear in her voice over losing her most prized possession was enough to break even the strongest man's heart. Peeling her fingers from his arm, Donovan said, "It's gone, Tally. The guards have it and we can't risk trying to get it back. I'm sorry, really I am, but it's gone."

Her sea-green eyes went wide and she threw herself at the guard's table, pushing papers and empty plates and tankards to the floor. They clattered and clanged with a deafening sound, one that had not gone unnoticed by the guards returning to their posts as the sound of stomping boots became all the more pronounced.

Donovan tried to grab her only to have Tallis push him off. Dropping to the straw-covered ground, Tallis frantically continued searching for her mother's ring as the heavy steps of the running guards became louder and louder.

Tomas's heart broke dozens of times over to watch her crawl through the filthy straw in vain attempts of finding a ring Donovan had already told her was gone. It was as if she refused to believe that her mother's ring could simply vanish. They were risking getting locked up again if they did not leave immediately, but neither Tomas nor Rosslyn seemed capable of crushing Tallis's spirit any further.

Cursing to himself, Donovan yanked Tallis to her feet and roughly tossed her over his shoulder. She began thrashing and yelling as Donovan ran with her. "No! Donovan, put me down! It can't be gone, it can't … it must be here. Donovan, stop it! Put me down, please!"

Tallis did not care they were in a dungeon surrounded by knights with instructions to imprison her; she refused to be parted with the ring. Tomas watched her thrash and beat on Donovan's back, all in vain; the big knight was more than willing, and capable, of saving his cousin's skin, whether she wanted him to or not. It wasn't until the pale morning light hit her that Tallis gave up. A look of despair and defeat settled on her face as she limply allowed her cousin to carry her to safety with Tomas and Rosslyn doing their best not to meet her eyes.

ᏮHEY HAD JUST managed to duck into a filthy alley when the alarm sounded at the prison. The group crouched in the shadows listening as the booming bells echoed across the city, letting their sound drown out Donovan's panting and the way Tallis seemed to whimper as she breathed.

Tallis's heart was hammering, and not entirely from their flight through the brick and stone building. Guilt twisted in her gut, causing a rancid taste to creep up the back of her throat. Tallis desperately needed to focus on anything else other than the cold, naked feeling she had without the ring around her thumb. Through the loud noise, Tallis asked, "So how did you get out?"

Tomas and Donovan exchanged wary glances before Donovan said, "Uncle Jon … I thought he had perished in the attack on Kincardine. Looks like he was able to get out after all. He said he overheard Raghnall say your name as he came to arrest us. Uncle Jon came and talked to some of the knights … apparently, they didn't like the idea of keeping a fellow knight locked up for no reason they understood, so he managed to get them to give him the key to our cell."

Despite her strained relationship with her father, hearing that he was alive sent Tallis's heart soaring. "My father lives? Where is he? I should see him before we leave and tell him I'm all right."

Tallis noted how Tomas's shoulders slumped and Donovan dropped his gaze as she mentioned seeing her father. Growing suspicious, she asked, "What?"

Donovan scratched at the stubble on his chin while mumbling, "He ... well you wouldn't want to see him, Tallis. He didn't come to save you, just me for my da's sake. He was unkind, even for Uncle Jon."

Tallis blinked slowly as understanding settled on her shoulders like a mountain. Pursing her lips, she looked out over the slowly waking city as she tried to put her father from her mind once again, wishing she could still go on believing he had died.

Gingerly, Tomas put his hand on Tallis's shoulder as they crouched in the shadows. Her heart sunk further as she guessed that Tomas was now privy to her dark secret about being found in the forest. If she was correct in what Donovan meant when he said her father was being unkind, then he had denounced her as his daughter in front of Tomas.

Exhaling deeply, she nodded and Tomas slowly took his hand away. "All right, well, that's fine. We need to focus on getting out of Fordoun, anyway. If

Raghnall and Henrik know we're here, then it's safe to assume they'll now be hunting us down."

"All of our stuff is back at the tavern. I don't think they'll just let us waltz in there and get it," Rosslyn said as she glanced back towards the Blind Mule Inn, fidgeting with her dusty, heavy, dark-blue skirt, tawny-colored vest, the sleeves of her deep brown tunic, and the white drawstring that peeked beneath the vest.

"No," Donovan said. "Certainly not after that stunt you pulled. What in Wodan's Pits were you thinking, Rosslyn? Getting in a fight like that … I didn't think you were so stupid."

"Oi!" Rosslyn said, pointing an accusing finger at Donovan's face. "It wasn't my fault! And I already apologized to Tallis."

Before they could continue bickering, Tallis shoved them hard against the wall, her eyes burning with a boiling rage and hurt that left no room for patience over their childish bickering. "If you insist on fighting, I'll have you tossed back in that dungeon and me and Tomas will do this alone. I've had it with your fighting. Now stop it, or I swear the tremps will be the least of your worries."

Rocking back on his heels, Donovan rubbed his temples, careful not to touch his swollen eye. "We have to split up," he said reluctantly. Holding up his hand before Tallis could protest, he continued, "I don't like it, either, but it's the only way we can get our things and get out of here without being seen by the guards."

Donovan crept to the edge of the alley and looked around. Waving the group over, he said, "Tomas, I need you to go back to the Blind Mule and get our things. Unlike the rest of us, if you go back, I don't think they'd recognize you. I'll see if I can get some horses. Maybe someone at the stables will honor my knighthood from Kincardine and give me a mount or two. If not, then it doesn't matter. Rosslyn, try and see if you can replenish our food for the journey ahead, and for the love of Wodan, stay out of trouble."

Tallis looked at her cousin. "What about me?"

Hanging his head, Donovan said, as if uncomfortable with his own plan, "You need to get out of Fordoun ... now. The knights and the baron's men will be looking for you hardest of all, especially with Uncle Jon aiding in tracking you down. We'll meet you on the shores of Lake Celebrain, just outside the city, as soon as we're all able. We'll stay there until morning to give everyone ample time to get out."

Tallis could feel the steady stares of her friends on her face as she looked down at the ground. She hated the feeling of running away like she was a coward. But if they wanted any hope of getting out of the city, then Tallis knew they could not be seen together. Tallis rolled her shoulders so they gave a loud pop. "All right ... I can do that, I suppose." After a moment of uncomfortable silence, Tallis pressed on with forced confidence, "This will work. We'll meet on the shores of Lake Celebrian outside of the city. It'll be fine."

She wasn't sure if she was saying it to convince the others or herself. Either way, it did not matter now. Meeting their eyes briefly, Tallis wrapped her wavy hair on top of her head in a messy bun, whispering as she disappeared in the fading shadows of the morning light, "Good luck and see you soon."

33

# *THREE*

ᏮALLIS WALKED AS casually as she could through the sleepy streets. She wanted to run; she wanted to fly as fast as she could out of the city and its gregarious splendor. She wished she had never come to this place, and that they had been brave enough to take Tomas's suggestion and stay out of Fordoun to begin with. As she thought about Tomas, she couldn't help but think of the grateful hug he had given her when he had finally managed to open her cell door.

Her skin started to tingle when she imagined the soft pressure of his embrace, and she imagined she could almost feel the rapid pounding of his heart. She wondered what he was about to say when the fight broke out, which made her hear the breathless way he said she was beautiful. She could feel herself starting to smile as she walked through the slowly waking streets, her thoughts getting lost to daydreams, when she shook her head and growled to herself.

What did it matter what Tomas was going to say? His heart was pounding as hard as it was because he was busy picking a lock under a high stress situation. He hugged her because he was just glad he was able to get the door open. The rest, Tallis convinced herself, was just in her head and not worth even thinking about, especially not now. Wrapping her arms around her stomach, she kept her eyes down and stooped her frame, hoping she looked just like a lost child rather than a woman who just escaped prison. She hoped that the plum-colored tunic with its low-cut neckline, and the drawstring clinching her stomach as well as the formfitting leather trousers from her old, first set of armor did not make her stand out in the sea of hungry, dirty faces she was trying to lose herself in.

She was walking for hours, heart racing like she had been running nonstop. She knew it was the adrenaline pulsing through her veins that kept her moving when she hadn't slept at all. Each time she came across a knight, she was careful to inconspicuously attach herself to another group of refugees crowded around a small fire, or she hid herself in the shadows of a makeshift shelter. She was careful not to draw attention to herself, something she had learned by watching the other refugees, as they, too, shied away from the knights, avoiding eye contact, staring at their boots, walking with a purpose.

Tallis watched their patterns, trying to predict what they would do so she could avoid them all the better. It wasn't long, though, before the knights stopped running around blind and became more methodical about the search. Soon they were stopping any woman with blonde hair or any girl with Tallis's same body type. Occasionally, they stopped groups of four, which made Tallis glad that Donovan had suggested they all momentarily part ways.

The knights also became more thorough in

questioning the throngs of refugees. Tallis could hear them asking the groups of people they stopped pointed and specific questions about her. She assumed Henrik must have told everyone just who she was, and now it wasn't just the baron's son who wanted her found, but Duke Alec himself.

It was midday when she finally came across Lake Celebrian. The lake was so large it managed to connect Fordoun to Isildor, making it the safest lake in all of Selkirk. Not that it mattered for Tallis now.

She stood near its shores and watched as the knights tightly monitored who came in and out of the city. They seemed to be stopping everyone, rifling through their things and making inquiries, and Tallis could only assume it was about her. As it was, she was far too exposed right now to be able to get out of the city; she had no hood to hide her face behind and no group of people to lose herself in.

She also could not swim through the lake to get out of Fordoun. While it served as a major thoroughfare, Lake Celebrian was heavily guarded, with a wall that extended the length of the lake, as well as a grate that reached to the very bottom. Even if Tallis believed she could swim the distance unseen, she had no way of getting through the grate.

Glancing around, she decided the best course would be to climb the ramparts and hope that the dark shadows climbing the walls this time of day would be enough to conceal her. The wall nearest the lake was the easiest to climb and the least fortified. Most people stuck to the roads, which forced the knights to pay attention to the throng of people milling about them rather than watch as Tallis began scaling the rough stone walls. Not that any of the people currently entering the city were looking to sneak out the way she was. They sought shelter from their liege lord, whereas Tallis was hoping to avoid his grasp.

Tallis had just reached the top of the wall when she heard a shout of alarm from far below. Cursing, she hauled herself up on top of the wall and ran as fast as she could to the other side, where she could climb down again before any of the knights on the wall could reach her. She could hear their steel-covered boots scuffling as they ran to cut her off before she hit the ground. Thankfully, the mass of people around the city gates kept them from getting to her as quickly as they would have liked.

Dropping the last few feet, Tallis ran as fast as she could over the bridge that went over the raging Noldor River that fed into the lake this close to the city. She could hear at least two knights chasing after her and she prayed to Wodan to lose them in the forest. Tallis was disappointed, however, when she turned to find the two young knights still chasing her, shouting at her to stop and surrender herself.

She could not risk the knights catching her, nor could she risk going much further without worrying that she would be too far from the rendezvous point with her friends. She dreaded the idea of having to do harm to these men as they followed her farther and farther away from the city. She knew they were merely following their commander's orders and probably did not even stop to question why.

Hiding in a cluster of trees, she listened intently for their footsteps and any sign that more would be coming after her. When she was satisfied it would just be these two, Tallis picked up a stone and tossed it, hoping the two knights would go and inspect the sound, giving her enough time to slip deeper into the forest unseen, so she could return later when they had gone.

She heard the knights stop and mumble to each other, one going to investigate the sound while the other continued heading towards where Tallis was currently hiding. She held her breath and tried to stay as still as possible, silently praying the knight would not see her and keep on walking. For a brief moment, she thought that was exactly what had happened. Until a flash of steel lurched around the tree as the knight attempted to bury the sharp blade up to the hilt into her side.

With uncanny speed, Tallis rolled away before the killing blow could connect with her exposed flesh. Hastily, the knight tried stabbing at her again as she danced to her feet. Before the knight could call for his partner, Tallis darted forward, snatching one of the daggers hanging loose at the knight's side and slipped inside his grasp. Grabbing the knight's wrist so he could not turn his sword on her a third time, she pulled his arm forward and pushed her back against his chest. Tallis thrust the dagger upward and sank it up through his exposed chin and into his head. He gave a loud gurgle as he fell, blood bubbling from his open mouth.

Tallis watched the life slowly drain from him and frustrated tears welled in her eyes. She had not wanted to kill this man; she had wanted them to turn around and cease in their pursuit. Instead, these knights insisted on pursuing her rather than aiding her in reaching her destination.

She crouched beside the dying man as his life

ebbed away; more tears began to fill her eyes and cloud her vision. Tallis wanted to comfort him, she wanted to stop any pain the knight may still be feeling. But she could do none of those things. Instead, she whispered in his ear as the last of his life fled, "I'm sorry, I'm so sorry. Please forgive me."

Just as she freed the dagger from his head, the other knight rushed towards her. He stopped in his tracks as he stared from his dead partner to the bloody weapon in her hand. He took out his short sword with a trembling grasp and Tallis realized he was just a young boy, barely a man. He was a new recruit and not a seasoned knight like Donovan.

She held up her hand and said before he could rush at her, "Please, I didn't want to kill him. I just want to go. Just let me leave Fordoun and pretend like you never saw me. Whatever it is you've been told about me, please believe me when I tell you it isn't true. I'm nobody, just a girl from a small town. I'm sorry, just let me go and we don't have to do this."

For a moment, the boy seemed to consider her words as he looked at his dead friend bleeding at her feet. The young knight swallowed and slowly sheathed his weapon. Looking at her skeptically, he asked, "You're this Tallis woman everyone's talking about? You don't look like some fearsome warrior in bed with them elves. Why do they want you?"

Tallis almost laughed in her sudden relief that this man seemed to want to reason with her. Tallis put the dagger on the ground in a sign of good faith. "I don't know. I really don't, trust me. The tremps, they all just attacked one night and my mother screamed my name as I killed one. I think that's why, but I can't be sure.

Please, just say you couldn't find me, that some feral elf got your friend and don't come after me."

The young knight scratched at his smooth chin as he carefully considered her words. He looked at the dead knight once more before meeting her eyes. It was the only time in her life Tallis hoped she looked as weak and pitiful as she felt, so this knight would not see her as a threat and would let her go. "But you killed him, it wasn't some tremp, it was you."

Tallis's heart sank and she put both of her hands up defensively. "I didn't have a choice; he was trying to cut me down before I could say anything. I was hoping you'd both follow the stone I threw. I didn't … I just wanted you both to go the other way so I could leave in peace. I didn't want to have to kill him."

Tallis wasn't sure if it was her pleas or if the young knight was too scared to fight someone who had taken down a fully armored knight with nothing but a small dagger. Either way, he nodded and said, "Fine, I'll tell them knights that some tremp got to him. Just don't come back, all right?"

Tallis smiled wildly. "I swear, you will never see me again."

Tallis waited until she could no longer see the knight before she exhaled. As she picked up the dagger and any other small knife she could put in the hidden place behind her steel-capped boots, she couldn't help but stop and look at the dead knight at her feet. A wave of guilt and frustration overwhelmed her as she stared down into his vacant dead eyes.

She wished they had just left her alone, or at the very least, began questioning why their duke was so intent on catching a woman the elves so desperately wanted to get their hands on. While she expected no help from anyone but her friends, she hoped she would not have to face opposition at every turn. And while she had wished she would never have to take a human life, she had been given little choice. Tallis felt ashamed over what she had done, but, all the same, she was angry the knights had given her no other alternative.

It felt different to kill a person rather than an elf. Of course, it felt the same if she closed her eyes and didn't think about it, but the elves were mindless monsters who would not hesitate to sink their teeth into your flesh and eat you while still alive. This knight would not have done that. No man, no matter how vicious he was, would have. But she had still killed him.

She kept telling herself that he had to die, that he had left her no other option. And while that was true, it did not make it any easier to bear, nor did it assuage her anger and frustration at being put in a situation where she had to take a human life to begin with. After a while, she numbed her senses to the dead body at her feet and, instead, hid him from view in case the young knight did not keep his word about having no more guards come after her. She doubted they would; if the young knight told them they had been attacked by elves, then no search party would come to reclaim the fallen knight, leaving the young man's family with no body to bury.

As she finished hiding the knight, all she could think about, besides her own burning anger and guilt, was how Tomas would look at her when he found out she had killed a man. Would he see her as a murderer?

---

Or would he believe she had no other choice? Tomas a was man of Wodan, his faith and principles were very clear and very important to him, and she had just broken one of the most sacred of morals Wodan had laid down for His people.

She desperately wanted to believe that the knight's death was entirely self-defense, but more than anything, she wanted Tomas to believe it as well. She did not stop to think what Donovan or Rosslyn might think of her actions; somehow, she doubted they would care, but even if they did, she found that their opinion of her did not matter as much as Tomas's. It was a strange realization, one that would have normally sent wild butterflies raging through her gut. But she was too scared by the idea that Tomas would no longer look at her with those same kind green eyes and shy smiles to allow for the butterflies to soar within her.

Lost in thought, Tallis stuck to the tree line as she moved back towards Lake Celebrian and hid herself in a willowy tree. It allowed her a clear view of the lake and the city walls where her friends would come from. She hoped she did not need to wait too long; she did not want to be left alone with a dead body and frustration as her only company.

TOMAS HAD EXPECTED to be stopped immediately as he entered the Blind Mule Inn. He thought his misdeeds were written plainly across his face, and anyone who saw him would know he had just escaped from the local prison and set his friends free as well. But hardly anyone gave Tomas more than a passing glance as he went upstairs and back to the room Rosslyn had won and none of them had slept in.

Few of the serving staff from the night before were currently working, and those who were present didn't seem to care or notice if Tomas was one of the several people caught up in the brawl from the night before. If they did recognize him, they assumed he had spent the night in the drunk cages and had been released; none of them seemed to know yet that he was one of the people they were tolling the alarm bells for.

Nervously, he pushed open the door and began tossing Tallis and Donovan's armor back in their bags, shrugged into his heavy-hooded beige cloak he had taken from his monastery, and stuffed the rest of the discarded clothes back where they belonged. Warily, he glanced over the bulging packs and wondered how he was supposed to carry all of their gear in one trip without any help.

He finally managed to fashion a type of sling with one of the bed sheets that allowed him to carry Rosslyn's pack on his back, and the rest of their more important possessions in the sling that crossed diagonally over his body. Feeling proud of his quick thinking, he pulled his hood down low and exited the inn just as the knights were sent into a frenzy as they tried to locate their lost quarry.

People tended to leave him alone as he quickly walked though Fordoun. Most refugees carried everything they had with them and left nothing unattended for any length of time. Seeing a young man heavily burdened with possessions was now a common sight, one which people preferred not to look at too closely, as the image brought up their own misfortunes all too well.

Avoiding the main market where Rosslyn would be replenishing their food and the stables where Donovan would be heading, Tomas found himself in the part of the market dedicated to the craftsmen of Fordoun. As much as he tried to simply focus on getting out of the city as quickly as he could without getting caught, Tomas could not help but marvel at some of the goods that were on display. Growing up in the monastery, he had never been allowed to experience walking through a bustling market; the brothers always had their goods personally delivered to them by the merchants. Even under such strained circumstances, he could not help but take a small delight in ambling through such a lively place now.

His eyes began idly scanning the various market stalls and glancing over their innumerable items for sale. He was coming to the end of the market when he stopped once again to gape at one of the makeshift tables and the merchant hovering protectively nearby.

Standing next to a rickety old table was a broad-shouldered woman with an odd assortment of cheap and antiquated jewelry littering the moth-eaten piece of cloth she used to hide the decay of the table. Nothing about the jewelry was anything fine or noteworthy, except that in the midst of several old and tarnished rings, sat none other than Lana's wedding ring.

The woman saw him eyeing it and gave him an overly friendly smile, the kind of smile that was so forced it looked painted on. "It's a lovely ring, real topaz, too." She maneuvered to stand next to Tomas.

45

"It would look lovely on a young lady's finger."

She was a middle-aged woman with brown hair that looked like it belonged on a broom, wearing an old maroon bodice with thick black sleeves, and a faded maroon and white striped skirt that was ratty along its hem. Her brown eyes gleamed as she watched Tomas stare at the ring as if she could already see how much he wanted it and how much the ring would mean to him.

Tomas chewed the corners of his lip. He knew that if he somehow managed to bring this ring back to Tallis, she would be forever grateful. He could hear the heartbreak in her voice when she'd thought she lost the ring forever, and he could only imagine her delight if he were able to give it back to her. "How much?"

The woman's eyes twinkled in delight. "Oh, well, for a ring like this, with a real topaz and such high-quality gold…." She trailed off as if she were weighing the value of the ring. Tomas tensed, knowing she would overinflate the price.

He had seen Tallis's ring up close and knew it was nothing of staggering value. The gold was not of the best quality and the topaz was not of a particularly stunning cut, but it was priceless to Tallis. Tomas was not sure how much money there was in their gear, he just hoped he had enough to pay the woman and to continue on his way.

Scratching her course and frayed brown hair, the woman declared, "Two silver for the ring. You won't find a ring like this anywhere cheaper, I can promise you that."

Tomas glared at her and shook his head. "It's a sin to lie the way you do, mistress. No way is a ring with such a bland cut for a topaz worth that." Tomas was not the best when it came to haggling; still, he hoped his bluff was enough to get her to lower the price.

The woman crossed her arms over her chest and narrowed her eyes. "I don't appreciate being called a liar." She looked Tomas up and down, head to foot. "Fine. One silver and that's as low as I'll go. Take it or leave it."

Tomas fished through their collective gear for a moment, his face palling as he realized that all the money they had was with Rosslyn, tucked away in one of her many hidden pockets.

The woman appeared to guess that he did not have the money for the ring as she carefully put it back in the bowl with all the rest of the rings she was trying to sell. "How about a trade?" Tomas said hastily before she could put the ring back and he lost it once again.

She raised an eyebrow at him skeptically. "A trade? What makes you think you have anything I'd want to trade for?"

Tomas's heart began pounding in his ears as he fished out the book he had taken with him from the monastery; the book that he had thumbed through over a hundred times and had scribbled notes into all the margins. He doubted the woman would appreciate the book half as much as he did, but he also knew a book, no matter its condition, was worth far more than what the woman would have ever gotten for Tallis's ring.

He held the book for a moment in his hand wondering if it was really worth parting over just to buy back the ring. As soon as the thought entered his mind, however, it vanished. He thought about the joy and happiness it would bring Tallis to be reunited with something she thought lost forever and Tomas knew he would have gladly paid any price to bring her that. Meeting the woman's eyes, he said without a hint of wavering, "I think you'll find this more than adequate."

Pushing the book into her hands, the woman casually thumbed through its pages to make sure it wasn't hollowed out or full of blank paper. She glanced over the notes in the margins and inspected the cracked leather binding before giving Tomas a mischievous look. She assumed he did not know what he was parting with in order to purchase a poor man's wedding ring. But Tomas did know what he was parting with and knew exactly why, and if the woman had known that, she may have given him the ring free of charge.

Picking up the ring, she pressed it into Tomas's hand, "You have yourself a deal, young man. I hope it brings you your heart's desires." He could hear the barely veiled laughter in the woman's voice, but he did not care.

He protectively held the ring in his hand as he left the market, fervently hoping that it would, indeed, bring him his heart's desire once he was able to put the ring back where it belonged on Tallis's thumb. Thinking about the happiness he was about to bring her helped ease the regret and sadness felt over parting with something he had cherished for years alone in his room when the other brothers did not seem to appreciate his inventions.

The book had been a source of comfort and inspiration. While he yearned to hold it again, he knew he did not need it. He had studied the book so many times that he had it memorized, even the complicated medical jargon he had never had a use for. He didn't need it in order to make his smoking powders or his fire grenades; he knew how to do that by heart. He just felt better making it when the book was opened and his fingers caressed its worn-out pages. And while he would miss its familiar weight on his back, he couldn't help but be excited to see the reaction on Tallis's face when he was reunited with her once again.

Tomas left the market behind as fast as he could after that. He tried to not draw attention to himself and practiced what he would say if he was stopped by a guard inquiring about who he was and if he knew of Tallis or any of her companions. He would tell them he was traveling from Linlith and heading for the town of Berwick, if he could. If the town was in the same disarray as all the rest, well then, he'd settle for Isildor or Hadding.

He thought he had the tale down perfectly and had gotten rid of any nervous twitches or tells that would give the lie away. Tomas was partially hoping that a knight *would* stop him just so he could rattle off the story he had practiced. But when he was barely stopped at the city gates, he could not completely say he wasn't relieved to be done with the ordeal.

The knights were distracted by a disturbance that had erupted near the markets and was rippling throughout the rest of the city. Idly, he wondered what the cause of the unrest was, but he took the opportunity to slip from the city and carefully make his way across the shore of Lake Celebrian, hoping to find Tallis waiting for him.

ᏩALLIS HAD BEEN sitting concealed beneath the willowy branches of her hiding place for a few hours when she saw a familiar figure striding towards her. Rising to her feet, she wiped away the last remnants of her frustrated tears with the back of her hand and poked her head out of the tree branches. Giving a soft whistle to get Tomas's attention, she smiled and waved him over. His face lit up like a candle when he saw her and he ran the last few feet to where she was concealed behind the tree branches.

Tomas unceremoniously dropped the gear he had been carrying, the concealed handmade crossbow within his pack making a loud thud as it hit the ground. Rubbing his neck, he smiled at Tallis and bravely took her hand. "I can't tell you how happy I am to see you. I was worried—well, I'm just glad you got out of the city all right." She nodded her head and looked down at their hands, wondering if he would notice the blood still caked under her fingernails.

Clearing his throat, Tomas gently dropped her hand and began fishing in his pocket for something. Tallis couldn't focus on much else above the thundering of her heart in her ears; she wasn't sure if it was because of how Tomas had held her hand, or if it was her fear over telling him what she had done.

Timidly, she began chewing her lip, debating whether or not to even tell Tomas about the man she had killed. If she never told him, then she would never need to worry about earning his disapproval—or worse. Still, she did not think she could hide something like that for long. Even if she had not been tired from lack of sleep or her recent ordeal, she didn't think she would be able to forget what had happened enough to never speak of it again.

Tomas found whatever he was looking for and held it protectively in his hand. Just as he was about to show her his prize, he finally noticed her bloodshot eyes and the pallor of her skin. Frowning, he kept his hand firmly shut over his treasure. "Tallis? Are you all right?"

Meeting his eyes, Tallis couldn't help but seem to fall endlessly into his concerned and trusting gaze. She could not understand what it was about Tomas that made her want to be nothing but honest with him, what made her want to protect him furiously, and allow him to attempt to do the same for her.

He had always been kind to her and had even left her blankets in the monastery library on cold winter nights when he could have just as easily locked the window and kept her out. He never demanded anything from her; he merely listened to her prattle on, and always indulged her whenever she asked questions about his inventions or lessons about Selkirk. Even when she knew it might be better to hold her tongue and speak no more of the knight she had killed, she had no desire to hide anything from Tomas.

Hanging her head, she dropped her gaze and said in a low whisper, "I killed a man, Tomas." The silence that fell between them was heavy like cold molasses, but not nearly as sweet. She wasn't sure what she expected him to say, but she could not bring herself to look him in the eye.

Sitting down beside her, Tallis became acutely aware of how little space there was between them. The slight void seemed to quiver and spark as if it were alive and trying to close the space between them. Before she could focus too long on the growing tension, Tomas asked, "What happened?"

Balling her hands into tight fists, Tallis became frustrated all over again. Quickly, she told him about how she had scaled the wall and the two knights who had pursued her into the forest. She told him how she tried to get rid of them and how it hadn't completely worked and she was forced to kill one of the knights before she managed to convince the other to leave her in peace.

"They don't seem to understand that I didn't do this, that I didn't want this. I don't want the tremps to go to war and kill everyone any more than the next person. But in their fear and cowardice, their commanders and their lords all want the easy way out by just handing me over to the first elf they see. They think that's all it's going to take to end whatever it is that's going on. No one seems to stop and consider the fact that if the elves are so desperate to get their disgusting hands on me, that maybe they should do exactly the opposite. It's just so maddening, Tomas.

"I didn't want to kill him, but he didn't give me a choice, and I really don't want to have to do it again. But somehow, I think that if another knight or some little lordling catches me, I won't have that choice." Tears of frustration once again started to fill her eyes.

Laughing ironically, she added in a rush, "And, of course, to top it all off, some arrogant prat of a guard takes my mother's ring. He said I could pick a lock with it, but didn't even really bother to search all the hidden pockets in Rozy's skirt. I know he just went off to sell it to some vendor on the street so he could afford more ale. I heard him and his partner talking about it, saying how they could make me ... *beg* for it. Oh, and let's not forget the fact my father is in Fordoun and would rather have me rot at the hands of the same knights who would steal his wife's ring rather than see me again."

Tomas shifted beside her, still clutching something tightly in his hand. Tallis dreaded what he would say, but still wished he would say something. Looking up, she scanned his face for any sign of disapproval or disdain at her confession. To her surprise and relief, that was not the expression he gave.

Instead, he lowered his head in an attempt to hide the smile starting to spread across his face, and the ironic chuckle emanating from deep in his chest. Tallis opened her mouth, about to retort, when her eyes once again settled on his clasped hand.

Suddenly, she could feel the gentle breeze of his breath as he sat facing her with his eyes downcast, and she realized with some surprise just how close, how physically close, they were to one another. She tried to focus on anything else besides the electricity prickling between the two of them when Tomas said, "You cannot fault yourself for his death, Tallis. It was self-defense, Wodan forgives such things. I know you don't really blame yourself, anyway. I know it's really just the circumstances around our time in Fordoun that has you this upset, but still ... I don't know if that makes you feel better at all, but if it doesn't, I hope this does."

Tomas slowly opened his hand and showed its contents to Tallis. Nestled in his palm was a ring that looked as if two golden bands were twined around each other, with a small blue topaz in its center. It was none other than her mother's ring, not a close imitation, but her mother's actual wedding ring.

Tallis's eyes widened as she snatched Tomas's hand and tenderly took the humble, yet priceless piece of jewelry from his palm. She held the ring as if it were a gentle butterfly perched on her finger, marveling at its beauty as well as her own good fortune. Breathlessly, she asked, "Where did you find it? How did you get it back?"

Tomas grinned. "It was an accident, really; I just found some woman selling it, so I got it back for you." Before he could say more, Tallis leaned forward and kissed him full on the lips.

Of all the disappointing and terrible things that had happened in Fordoun, she had never expected Tomas to bring back the one thing she had thought lost. Donovan would never have done that; when he said it was gone, he had meant it, and the matter had ended there. But Tomas had brought her mother's ring back to her, even when he did not need to. She may not know what she and Tomas had, but she was glad to have him, if even briefly.

Wrapping her arms around him while breathing heavily, Tallis broke off the kiss and gently rested her forehead against his. Tomas pulled her close so that Tallis was sitting on his lap as he wrapped his arms around her waist, their bodies rising and falling in time with each other as they tried to catch their breath.

Tallis didn't know what to say, she had not thought anyone would ever care enough about her to sacrifice anything when they didn't need to. She also was not sure she should have kissed Tomas the way she did, but at the moment she wasn't listening to her brain, but rather to the pleas of her pounding heart.

Tomas cupped her chin with his hand and brought her face up to meet his eyes. He had a dreamy look to his strong face that made Tallis's breath catch in her throat. Tallis had always thought Tomas was handsome, but she had never really looked at him as a man until now. As an initiate in the monastery, he had always seemed off limits to her. Even when he left his home for her, she always just assumed one day he would go back. But Tallis was finally starting to realize that Tomas had left the monastery to *be* with her, and in every sense of the word.

He boldly ran his fingers through her hair, Tallis's lips parting again as Tomas leaned in to kiss her once more. Tallis melted into his embrace as their lips met. She wanted to pretend there was nothing else in all the world but Tomas, this moment, and his solid body as it held on to her with a hungry protectiveness. Breathlessly, he murmured against her lips, "Tallis, I—" but he never got the chance to finish his thought as they heard the sound of someone approaching.

Tallis's eyes widened at the coming steps as she gracefully detangled herself from Tomas and rose to her feet to see if the arrival was friend or foe. For his part, Tomas watched Tallis with longing plain on his face as she slipped once again from his grasp.

ROSSLYN SULKED THROUGH the market sniffing at the tantalizing smells as fresh made food began to assault her senses. She had been careless, and knew her pop would have smacked her for getting her friends into trouble. That was not to say she thought she was wrong to have cheated the way she did, she had followed her Galon Sipsiwn, and no Sipsi would ever fault her for heeding the call of the Sipsi heart; she was mostly angry that her sloppy behavior had gotten her caught. It was why she now decided that for the time being, she was going to be honest in her dealings with the merchants.

Normally, she would have done her best to pilfer and cheat vendors out of their food. They had plenty to spare and she would have only taken what was needed for their journey. But the fear of being caught without her friends to save her, and the shame of her antics from the night before, prompted her to take the money she had won and actually pay for the provisions. Her pop may have laughed at her, but for the moment, this was the only way to ensure her safety.

Rosslyn stopped at a few of the stalls, and when she could not get them to lower their prices for old meat or produce that had been nibbled on by insects, she would move on. She never lingered at a stall too long if they did not come down in price quickly enough. While she wanted to buy the best of what she could, she did not have the time to haggle with testy shop owners who might recognize her or delay her long enough for a guard to catch up.

As she went, Rosslyn would listen in on the bits and pieces of the merchants' angry conversation as they bitterly complained about the knights harassing them over the location of some escaped group of criminals. None seemed to really know what the knights wanted with these people and none cared. They had been bullied by the knights since the mess with the elves had started and were growing fed up with their brutality.

Eventually, she had managed to procure a shank of stringy beef that would be perfect for curing, as well as several slices of goat jerky and smoke dried haddock. Rosslyn also bought a large bag of dried fruits, nuts, and berries to replenish what they had already consumed on their journey. Last, Rosslyn managed to buy a few potato spuds, a small wheel of hard cheese made of goat's milk, and a large loaf of hard brown oat bread. It was arguably the most food Rosslyn had ever carried at any one time, but if Donovan managed to get them horses, then she doubted they would have much time to stop and hunt for more, as they would be moving too quickly for her to catch anything.

Rosslyn carefully packed away all the provisions she had purchased and counted the few copper coins she had left, hoping they would have no need of them as they followed their journey to its bitter end. As she stuffed the money back in her pocket, a commotion broke out at one of the vendors she had spoken to but had not purchased anything from. Seeing the knights, Rosslyn moved into the shadows in order to hide herself, but her curiosity over the scene prevented her from leaving.

Three large knights surrounded a small bronze-skinned merchant clad in a black coat, gray tunic, and gray trousers as he stood boldly by his little shop of fresh berries. The man was short and squat, with dark brown hair, and darker eyes, made all the more so by his defiance.

"Come now, Kester," one of the knights said. "Bunch of blokes saw you talking to one of the people we're looking for. Stop making a fuss and give us a look around the stall."

Kester crossed his arms over his barrel chest and sneered. "I don't know who you been talkin' to, but there be no woman hidin' in my stall. You plonkers can go piss off and leave me alone—now."

The knight ground his teeth. "We have it on good authority that you were talking to someone who matches the description of who we're looking for. Don't make this harder than it has to be."

Kester did not move. "Aye, I'm sure I did. Not much of a description you have to go on. I talk to lots of people. If you haven't noticed, this here be a market."

Losing his patience, the biggest of the three knights pushed Kester roughly out of the way, and without regard for his fresh and fragile berries, flipped over the little makeshift stall. Kester gave a loud yell in protest and roughly shoved the big knight as he began tramping over the berries as they littered the ground.

Cursing the knights, Kester attempted to save his berries from their feet. "I told you I was hidin' no one, you horse's arse! You goin' to pay me for the damages, or you just goin' to stand there like the curs you are?"

The knight who had tried to reason with him earlier, shook his head, and turned his back as one of his companions roughly picked Kester up by the scruff of his tunic and punched him squarely in the gut, doubling him over in pain. "That'll teach you to call me a horse's arse."

By then, a crowd had gathered to watch as Kester

had his meager crops destroyed all about him. But when the knight punched him after it was clear they had made a mistake in accusing him of harboring a fugitive, the mood darkened.

They began to crowd around the knights and shout at them to leave Kester alone, that he had done nothing to deserve this, and that they were all tired of being treated in this manner. Rosslyn knew she should leave before the situation got worse, but found herself captivated by the scene and caught up in the growing ire the people had for the knights of Fordoun.

The knights attempted to shove everyone out of their way as they left Kester sputtering on the ground surrounded by his destroyed berries, but the wall of ordinary townsfolk, shouting and hurling insults their way, would not part.

The biggest knight had a temper, and was not afraid to let it flare when the people gave him a hard time. He began knocking people down, tossing them into other stalls, or roughly throwing them to the floor. It did not take long for people to shove back.

Growing increasingly frustrated, the knight completely lost his temper and unsheathed his sword. The next time he felt himself get shoved from behind, he quickly turned and sank his blade all the way through a middle-aged man's soft belly.

A hush fell over the crowd. As the knight yanked the blade from the man's gut, and he sank to the floor, there was a brief instant where the market appeared as if it were moving in slow motion. The market seemed devoid of all noise as the dying man clutched at his stomach, eyes widening in disbelief before he fell, never to rise again. It was then the silence erupted with indiscernible cries of shock, fear, and pure anger.

The destitute people of Fordoun jumped the knights and brought all three to the ground. They clawed at their faces and kicked at their sides as the knights frantically called for help. Rosslyn watched in horror as the knight who had vaguely tried to talk to Kester had his face kicked in until it became nothing more than a bloody pulp.

As the refugees began taking up the angry cry of civil unrest like dry grass catching fire from lightning, Rosslyn fled from the market. Protectively, she held on to her food as she shouldered her way through the riot that was spreading through the market and the impoverished areas of Fordoun.

The knights were far too busy trying to quell the riot to notice another dark-skinned girl with unruly curly black hair as she fought her way from the market with the other citizens who simply wanted nothing to do with the ruckus. Several times, Rosslyn found herself bumping shoulders with knights as they roughly pushed passed to get to the disturbance that now had encased Fordoun's entire market district and looked to soon spill over into the other shops and taverns. But none gave her a second glance.

As she approached the city gates, Rosslyn turned to see just how far the riot had spread, and she could see several homes were already engulfed in flames. She could hear the screams of citizens as they fled through the streets and the distinct clatter of steel flashing through the city as the knights attempted to regain control of the situation.

Rosslyn grinned while she slipped through the gate as the knights distractedly interrogated any group of four that passed by them. Sliding passed them virtually unseen, it took all of Rosslyn's resolve not to run for the shores of Lake Celebrian upon exiting the city. Instead, she stuck to the main road that would lead to Isildor before losing herself in the surrounding trees.

By the time she got to where Tallis was supposed to be, the sun had just begun its downward trek. Briefly, she looked back towards the city walls and grimaced as she saw the smoke of the fires that still raged within.

Rosslyn carefully walked along the shore, stopping every time she heard a branch snap. She was paranoid that someone was following her, or worse, she would be snatched by an elf just like what had almost happened to her baby brother. She was beginning to worry she had come to the wrong place or that something had happened to Tallis, when she finally saw her friend's pale and lovely face poke itself out of a curtain of leaves from the willow tree she was hiding beneath. Smiling in relief, Rosslyn trotted over to where Tallis was waiting.

Pushing her way through the tree branches, Rosslyn stopped and glanced at Tallis and Tomas. Tallis's hair was disheveled and Tomas looked as if he were waking from a dream, his eyes half-lidded in happiness and a gentle flush to his cheeks.

Tomas noticed her questioning stare as he cleared his throat and dropped his gaze from Tallis, where it had been resting. Rosslyn was sure something had happened between the two of them, but before she could ask as to what it was, Tallis interjected, "So? What did you get from the market?"

Grinning from ear to ear, Rosslyn showed them

what she had managed to get from the vendors. "And all without having to cheat or steal any of it, I'll have you know."

Normally this would have amused Tallis, but her lips did not even twitch upwards in a smile. Clearly, it was too soon to joke about their situation. Lowering her gaze, Rosslyn sat down and began curing the beef shank she had purchased while telling Tomas and Tallis about the riot that had erupted in the streets.

Tomas stopped organizing their gear into neat piles. "So, that's what was going on. I didn't get here much before you did, and even by the time I managed to get to the gate, the guards were distracted by something happening over in the market."

Rosslyn nodded. "Aye, by the time I got to the gate, the riot had claimed a few houses as well. Hopefully, Donovan can use the distraction to get out of the city all right. They seem to be stopping every group of four they come across, even if it's a group of all men."

Tallis nodded and Rosslyn noticed how she seemed to be avoiding Tomas as much as possible, but failing all the same. Each time Tallis was caught looking at him, a light pink blush colored her cheeks before she hastily dropped her gaze and turned away. Each time Tomas caught her glancing at him he would smile and open his mouth to speak, only to have a look of confused disappointment replace it each time Tallis turned her back.

She wanted to ask what was going on, but Tallis did not give her the opportunity, as she quickly grabbed her leather and chainmail armor from the pile Tomas was going through and walked to the backside of the tree. Rosslyn noted with some amusement how

Tomas's eyes lingered where Tallis had disappeared behind the tree's trunk.

Rosslyn gently took Tomas's arm, causing him to jump lightly in surprise. Rosslyn cocked an eyebrow and waited for him to explain himself. But much to her surprise, Tomas did not even try to hide what he was doing or make an excuse for it. He opened his mouth to say something before firmly shutting it once again. He jerked his arm out of Rosslyn's hand and finished reorganizing their gear before he set to work making more crossbow bolts.

She watched him work for a moment before shrugging it off. Tomas was no good at keeping secrets, and eventually she would get the truth about what happened from either him or Tallis. For now, though, she was content to let them both act painfully awkward around each other as she went to work preparing their food for the trek ahead.

THE STABLES WERE much farther into the city than Donovan had anticipated. He tried to keep his head down and to avoid eye contact as much as possible, but it seemed as if he had *knight* written all over his face, as people tended to give him a wide berth.

He felt naked without his armor and sword after wearing both for so long. He felt vulnerable and small without the heavy steel hanging on and from his body. So much of his identity was tied into his armor and small status as a knight of Kincardine that he wasn't sure how to act or behave now without it.

Donovan stuck to the shadows and tried to look dumb and ordinary whenever he was stopped by a knight. He tried to hide the way he spoke, as if any other knight would be able to discern a secret code in his words that would oust him for who he really was. Donovan may have been acting overly paranoid and cautious, but given the kind of trouble that followed in Rosslyn's wake, he did not think being overly vigilant was necessarily a bad thing.

By the time he reached the stables, chaos had erupted back at the market district. Casually, he watched as the knights flew past to quell whatever civil unrest had gripped the city. He chewed the inside of his cheek as he watched before shaking his head and pressing on, making a silent bet to himself as to whether or not the disturbance was also Rosslyn's fault.

Very few horses were left at the stables by the time Donovan shouldered his way into the large barn. The knights had been barking orders at their timid squires for the past hour as they made their way to restore order to the city before the situation got worse, leaving the building barren of most mounts and men of authority.

Using the chaos to his advantage, Donovan approached a bashful looking young squire. "I need two horses so I can help deal with the ruffians in the market." Now he hoped his demeanor and stance would portray him as the knight he was even without his armor.

The young boy blinked at him stupidly for a

moment before stammering, "Who are you? You're not a—you're not a knight, are you?"

Donovan did not want to be mean or overly harsh with the boy, but he knew if he wanted to convince the squire he was there on official business, he would have to be. Donovan barked down at the child, raising his hand as if he would strike him, "Don't be daft, you little muppet. Of course I'm a knight. Don't you see what those peasants are doing out there? They caught me unaware"—he gestured at his bruised face—"but that won't stop me from ending this madness before it gets any worse. Now give me the horses or I'll report you to my Lord Maric and have you flogged." By evoking the Baron of Kincardine's name, Donovan had won the lad over.

Dropping the pail of muck he had been holding, the squire darted to the nearest stall and brought forth two horses already saddled. Donovan hastily mounted a squat, brown horse that had a short dark-brown main and stocky legs. Its head was much larger than the horses he normally saw in Kincardine, making him believe this was once a wild horse they had caught and recently broken.

He took the reins of the second horse, a dappled mare with a long gray main and tail that nearly draped on the floor. The horses snorted at each other and tramped the floor of the stable in agitation, the smell of the fire upsetting them.

Just as Donovan was about to lead the horses from the stable, the young squire stopped him once again. "Pardon me asking, ser, but why you need two horses?"

Donovan tried to keep his face impassive as he

quickly tried to come up with a lie that the young man would believe. Shifting in the saddle, he said, "The mare is for the baron's son, Henrik. He wishes to take part in restoring order. Now back to work, lad." The squire hastily bowed and scuttled back into the stables to clean the mess from his dropped pail. Donovan couldn't help but smile to himself, hoping that if his lie were discovered that it would at least put Henrik in a difficult situation with his father and Duke Alec.

Donovan left as quickly as he could after that. He knew that had a more experienced squire been left behind to tend the stables, his story would not have held up and he had no desire to be in the city when his ruse was discovered.

Luckily, most people dove out of the way as he pushed his horse to a trot and led the dappled mare by the reins through the streets. He shouted occasionally at people to get out of the way, but otherwise did not stop for anyone or anything. Thankfully, the civil unrest had grown so large that people fleeing the market district were just as common as those who were rushing to join the fray in one capacity or another.

He reached the city gates as dusk began to fall only to find them deserted. He puzzled over it for a moment before he realized that the gates were empty because the few knights left to guard the walls were closing the city for the night.

The loud cranking sound of the gate slowly lowering frightened the horses and took him precious moments to control. Kicking his horse roughly in the side he spurred them on and managed to get out of the city before he could be stopped. He heard knights shouting at him, their threats lost under the sound of the horses' hooves as he pressed them forward.

Donovan heard the loud bang as the gate shut and knew that no one would pursue him. Considering what had happened earlier in the day, they had bigger worries than a lone man leading two horses out into the quickly approaching darkness.

He slowed the horses to a light walk as he followed the banks of the lake, hoping that it would not take long to find Tallis. He hoped that everyone had managed to get out of the city, and vaguely hoped he was, indeed, the last to make it out. If he wasn't, then they would not be able to get out of the city until morning, and he wasn't sure he wanted to risk spending another day this close to Fordoun now that they were all wanted by the baron and the duke himself.

Donovan heard them before he saw them, heard Rosslyn's deep, yet still feminine voice as she spoke of food preparation and heard the scraping of wood as Tomas busied himself with making more of his crossbow quarrels. Giving a low whistle so as to not frighten them, Donovan dismounted and waited for his companions to show themselves, so he wouldn't blindly lead the horses over unsure ground.

Tomas was the first to poke his shaggy blonde head out from beneath a willow tree's protection and wave Donovan over with a look of surprise and relief. Grinning lopsidedly, Donovan went to rejoin the group, immensely relieved that Wodan had chosen now to smile down on them and see that they all safely got out of Fordoun.

Rosslyn inspected the horses Donovan brought with a look of open admiration. "Well, I'll be...," she said as she gently stroked the mare's large gray head.

"I always thought you'd get out of the city, but I didn't think you'd actually manage to get horses in the process. This is going to make getting to the clan not just easier, but much faster, too. I was getting tired of walking for days on end through these bloody forests."

Donovan rolled his eyes as he led the horses over to the lake to feed and water. "I had help. There's a riot of sorts going on in the city. I assume I have you to thank for that?"

Rosslyn folded her arms over her chest and feigned indignation. "Me? Have something to do with a riot of that scale? What kind of person do you think I am?"

In the growing darkness, Rosslyn could not see the dark look Donovan gave as he shot an accusing finger at her. "Aye, I know the kind of person you are. You're the kind who thinks keeping a low profile means starting a brawl in an inn and then getting us thrown in prison. So tell me, did you cause the riot in the market? After all, that's where you were supposed to be today."

A hush fell over the group as the teasing atmosphere dissipated under the sudden scathing anger Donovan had for Rosslyn. They all knew his irritation was justified to a degree; Rosslyn had cost them precious time, and could have sent Tallis to her grave had Henrik had his way and convinced Duke Alec to give her over to the elves. But that had not happened.

They had gotten out of the city and managed to replenish their food, as well as make out with a few horses. It was likely that had they not been fugitives, none of that would have been possible. But it did not matter to Donovan.

All Donovan could see as he stared at Rosslyn's shadowed face was a careless cut-purse who did not understand the gravity of their situation. If Rosslyn was hoping to escape her guilt because Tomas and Tallis had other things occupying their minds, she would not escape from him.

Rosslyn dropped her gaze and kicked idly at the ground, looking unsure what answer might exonerate her from her past transgressions. Giving up, she dropped her hands and gave a defeated shrug. "I didn't start that business in the city. Some fool knights were bullying a man I had spoken to about his fare, and they wouldn't let up. A fight broke out and someone was killed and that's when chaos broke loose. I should be flattered you'd think I was capable of orchestrating such a thing but ... look, I'm sorry all right? For that mess back at the inn. I didn't mean for it to happen; I just lost my head for a moment. I don't know what else you want me to do or say, it's done now. I'll be more careful in the future, I promise."

Donovan shook his head angrily and placed his fists squarely on his hips. "You don't get it," he grumbled, "it takes one moment, one heartbeat of lapsed judgment, and you don't just put yourself in danger, you put all of us in danger. You can never let your guard down. *Never.* You always have to be vigilant and think about what consequences your actions have. If you get in a pinch like that again, Rosslyn, don't expect me or anyone else to come for you. At some point, you're going to have to make up for all of your mistakes."

"Oi! You make it sound much worse than it is. It's not like I killed anyone."

"No," Donovan retorted, "but in a country at war, anything that gives people an excuse to notice you, to hate you, that's as good as signing a death warrant."

Rosslyn took a step towards Donovan and Tallis stepped between them, gently placing her hand on Rosslyn's wrist. "That's a little fatalistic of you, cousin. Rosslyn said she was sorry, and I'm sure she means it. It helps no one to make her feel worse about it with all your shouting."

ꙦALLIS HAD A natural ability to diffuse tension whenever it arose. Growing up with a father who constantly disapproved of everything she did, and argued continuously with her mother about the usefulness of their daughter, had given her a low tolerance for quarrelling between people she cared for. Fighting tended to make Tallis irrationally nervous, causing her to forgive easily and sometimes before her anger had truly abated. But in situations like this, it served her well for settling disputes amongst her friends, especially when they had no time to turn against each other.

Donovan and Rosslyn did not speak after that. Instead, Rosslyn returned her attention to packing up their food, and Donovan returned to the horses. Tallis glanced at the now nearly black sky and sighed. She waited a moment before saying, "We can't stay here. We need to move further down the lake."

Donovan turned his attention to Tallis before continuing with what he was doing. "It's too dark to get anywhere tonight, Tallis. We'll be fine here." As if that ended the discussion, he started to hitch the horses to the tree they were camping beneath.

She chewed her lip momentarily as she debated whether or not she wanted to tell him what had happened. As she made her choice, she snatched the reigns from Donovan's hand and said, "We can't. I didn't get out of the city as neatly as the rest of you. We just need to go a little farther in, that's all. It won't hurt the horses to walk a little in the dark."

Donovan did not let go of the reigns as Tallis grabbed them. Instead, they had a silent game of tug as they tested to see whose will was stronger. As they came to an impasse, Tallis blurted out, "There's a dead body of a knight who followed me not far from here. I'd prefer not to set camp right next to him."

"You did what?" Rosslyn blurted.

A moment of silence passed as the group stood and stared, waiting for Tallis to respond.

"I had to scale the walls to get out of Fordoun. The guards saw me and two of them managed to follow me here. One caught me by surprise and I … well, I didn't have much of a choice and I … well, I killed him. The other one I was able to convince to just leave. Please, there's a cluster of birch trees not far from here we can hide in pretty easily. It's not as concealed as all this, but at least it's not practically on top of the boy I killed." Tallis began praying she was right in her assumption that Rosslyn and Donovan would not begrudge her for killing someone.

Without a word, Donovan dropped the reigns and helped gather their things. Tallis breathed a sigh of relief in the darkness as she realized she did not need to justify or explain herself any further. Rosslyn was in no place to judge anyone at the moment, and Donovan was a knight, trained to kill, and a man who more than understood the necessity of self-defense. He may not have cared if they camped near a dead body, it did not seem to bother him the same way that it did Tallis, but he understood her desire to put literal distance between her and the first human she had killed.

They walked in silence as Tallis carefully led them through the deepening darkness to the cluster of silver birch trees she had mentioned. It was not far and they could still vaguely see the outline of the willow tree they had just been under, as well as the faint glow of the city as the riot still raged within. They may not have been all that safer a few yards away as they were still within the shadow of Fordoun, but it calmed Tallis's nerves and that was all that mattered at the moment.

# *FOUR*

ꚌHAT NIGHT, THEY ate particularly well and Tallis appreciated it. It might have been the excess of food Rosslyn bought, or it could have been the last remnants of her guilt over what had occurred the night before, but either way, Rosslyn prepared a feast.

Taking the last of the rabbit and quail, one of the potatoes, a large hunk off the cheese she bought, as well as a handful of the fresh herbs they managed to collect along their journey, Rosslyn managed to make a wonderfully thick and hearty stew. She swore it was nothing compared to what her mother was able to make, but it was delicious all the same. It seemed to delve deep into their guts and warm their tired spirits and aching bodies. It was food that helped the soul as much as it did the body.

But despite the hearty fare, tension clung to the group like a wet cloak. Tallis was not speaking much to anyone and was avoiding all contact with Tomas. Donovan was still cross with Rosslyn, and she was upset at him for being cross at her. All the while Tomas stared at Tallis, trying to catch her eye, as if he would speak to her with his stares alone. Even the horses seemed to feel their tension as they shifted restlessly from foot to foot.

Eventually, weariness settled over them and Rosslyn issued an over-exaggerated yawn. She stretched out to sleep before anyone could object or volunteer her for the first round of watch. Donovan was about to get up to take over the duty when Tallis stopped him. "I'll take the first watch." She rose to her feet, scuttling away only to find Tomas following her.

"I'll help," he said.

Tallis turned quickly on her heel and was about to stop him with a hand on his shoulder before she caught herself. Too quickly and a little too loudly, she said, "No! I mean, no, it's all right. I can manage by myself for now."

Donovan glanced between the two of them as if he were intruding upon a private conversation. A grin tugged at the corner of her cousin's lips and Tallis could feel her cheeks redden, but before she could ask him to convince Tomas to stay put, Donovan turned away and reclined against one of the birch trees, pulling the hood of his cloak down over his eyes.

Gawking at Donovan as she realized he wasn't going to speak on her behalf, she reluctantly met Tomas's eyes. She wondered if she would have treated Tomas differently if he had not been destined to become an ordained brother in the monastery, devoting his life to quiet servitude for Wodan. She wondered if she would *still* treat him differently if he were planning on returning to the monastery at some point. While she regretted plunging him into such uncertain danger when she convinced him to run off with her, she would be lying to herself if she said that was not what she had wanted to happen all along.

While most women found men like Donovan, men who could easily pummel any foe to the ground, to be the epitome of manliness, Tallis looked at Tomas and found his mind to be far more impressive and useful than being able to swing a sword. Tallis could do that well enough on her own, she did not need another bloodstained warrior in her life.

Tallis began to wonder if he had had parents that kept him and allowed him to grow up with no predetermined destiny, if the girls of Kincardine would have come between them and kept Tallis from ever really meeting Tomas in the first place. Tallis liked to think they still would have become friends, but she was not positive. Thinking about that made her wonder just when his feelings for her had changed, and when had hers?

She could not speak for Tomas, but if she really thought about it, she knew when she first started to notice his actions towards her becoming more than just friendly. It had started for her with the way he shot Raghnall back at the Lonely Tavern, and continued through him trying to bring her fresh food, taking care of her when she had fallen ill, doing his best to protect her from everything and anything that wanted to do her harm, even the way he stammered through being polite whenever he spoke was becoming increasingly delightful for her to watch.

She could feel herself falling easily for Tomas, letting herself slip into an easy companionship with him. She wanted to know what it felt like, what it felt like to be in love with someone and have them love her back free of the animal lust that usually caused men to paw at her back in Kincardine.

But she couldn't.

Much of what Donovan said earlier to Rosslyn about being forever vigilant also applied to whatever it was Tomas and Tallis had. To lose herself to this would only lead them into danger and be an unnecessary distraction. *No,* she told herself, *better to end this now.*

Moments of awkward silence had trickled between the two of them as Tallis's mind went racing through these thoughts. Tomas gave her another questioning glance before Tallis jutted her head to the side, indicating for him to follow her so they could speak without being overheard.

They walked a short distance away before Tallis turned to face Tomas. In a barely audible whisper she said, "We can't do this."

ᏀOMAS'S FACE WENT ashen as Tallis's words hit him. He was glad she could not see his pallor in the darkness, and he hoped his voice did not betray his hurt and the sound of his heart plummeting to his feet. "Why? I don't understand ... you kissed me."

"I know and I'm sorry for that. I shouldn't have. But it's like Donovan said, if we aren't careful at all times we could be caught unawares, and those consequences will affect more than just us. As much as I—" Tallis cut herself off and began again. "It's not a wise decision to start something like this. Not here, not now. You of all people should know that."

Tomas was silent for a moment as he thought about what she said. Tallis wasn't wrong; it would be unwise for them to let their feelings stand in the way of stopping the elves as they continued to purge the towns surrounding the big cities. But that was assuming it was even something they could stop, that was assuming that the elves would care about what they felt for one another, and it was assuming that neither one of them could control themselves around each other. It was a lot of assumptions he felt should have no real impact on them at this very moment.

Drawing in a deep breath, he took a step towards Tallis, and—while immensely grateful when she did not back away—said, "You're right. Letting this interfere with what we have to do would be foolhardy. But that doesn't mean we can't … I mean, as long as we are careful and don't let ourselves get carried away, I don't see the problem."

He hoped she could not hear the pleading in his voice. He did not want Tallis to get the impression he was desperate for her affection, even if, in a way, he was. He had been tormented by the sight of her night and day for the past six years, and part of him refused to let either of them be sensible about it now.

If he had been sensible, he would have never followed Tallis out of his bedroom window in the monastery and come here in the first place. But he had. Tomas was realizing how short and fragile life could be, and he did not want to meet Wodan one day without ever knowing what it felt like to openly love someone and hold them in his arms.

—

TALLIS COULD FEEL how close he was to her. Close enough for her to gently feel his breath as it pushed its way across her hair. She wondered what it would feel like to take a step closer and hold Tomas the way you were supposed to, the way Donovan held Nessa.

She knew it was strange for a girl her age to have never been with someone before, to never having actually been kissed. She should not be afraid of that kind of intimacy, but part of her was.

Tomas was different, though. She could look at him and see glimpses of a future where it was akin to what Donovan and Nessa had, a true and equal partnership between two people who had seen the ugly side of their lover and took their hand all the same. All she had to do was take one step closer and she could finally see what it was like to have something true and pure for the first time in her life.

But she stopped herself. "How do you know we won't get carried away and consumed with one another? I'd much rather do that than tramp through the forest to stop the tremps from murdering in my name. I want that more, well, more than I can honorably say. But I don't trust myself to know when to stop, when to tone things down so Rosslyn and Donovan don't notice a single missed step as we continue on."

Tomas moved a little bit closer and Tallis swore she could feel the air heat up between their bodies. He lightly touched her cheek and she could feel him trembling; he was just as unsure of himself as she was.

"That's not fair, and not just for you; it's not fair to me. You can't tell me that kiss was just a *thank you* and it meant nothing. You cannot just pretend it never happened. Why can't we act our age for once and indulge in something that could turn out to be truly amazing? Don't we deserve to have just one good thing for ourselves?"

It would be so easy for Tallis to admit he was right and to let herself fall into his arms and pretend like they were the only two people that mattered in the world. But she knew she couldn't, and if that meant breaking Tomas's heart, then she would, even if that would kill her as surely as an elf would.

"It doesn't matter now; we can't let it happen again." Tallis turned and walked back to camp. It was one of the hardest things she had done to date, and she couldn't bear to see what her words had done to Tomas.

She felt shameful and filthy for hurting such a good man, a man who deserved the best she could give him. In her disgust, she wondered what a man like Tomas would even see in a girl like her. For, in that moment, she did not feel that she deserved any of his affection.

Tallis climbed one of the trees to give her a higher vantage point of the area around them. She found it much easier to keep watch this way. She could see Rosslyn and Donovan below her, softly snoring in their light slumbers. Eventually, she heard Tomas slowly make his way back to them. Throwing himself down on the ground, the defeat and despair emanating from him was so palpable that Tallis wondered how it did not send Donovan and Rosslyn into fits of tears.

Tallis told herself she would make it up to him later. She wasn't sure how, but just because they could not indulge in the secret feelings of their hearts did not mean they couldn't be friendly towards one another. Or at least she hoped it didn't. A cold fear gripped her as she wondered if perhaps she hadn't just lost Tomas as a potential lover, but as a dear friend as well.

# *FIVE*

DAWN CREPT THROUGH the trees to gently rouse the sleeping group. Tallis watched as Donovan and Rosslyn groggily got to their feet as Tomas quietly moved around them. He moved like a ghost, as if the life in him had fled with the darkness. He moved impassively, eyes never lingering on anything for long, and his mind far away, somewhere no one could hope to reach him.

The elves had been clicking to one another all night. It made everyone tense and anxious to be on their way to where they hoped to find the Sipsi clan. If they were where Rosslyn thought they would be, then they had a good day's ride ahead. The trick would be getting there while avoiding any of the elves who might still be lingering in the area just out of sight.

Tallis's strange connection with the old trees had protected them so far, offering guidance without words and pledging a handful of animals to watch over them to combat those under the tremps's thrall, but that had largely been when they were stationary and much farther away from the Guldar Forest. They didn't know if the help would remain as constant as it had been the closer to their destination they got, nor did they know if it would help when they were moving at a quicker pace now that they had the horses.

It was something Tallis knew they were all thinking and she wished she could ease their minds with a definitive answer one way or another. But the truth was, she simply did not know. It was easy to pretend she had all the answers, that she knew what lay ahead for them, and that they were as safe as anyone could be with the help of the forest. But in her heart, she knew that was not the truth.

Detaching herself from the group, she made her way over to one of the ancient birch trees. As she approached, she could feel the familiar, tingling of power crawling up through her toes and all the way to the top of her head.

Tallis had been trying to avoid delving deeper into the mysterious connection she had with the trees ever since Tomas had recounted to them the legend of the demon. While she sincerely doubted such a story was true, she did not wish to explore her connection any further.

Part of her hoped if she ignored it, then it would dissipate. Then she would not have to hide a secret that would have her tossed into the mad houses in Linlith if anyone outside of her friends ever found out. But she could not deny the connection any longer. As her heart continued to plummet further than she would have ever felt possible after what had happened with Tomas, she needed to be connected to something that offered her nothing but warm acceptance.

She was always amazed that the trees all seemed to have distinct personalities. While all seemed glad to have her around, some were more frightened than others. While some were generally content and offered nothing but warm affection, much like a grandmother would, others had been driven mad by the loss of what they all referred to as their children, and clung too tightly to anyone that could return what was lost back to them.

She wondered what this tree would be like, and hoped that it offered the kind of solace when she had first clung to one of these ancient trees shortly after her mother had died. Glancing over her shoulder once more to her friends, she turned her attention to the elderly birch and gingerly placed her hand on its moss-dappled trunk.

Tallis did not have to wait long to have the tree grip a hold of her mind, melding its emotions with her own. The tree was nervous; it could feel the lost children nearby, but it could not reach them. Tallis could sense the plunging feeling of desperation as the tree tried communicating with her in a way that was much more direct than anything she had ever before experienced. It almost sounded as if the tree had a voice but was unsure how to use words. Snatches of wordless melodies in a distant baritone flooded through her mind along with the sensations the tree was drowning her in. It felt almost like the dream she had where the forest had warned her of the tawny owls that were watching them as they slept, but the tree could not form the words to speak.

She tried to send soothing thoughts back, as she could feel the frustration pulsating through her hand and into the rest of her body. She was not sure if it was working, as the tree gave up with trying to formulate

actual words with which to speak. Eventually, just as
Tallis was about to rejoin the group, she began to see
flashes of an impossibly old yew located in a damp
clearing of the forest.

Tallis could almost smell the crisp clean scent of
decomposing leaves and the rich earthy aroma of damp
soil, as if from a recent rain beneath her feet. Soft green
grass grew around the tree in an almost perfect circle,
separating the little yew from its much more majestic
oak brethren. The yew was not the biggest of trees she
had come across so far, but it had a trunk nearly as wide
as some of the tallest trees Tallis had ever seen.

The bark was almost bone white with age and it
made its dark green diamond-shaped leaves clustered
towards the top of the tree appear all the more vibrant.
The mess of foliage atop the tree gave it a bright-green
mane that cascaded down the back of the yew to nearly
brush the ground beneath it. The boughs were such a
tangled mess of interlocking branches that it was
impossible to see anything that could be hiding in the
top of the tree. But while the branches of the yew were
so cluttered with tightly-packed leaves, the rest of the
tree was surprisingly bare. Unlike the rest Tallis had
encountered so far, not even moss grew on the fat trunk
of the tree.

The trunk itself looked as if several trees had at one
time grown on the same spot. It caused gaping holes
all around the yew tree that created a dark cavern in the
center. It was impossible to know if it was merely age
and rot that had caused several places of the wide trunk
to cave in to show what otherwise appeared to be a
hollow center, or if it was actually the remnants of
other yew trees that no longer existed as individuals.

One such gap looked like a mouth screaming in perpetual agony. And while such a sight would normally leave Tallis feeling chilled to the bone, the birch tree reassured her that the yew she was seeing was something important, as if it were a long-lost friend worth finding, one that could help and provide answers to the questions burning in Tallis's heart.

Tallis tried to tell the birch that she did not understand its meaning, nor where this old yew tree was even located. Selkirk was full of yews, and who was to say this particular yew, while very distinct in the way it appeared, would be easy to find, or if it was even nearby. But the tree either did not understand her, or it did not hear her the same way she heard it. Instead, it kept portraying the feeling of urgency in its distant baritone melody and that Tallis needed to find this particular yew. Unfortunately, Tallis did not recognize the area the tree was showing her, and she was not sure if she could find it.

She took her hand from the tree and stared at the place on the bark where her hand had just been. She had never known the trees to try so hard to actually speak. Beyond the one instance where the tree took over her dream with its dire warnings, they seemed perfectly content to share their slow-moving emotions with her and have Tallis extrapolate any meaning she wanted to from those fragments. But much like the rest of her journey so far, this was something she had never before experienced, and she was unsure what to do with the information she had just been given.

Turning her back on the old birch, Tallis, deep in thought, slowly made her way to the group. The image of the yew tree was still burning in her mind's eye; it

85

had been so clear and distinct that even the aroma's she thought she had smelled still lingered.

She glanced about their camp as if she expected to see this ancient yew nearby, but when she did not, she was hardly surprised. The tree stood alone in a little clearing in one of any number of forests all around Selkirk. It would have been too much to ask for the one tree she was supposed to find to already be within arm's length.

Tallis's reprieve was broken when Rosslyn handed her a piece of smoke dried haddock and a hunk of the brown oat bread purchased the day before. Tentatively, Tallis chewed the fish as she watched Donovan prepare the horses for the journey ahead as she tried to take her mind from what she had just experienced. She would not forget what she saw, but for now, she had other things to focus on.

They would have to double up on the horses, and since Donovan was the largest of their party, and Tallis the smallest, it made sense they would need to ride together to help balance out the load the horses had to carry. At least it saved her from an awkward situation with Tomas once again. Though she was not sure how he would take to having to share a horse with Rosslyn.

Donovan led the two horses over and Tallis was finally able to give them a true appraisal. The stockier brown horse, while shorter, seemed much stronger than the elegant dappled mare. The brown horse had once been wild and it stomped its foot in impatience, its spirit used to running free and not being tethered whenever it wished to roam unbridled. The mare was much gentler; she had grown used to life in a stable where the great ladies of Fordoun would take her for pleasure rides around the city. Occasionally, she tossed her gray mane as if she found being out in the forest to be utterly beneath her.

Tallis stroked their heads and smiled. She may have been reading too much into the horse's behavior, and giving them personalities they did not possess, but either way, Tallis felt like Donovan could not have picked two better horses for their journey.

"Do either of you know how to ride?" Donovan asked Rosslyn and Tomas as they joined Tallis around the horses. As they both shook their heads in response, Donovan handed Tomas the mare's reigns. "Then you'll need to ride this old girl. She should be easy to handle for a pair of novices."

Tomas and Rosslyn exchanged glances with one another, neither of them looking keen on the idea of sharing a horse. Tomas glanced desperately at Tallis for just a moment, as if hoping she would take this opportunity to rescue him and give him one more chance to be with her. But in the brief instance their eyes connected, Tomas lowered his dusky green gaze to the ground, as if the memory of the night before was still too great to face and the pain of her words still too sharp for him to bear.

Unfortunately, Tomas's lack of subtly ensured that everyone saw the brief flicker between them. To break the awkward moment, Rosslyn gently bumped Tomas with her shoulder. "Don't worry, I won't bite. You aren't my type, anyway."

Tomas gave her a questioning stare for a moment before seeming to understand what she was talking about. Blushing, he looked down and stammered, "That's not ... I'm not afraid of that. I just ... I don't know, it just seemed...."

"What is your type, anyway, Rosslyn?" Donovan asked as they carefully got on the horses.

Rosslyn chuckled nervously as she gripped Tomas's waist to keep her balance as the gentle mare began to move. "Why do you want to know? Should your Nessa be concerned about your feelings for me, Donovan?"

Donovan shifted on the little brown horse as he got comfortable and tried to give Tallis as much room as possible. "Hardly," he retorted. "You just seem to not be all that particular over whom you spend your time with, if you catch my meaning."

Rosslyn scoffed. "Oi! I'll have you know, I do, indeed, have a type; I don't share my affection with just anyone. I'm just not as prude about it as the rest of you lot. In the clans, we encourage people to act upon their feelings, regardless of whether or not the couple is married. Even if that happens to mean it's two women wanting to spend a bit of time together. I just happen to find a variety of people attractive, both men and women. If they are witty, gorgeous, and have a mysterious allure, then I'm interested."

Rosslyn could feel Tomas tensing as she spoke. Laughing, Rosslyn said, "What makes you more uncomfortable, Ser Would-Be-Brother? The idea of me being with a man out of the marriage bed, or being with a woman in that way?" While Rosslyn's tone was light and teasing, it was still clear she expected Tomas to give her an answer.

"I don't ... I mean, I was just taught that kind of intimacy was wrong, but I ... I mean I don't think I really mind it or care. I don't know how you could be with another woman, but...." Tomas shrugged and gave up, his face a bright scarlet from being so uncomfortable with the conversation.

Rosslyn shook her head, her thick and tight black curls lashing around her face with the movement. "I can never understand you people. It's the one thing I really miss being with my clan. There, we treated sex the way it should be treated. Sure, you should do it with respect, but if two adults want to share in that, then they bloody well should. Sex is wonderful, fun, and one of the best things two people can share. You lot under your king and the strict laws of Wodan all treat it like it's a big dirty secret meant to be spoken of only behind closed doors and engaged in secret. It's truly a wonder any of you sods manage to have babies at all!"

Tomas scratched the back of his head, his face still burning with how uncomfortable he was. "Can we just stop talking about this now, please?"

Tallis glanced over her shoulder at him and couldn't help but smile; Tomas was wonderfully adorable when he was uncomfortable and unsure of how to act. Winking rakishly at him as if nothing had changed between them, she asked Rosslyn, "So, Roz, do you fancy me then? I have a wonderful mysterious quality, if I do say so myself."

Tomas's eyes widened in shock and surprise at Tallis's brazen behavior before he dropped his eyes and fixed them firmly on Donovan's horse.

Peering over Tomas's shoulder at Tallis, Rosslyn said with a slight purr to her voice, "Sorry, but no. Don't get me wrong, you are stunningly beautiful, Tally, but I need a woman who can keep up with me in a tavern, and you just can't do that yet. Maybe if you practiced more with our Ser Soon-To-Be-Brother, then, well, who knows?"

Tomas's face managed to pale under his embarrassed blush at Rosslyn's suggestion. The sight of his pallor sent Rosslyn into a furious fit of laughter at how successfully she was able to tease the young man and how easy it was for her to make him so uncomfortable.

Tallis couldn't help but laugh in return; Rosslyn's laughter had always been infectious like that. But one look at the hurt that was beginning to blossom on Tomas's face from having been a part of a joke he did not find particularly funny, caused Tallis's laughter to die in her throat. Giving Tomas an apologetic look, she turned around and kept her eyes forward, kicking the once wild horse to force him into a trot and put more distance between her and Tomas.

DONOVAN LISTENED TO the exchange with mild disinterest. While he had been curious about Rosslyn's preference, he did not care for the preaching. Regardless, he did not care who or what Rosslyn was interested in, she was a Sipsi at heart and he could not pretend to understand her kind. He only wanted to get the group focused on something besides the sullen atmosphere that was following them like a rain cloud as they moved forward. But he could tell with how quickly Tallis had stopped laughing and the way that she had pushed their horse on, that the conversation had found a way to strike too close to home.

Donovan glanced over his shoulder at Tomas as he struggled lightly with getting the mare to match the once wild horse's gait. When he was convinced that Tomas would not get thrown off the mare's back, and was still a little distance behind them, he turned to Tallis, "I like him. Tomas is a good man, despite the shite Rosslyn and I give him."

Tallis stiffened at her cousin's unexpected words and stuttered in response, "Pardon? Where did that come from?"

Donovan shrugged. "Just this banter and the hard time we've given him made me think of it. That, and you two are really awful at hiding how you feel about each other. I've known since almost the moment we started this journey that Tomas has had a type of fondness for you. Seems like you finally started to see him in the same way. Wouldn't have something to do with him retrieving Aunt Lana's ring, would it? Doesn't matter. I just want you to know that I think he's a good man. He'd be good for you when this is all over."

Exhaling slowly, she said in a soft whisper, "I didn't know it had been going on so long or that it was that obvious to everyone but me. But it doesn't matter what he feels or what I feel. It's too dangerous right now to even pretend like there could be anything between us. I told him as much last night and it … well, I think I may have officially broken my first heart."

Donovan could hear the sadness and loneliness in Tallis's voice. Even though this seemed to be harder on Tomas, he knew that Tallis wished that the situation had been different, and that she, too, could view love and intimacy with the same kind of candor that Rosslyn did.

But Donovan knew Tallis, and he knew that her sense of honor would never allow her to indulge in such feelings, even if they were mutually shared. If there was the possibility that the relationship may ultimately end up going nowhere, or that it might cause one of them more pain if their quest did not end well, then Tallis would not want to risk the potential hurt that would follow if she allowed herself to be open with how she felt.

Glancing over his shoulder once more to make sure Tomas could not overhear them, Donovan said, "I understand, Tally, but I think you're wrong. Yes, it is better to focus on the task at hand without distractions, but you don't have to be that cold to the poor man. I want you to have a real life when this is all said and done, and it may be nice if Tomas is a part of that. If you want him to be a part of your life, or if you want to even be able to have something with him when we get home, make sure he knows that and doesn't just think that your feelings are a mistake. Does that make sense?"

Tallis sighed. "What good would that even do, Donovan? It's not like we can do anything about how we feel. Would it not just be easier to kill it now so that...," she trailed off, her voice barely above a whisper, "so that it won't hurt more later if anything were to happen to him or me?"

Donovan shrugged, the action forcing Tallis to raise her head once again. "What would be the point of potentially saving all of Selkirk if you cannot have a life or a family on the other side of this crisis? What's the point in stopping these tremps from ripping apart the life we know, if you don't want to actually live at the end of it all?"

He asked without a hint of accusation or disappointment in his voice. He was seriously asking Tallis why she would do all of this if she thought that it would be pointless for her to have something good when things were put back the way they were meant to be. Donovan could tell by her silence that Tallis had never truly considered these things before, that she had never really given herself the opportunity to ask just what it was she wanted.

A gasp of laughter erupted from her, startling Donovan before Tallis gave him a hug. "You're right, Donovan. Nessa is a lucky girl to have a man so willing to risk himself righting the world just so he might have a true and happy life with her. And I think … I think I want that, too."

Donovan squeezed her hand and said quickly as Tomas and Rosslyn managed to get their mare to catch up, "Then make sure he knows that, Tallis. Just be sure you both know that it'll still have to wait until all this madness has passed."

TALLIS DID NOT speak to Tomas just then about what she and Donovan had discussed. Instead, the group largely remained silent as they passed through the shadows of the ancient trees, wary that the elves they had heard from the night before were still lurking nearby. They only dismounted when they felt it necessary to give the horses a rest, otherwise they never paused in their long trek up the Noldor River to where it split off and became the Elwe River. But despite the rest stops and Tomas and Rosslyn's timid horse riding abilities, they were still making good time, and Rosslyn predicted they should reach the clan early the next day.

As they went, Tallis watched the scenery change around her. She noticed that the Noldor River was not as brown and murky as the Inglar River had been, as the refuse from the refugees and the ashes from the burnt towns infiltrated its normally clear water. It gave Tallis hope that perhaps the wake of devastation the elves brought with them had not come this far north. In fact, if Tallis ignored the unsettling clicks of the elves from the night before, this part of Selkirk was exceptionally peaceful and beautiful.

The trees in this part of the Uldor Forest all carried the ancient connection that had become a constant form of peace and safety as they progressed across the island. It made the gentle breezes that came through their branches tinkle with soft music and give fresh life to everything around them as the tree boughs gently swayed as if waving the group forward.

With Lake Celebrian and the main road being the preferred method of travel for those going between Isildor and Fordoun, this stretch of Selkirk was untouched by man. The animals seemed less skittish, the trees were free of any marks of cutting, and the ground was covered in dead leaves that hadn't been disturbed in centuries. With each step the horses took, Tallis could smell the rich and earthy fragrance of the leaves as they were pushed into the soft ground under their weight.

The quiet and natural beauty of the area gave her a feeling of true peace, and a sense of belonging that had been absent growing up. She knew in the back of her mind that such thoughts and feelings should be wrong, that she should have felt at peace back amongst the people of her hometown, but there was something familiar about this place, even though she had never been here before.

They stopped once more as darkness began to make the shadows outnumber the sunbeams that filtered through the trees. Rosslyn was impatient; she knew they were near the clan, and after having missed them once already, she did not want to tempt fate again and find that the clan had moved on once more. As much as Tallis wished to give her friend the solace she sought in pressing on and arriving at the clan that night, she could not risk the horses not being able to see where they were going. Coupled with navigating their way through territory that seemed to have the most elven activity since they had first left the Brethil Forest, Donovan and Tallis decided they needed to stop for the night.

"Why don't you stop whining about it," Donovan snapped. "And instead, help us prepare for what we can expect when we reach this clan your brother spoke of. What're they like?"

Rosslyn glared at him before relenting. Plopping down on the ground, she began fishing in her pack for various food items from which she could make their supper. After finding what she was looking for, she said, "From what Munro said in his letter, this is like no clan he has ever come into contact with before. Years ago, my pop spent some time with a clan that sounds like them, and if they're one in the same, we'll need to be careful."

Tallis helped Donovan secure the horses for the night before joining Rosslyn on the ground. As she helped her light a fire, Tallis asked, "Why's that? Are they truly so different from your family's old clan?"

Rosslyn did not look up as she spoke; instead, she focused her gaze on the food she was attempting to make. "There are only a few clans who have an alliance with the tremps, and all of them are very dangerous. For whatever reason, they feel kindred towards those nasty aresholes and would rather have dealings with them than anyone else. They don't even venture into the towns and cities for goods like the rest of the clans. Instead, they trade with the elves and, if my pop can be believed, sometimes that includes trading unwanted children to the tremps. Though I suspect he only said that to keep me in line."

She paused for a moment as if she were unsure how to go on. Then, with an uncharacteristic air of solemnity, she said, "This clan is one even the others who claim to be friendly with the tremps fear. Their disregard for the laws of your King Ailbeart goes so far as to be openly hostile to any outside of their clan. My pop even once said they could understand the elves and all their clicking; though, I don't know if they could understand *everything* the elves said.

"They'll camp near the cities and even Isildor on occasion, and for no other reason than to show opposition to the laws of the land, and then they'll raid any trading caravan they happen to come across. They live by a perverted Sipsi law that no other clan recognizes, and all of us shun to varying degrees.

"It's … it's very strange they decided to answer my brother's message at all, let alone invite us to seek them out for answers. I'd say we need to be cautious when we find them, but I think that goes beyond saying. Don't eat or drink anything you didn't watch them prepare for yourself, and sleep as lightly as you can. Any clan that claims such close kinship with those feral beasts cannot be trusted, even if they have the answers we're looking for."

A weighty silence followed her warning as they digested what she said and its heavy meaning. After what seemed like ages, Donovan asked through gritted teeth, "And why is it, exactly, that you're only telling us this now? Did you not think this might've been important for us, as we ventured closer to this clan every day?"

Rosslyn shut her eyes tightly and as she slowly opened them again, she said, "I didn't want you to think we were all like that. And I was hoping I was wrong, that the clan we were looking for wasn't the one my pop used to tell me scary stories about. Now that it looks like they are one and the same, well, it became more pertinent.

"We Sipsis are good people. We just don't think living under the laws of your king is the right way to live. We don't mean anyone any harm, nor do we judge anyone for the way they live. We're supposed to be nonjudgmental, and we let everyone live their lives the way they want to. Even when we moved to Kincardine, my parents tried to make sure we always kept true to that. They encouraged me to keep my Galon Sipsiwn, even if it got me in trouble.

"This other clan … is rooted in opposition to everything the Sipsi clans stand for. I'm not saying any of this is a good reason for not saying something sooner, but that's the only reason I've got."

Donovan's face reddened as his anger continued to grow. Silencing him with a hand, Tallis said, "It doesn't matter now. We'd have had to go and see them one way or another, anyway. Is there anything else we should know? Anything we *should* or *shouldn't* do when we get to this clan?"

Rosslyn shrugged. "They will insult your way of life and your beliefs. Don't give in to it and argue back with them. Be polite, and keep sight of your possessions at all times. My pop didn't have any particular trouble with them when he was there, but that was a long time ago. I can't say more beyond that; I really don't know what it'll be like."

Donovan was still not ready to let the matter drop, but no one wanted any more of Rosslyn and his bickering—especially Tallis.

Putting his hand on Donovan's shoulder, Tomas said, "Come, help me with the traps for tonight. With all the elven activity going on, I'd like to have them doubled up." With a muffled grumble, Donovan nodded and willingly went to help.

Tallis watched them go, momentarily upset she would not be given the opportunity just yet to speak to Tomas about what she and Donovan had discussed. Still, her heart felt lighter, and she did not worry over not getting the chance to speak with him, nor if he would forgive her. Something told her that Tomas was not lost to her just yet, and if she did not get the opportune moment to speak with him tonight, she would soon. Besides, Tallis had other things to concern herself with, like the nausea and headache that had plagued her around Lake Mithrim starting to return.

She had hoped to be free of this mystery illness, but it seemed that whenever they began to make their way to the Guldar Forest, her illness was ready to rear its ugly head. It was not so bad yet where she thought her insomnia may return, or if she touched one of the trees that it would shrink from her touch and deny her the protection that had kept them safe so far. She just hoped that whatever answers this clan had, the origins of her lingering sickness would be one of them.

Keeping her illness to herself for the time being, Tallis helped Rosslyn as she sullenly prepared their food. Tallis was a little upset that Rosslyn had not warned them before now about what danger they may be walking into, but at the same time, Tallis knew it would not have changed anything.

Regardless of how dangerous this clan was rumored to be, Tallis would still go to them and see what they knew about the elves and why they all of a sudden retained some of their ability to speak. She had come too far to allow a story to scare her off now.

# THE PRICE OF KNOWING

## SIX

TALLIS DOZED LIGHTLY that night. Her stomach was churning and her head had begun to throb the longer they stayed this close to the Guldar Forest. She was trying to take advantage of any sleep she could get before her crippling pain returned, but she was doing a poor job of it. She was uncomfortable, which made sleep illusive no matter how hard she tried.

Every sound seemed to jar her awake just as she was beginning to fall asleep. She tried to calm her nerves by telling herself that Tomas was keeping watch, and between him and the traps, nothing would be able to take them unawares. Still, she was feeling uneasy, as if she could feel countless eyes watching her as she tried to force herself to sleep.

Tomas must have felt the same, as she heard him lightly get up to inspect something farther in the forest. She listened to his nearly silent footfalls as he walked farther and farther away. Tallis did not worry as long as she could hear him moving around. He thought he was being as silent as possible and Tallis never had the heart to tell him that he was not as sneaky as he thought he was—at least not for her sensitive hearing.

So amused was Tallis by the image of Tomas trying to sneak through the forest in his thick and clunky boots, that she was not sure just when she could no longer make him out. Holding her breath, she strained her hearing to differentiate between all the soft sounds of animals moving in the dark for the distinct crunch of Tomas walking. She counted the moments that trickled by as the silence around her began to thicken and stretch for what seemed an impossibly long time.

Exhaling slowly, she sat upright and peered through the darkness. She could see very little in the sparse moonlight that filtered down from the trees. But even in the dim light, she could not see any shape that even remotely looked like Tomas. Rising to her feet, Tallis gripped the hilts of her daggers and went searching, hoping that he had just gotten himself lost on the way back from relieving a call of nature.

Moving as silently as a fox, Tallis attempted to follow any trail she could find that would lead her to Tomas. Moving so silently was no easy feat; she had to deliberately place each of her feet in slow, arching steps, and crane her body so as to make sure the tight armor did not betray her. She no longer worried about the formfitting, hardened leather with its fur lining and dark gray color—even with its red studs where the leather was reinforced—creaking or making her stand out in the night, even the metal coverings over her knees and elbows did not cause any worry. It was her chainmail she was most concerned over. The short-sleeve chainmail tunic occasionally sounded as if a gentle rain had begun to fall, which would be fine if it was indeed raining. Each time she heard the soft *clink* of the chainmail, Tallis winced and gripped her wide, off-white leather belt with all its pouches and the rings holding her daggers to still her irritation. Creeping slowly ever forward, it wasn't until she reached Tomas's first ring of tripwires that she saw him.

Looming over a bound and gagged Tomas were five shapes of varying sizes. Tallis could not see their faces, as each seemed to wear heavy cloaks made to look more like walking bushes with patches of moss and lichen strewn over their backs and sides. One of the figures carried a long, cylindrical, rusty lantern that had a thick and squat candle burning away inside. The lantern had no doors, and was as far from decorative as any lantern Tallis had ever seen. One side of the lantern was open and the light the lamp gave was just enough for Tallis to see the figures and nothing more. But she at least took comfort in knowing that Tomas was not surrounded by elves.

Her heart began to pound in her ears as she watched the figures push Tomas around as he kneeled on the ground with his hands bound. Tallis was fighting the urge to burst from where she was concealed in perfect shadow to rescue him. But she did not know who these people were, or if there were more figures lurking just out of sight. She doubted they were knights, but she could not be sure. And until she had a better idea as to who they were and the kind of weapons they had, she could not risk bursting from her hiding place if it meant she could potentially get Tomas killed.

Silently, she tugged the hood of her armor over her

head ensuring no flash of light would reveal her bright blonde hair, unsheathed her trident shaped daggers, and moved around the tree she was hiding behind. She could hear a hushed murmur as the figures spoke in low whispers to one another, all of which was impossible for Tallis to discern. Just as she was beginning to think only five people had found their little camp, she heard thrashing coming towards her, and suddenly seven figures stood where there were once only five.

Holding her breath, Tallis swallowed the yelp of surprise that welled in her throat as the two other figures roughly tossed Rosslyn down next to Tomas. No longer trying to stay quiet, a large man the shape of a tree trunk said, "We got to the knight before this one even knew we was there. Lucky break that, 'cause this knight, you see, he could have easily taken us. Bloke's sword is nearly as broad as a house, it is. Couldn't find no one else, this must be that Tallis girl the clan leaders told us to get."

Tallis cursed herself and hoped that Rosslyn and Tomas had the presence of mind to play along for the time being. If they believed that Rosslyn was Tallis, then at least Rosslyn would know she was still free and would do everything in her power to rescue them. Tallis sent a silent prayer to Wodan in hopes that Donovan was not seriously hurt, and desperately tried to come up with a plan to free her friends from, what she assumed, were seven armed assailants.

"This ain't Tallis," a woman said as she pushed the hood back from her cloak to better look at Rosslyn. She grabbed Rosslyn by the chin and none too gently jerked her face around as she said, "Leader Alexine says the girls' got to be slight. *Slight*, Blane. This girl look slight to you? Leader Durell may not know a slight girl from a house, but Alexine … least Durell's got a smart wife or we'd all be dead."

The woman who spoke was almost as short as a child, with a mess of thick curly light brown hair and fierce dark brown eyes. She sneered down at Rosslyn and pinched her face roughly, "Who are you, woman? What're you doing here?"

Tallis held her breath as she continued to slide around the tree, trying to get behind the two biggest of the group, the man named Blane and another who had hazel eyes that looked almost bone-white in the lantern's glow.

Rosslyn spat on the ground at the short woman's feet and sneered. She gave the woman the once-over and said with anger coursing through her voice like a well-aimed arrow, "This is how you treat a member of another clan? If my leaders knew this was the kind of reception you gave one of your own kind—"

That was when the short woman backhanded Rosslyn and said in a low whisper full of contempt, "You ain't *my* kind, woman. You ain't nothing but piss to me. Now once more or I start taking fingers, who are you and what're you doing here?"

Another woman put her hand on her short companion's shoulder. "Tavie, no need to be rough. She does have the look of the clan about her. Maybe we made a mistake?"

Tavie swatted her hand away and sneered. "Don't be stupid, Freya. Course this is them. It was a clan member asked us about knowing anything about a human speaking to them trees, remember? With the elves finally taking back what's there's, who else would be camping out in the forest except Tallis and whatever group she's running with?"

Turning her attention back to Rosslyn, she took out a dagger and jerked it up under Rosslyn's throat. "So? Out with it, or maybe I give you to my partners Blane or Ivar here to have fun with before we give you over to our elven friends."

Tallis glanced at the two men Tavie mentioned. Blane may have been as wide as a tree, but he looked none too bright as his dark blue eyes stared blankly down at Rosslyn and nowhere else. He did not even seem concerned they may have been missing someone else from the campsite they had just stumbled upon.

Ivar was a different matter, however. His hazel eyes looked over Rosslyn with an evil hunger. He rolled his broad shoulders as he ran his tongue over chapped lips, as if he would rather eat Rosslyn than anything else. He was the oldest of the group, with hair that had already gone completely gray. Between the two, Tallis was far more concerned about Ivar than she was Blane.

Rosslyn jutted out her chin defiantly. "I have no idea what you're talking about. After getting separated when Dumfry fell, my husband and I were travelling with our hired bodyguard to get back to our clan. You want a clan war on your hands by abusing us like this, then go ahead. But it's your funeral, you trollop."

Tallis was expecting Tavie to backhand Rosslyn once again, but, instead, she spun on her heel and kicked Tomas in the gut, forcing all the air from his lungs. Tallis had to bite her lip to keep from screaming in fury as Tomas bent over, sputtering on his gag as he struggled to catch his breath.

Rosslyn began struggling like a wet cat. "You bitch! You leave him alone!"

Tavie stroked her chin and grinned wickedly. "He ain't your husband, woman. You may be from the clans, but that fool ain't. He's got no sense in his head when it comes to being out in these woods."

Motioning with her chin to the man holding the lantern, he silently moved to Tomas and grabbed him by his hair, forcing his head back. Tavie moved to Tomas's exposed neck and put her blade to his throat. "You tell me what I want to know, or I bleed him like a pig and give you to Blane and Ivar. Do we have an understanding?"

Rosslyn's eyes shifted to Tomas who was still trying to regain his composure. Tallis could see her brow crinkling in despair as Rosslyn tried to figure out what to do, for if Freya's nervous fidgeting was any indication, Tavie's threats were anything but bluster.

Tallis knew she had one shot to get this right if she wanted any hope of getting Rosslyn and Tomas out of there alive, but she was finding it hard to focus on a plan. Her head was pounding and her stomach churned like a tankard of water aboard a sinking ship. She wasn't sure if it was her mystery illness coming back in full swing, or the realization that the clan they had been trying to find this entire time was bent on capturing her as well.

She needed Tavie to move her dagger away from Tomas's throat first and foremost, though, or he would be dead before she could get to him. The pounding of her nervous heart did not help the situation, and she was finding it hard to believe she was the only one that could hear its thundering.

"Oi! All right, all right. I'll tell you everything," Rosslyn said, eyes wide and frantic like a cornered deer. "I'm ... I'm Tallis. I'm the one you're looking for."

Tavie sneered and moved the blade away from Tomas's neck, only to slice Rosslyn along the cheek. "Don't lie to me. I know you ain't Tallis. She's got a very specific look and you ain't got it. You lie to me again and we begin the *real* fun."

That's when Tallis decided to take her chance.

Slipping through the shadows, she crept up behind Blane and Ivar and positioned her daggers firmly against their backs. Through gritted teeth, Tallis said with a tone that could chill a dead man's blood, "Let my friends go and I promise to let you leave this place alive. Hurt them again, though, and all bets are off. What've you done with the knight back at our camp?"

Freya covered her mouth to keep a squeal of surprise from escaping while Tavie stared at Tallis. She still could not see them all that clearly, but of all of those assembled, save Freya and a slight young man with bronze skin, dark brown hair, and shocking pale blue eyes, they all looked like they were born killers.

Licking her lips, Tavie purred, "Now *that* I believe. If you're what you're supposed to be, I doubt anyone is going to walk away from this unscathed. Your big knight is fine; you'd be better off worrying about yourself right now, lass."

"Let them go," Tallis repeated as she pressed her daggers further against Blane and Ivar's backs, causing their eyes to bulge in pain.

Tavie put her hands up. "How about a trade then.

You come with us and we let them go. More than fair, if I do say so myself."

"Why would I go with you anywhere?" Tallis asked with a grimace of contempt as she kicked Blane and Ivar in the back of the legs, forcing them to their knees so she could better see the rest of the group. She tried not to look at Tomas or Rosslyn, afraid that if she broke eye contact with Tavie, they would see the depths of her feelings for her friends and use that to further hurt them, or get her to agree to more of their ridiculous terms.

"Tell her, Kincaid," Tavie said, motioning to the man with the lantern who was still holding on to Tomas's hair with his free hand.

"Because we know what you are, Tallis," Kincaid said in a sing-song manner. "Our leaders, Alexine and Durell, know all there is to know about *who* you are and *where* you came from. They know *why* you can commune with the trees, and they know *why* the elves are now saying your name. You come with us, you get those answers. You don't, well, why wouldn't you come with us? After all, we know that's why you're here."

Tallis would not falter. She had no doubt they did, indeed, have these answers. After all, it sounded like they already knew a fair deal about her without them ever having met before. But Tallis also knew they were not interested in simply giving her this information and allowing her to continue on her way. No, if they had wanted to carry her off in the middle of the night, then they would have no intention of letting her go if she went with them, willingly or not.

Still not looking at Tomas or Rosslyn, even though

she could feel their eyes burning on her face, she looked at her would-be captors one by one, as if she were seriously considering the offer.

Freya was a sweet-faced young woman who looked to be about Tallis's age. She had strawberry-blonde hair and large hazel eyes set in the middle of a pale round face littered with freckles. One look at her and her nervous twitching, and Tallis knew that Freya would run away and pose no trouble.

Kincaid, however, looked as sleazy as he sounded. While he may have been able to purr with a charm that Tallis had no doubt found many unwilling victims suddenly agreeing to his schemes, he did not have the looks to match his magnetism. His face was covered in red pit marks and cuts from scuffles in his youth. He was also starting to go bald, making the few stringy black hairs he had look all the more thin. His harsh brown eyes held no sympathy or remorse, and the only comfort Tallis could take was that he would have to release Tomas or discard his lantern before he could defend himself.

Then there were the two other shrouded men.

One was darker than Rosslyn with a deep brown eye that seemed to get lost in his angular face, and a large scar running from the middle of his forehead down over the other eye, causing it to go milky white and completely blind. He looked like a capable man, but Tallis hoped she could use his blindside to her advantage before he was able to ready any weapons.

Lastly, there was the bronze-skinned man with the alarmingly pale blue eyes and dense dark brown hair that blended in perfectly with the night. The man gave Tallis a curious look, one Tallis could not quite discern. He appeared to be curious about her, but there was still something slightly dishonest about his stance. His hands hung limply at his sides as if he were trying too hard to look harmless. There was something about him that made Tallis nervous, though she could not say about what. Still, he only looked to have a bow, and it would take him time to fire anything at her.

Blane and Ivar would cause Tallis no trouble, as they were already at her mercy. Tavie, obviously, was a woman not only unafraid of violence, but one who, no doubt, reveled in it. She was already armed and stood between Tallis and her friends. Despite her short stature, Tallis knew she would be the most dangerous of those currently assembled.

Meeting Tavie's eyes once more, she carefully tightened her grip on her daggers and moved her feet into a better position so as to move quickly without anyone noticing. Sighing, Tallis tried to make it seem as if she were giving in, "You leave me very little choice."

Tavie smiled wickedly and lowered her sharp dagger, believing she had Tallis over a barrel. Boldly, she took a half-step towards Tallis as if she were going to grab her.

Then Tallis acted.

Pushing all her weight down, she forced her daggers deep into the spine of Ivar and Blane, forcing them to the ground with quick yelps of surprise, pain, and death. Landing on top of them, Tallis pushed down even harder, using the momentum to twist her legs up over her head and using the force to flip herself up and kick Tavie hard in the face with both of her steel-capped boots as she freed her daggers and righted herself.

As predicted, Freya screamed and fled into the night to return to wherever the rest of her clan resided. Kincaid dropped his lantern as he tried to wrench the rusty short sword from his belt—but he never got it free. Tallis flung one of her daggers which sunk deep into his throat, the two prongs that gave her dagger its trident shape further slicing open his neck as it buried itself up to the hilt into him.

By then, Tavie had recovered enough to struggle to her feet. Just as Tallis rounded on her, though, Rosslyn was already on the small woman, hitting her and clawing at her face like a wild animal. Tallis had never seen Rosslyn act so ferociously before, but it allowed Tallis to focus on the two remaining men.

The dark man with his one good eye had picked up his axe by then, and looked like he was about to rush at Tallis, when he suddenly fell forward as if pushed. Tallis's eyes widened as she saw the long shaft of an arrow protruding from his back as the bronze-skinned man stood behind him, bow pressed firmly against his face. He briefly met Tallis's eyes before lowering his bow, and standing awkwardly where he stood, making no other move.

Spinning her dagger in her hand, Tallis tore Rosslyn off Tavie only to find that Rosslyn had killed her. The ferocious way Rosslyn had been pounding the woman's head with her fists, and against the unyielding ground, had done its work all too well. Rosslyn's honey brown eyes widened in horror as she realized what she had done, but she soon recovered herself and spat on the ground once more near where the bloody Tavie lay and shrugged Tallis off of her.

Warily, Tallis watched the last man in the group as she carefully untied Tomas and took the gag from his mouth. Lightly cupping his cheek in her hand, she brought up his head so she could better look at him. They were so close their noses nearly touched as Tallis searched his face. "Are you all right? They didn't hurt you, did they?"

Tomas shook his head; it seemed as if only his pride had been hurt at needing Tallis to rescue him. Tallis gave a laugh of relief as she pulled him to her in a fierce hug and did not let go. "I thought they were going to kill you. I'm so sorry I didn't get to you sooner."

Swallowing, Tallis pulled back and quickly gave Tomas a peck on the cheek. His eyes widened and he opened his mouth to stammer some response or other, but Tallis stopped him with a shake of her head. "I know I've been cruel and I'm sorry. Donovan can be surprisingly wise when given the chance, and he made me realize that when this is all over and we can actually go home, that I … well, I want to see what it's like to be normal. And I think I'd like it if you were there with me. If you still want that, that is."

Tomas's mouth opened and closed like a fish gasping for breath. She could see the blush creeping up his neck and the joy twinkling in his dusky green eyes. Softly he ran his fingers through the hair on the back of her head, brought their foreheads together, and nodded.

Tallis smiled and briefly squeezed his hand before standing again and twirling her dagger as she addressed the man who still stood with his hands limply at his sides. Rosslyn hadn't once taken her eyes off of him and Tallis could tell by the ridged way she stood she did not trust him, even though he had shot one of his own companions in the back.

Tallis circled him as she retrieved her dagger from Kincaid's throat. "Who are you?" she hissed as she turned to face him once again, pointing her bloodied dagger at his heart.

The man looked to be about five years older than Donovan, but had a childish sparkle in his pale eyes. He would have been handsome, except there was something unsettling about the way he always seemed to be grinning, the smile strained, like it was hiding what he was really thinking.

He shrugged, but with the motion looking like a ripple had caused his arms to flap out uselessly at his side, instead. "Cullen," he said. "That was Rory." He indicated the man he had shot. "Shame really, I liked Rory. Always had a sweet or two hidden away for me. Always gave me a sweet if I was a good boy."

The way he spoke sounded like he was addressing both Tallis as well as some distant memory that was haunting at his side. He was a man walking the fine line of madness, but at the same time, seemed completely aware of everything he was doing.

Cullen's eyes shifted quickly to Rosslyn. "You killed Tavie. Good, good. Didn't like Tavie. She was mean, and would have worn your skin like a cloak, if you'd have let her."

He shifted lightly before addressing Tallis once again, "You are the Tallis? Yes, yes you must be. You move like fast water and you look like…," he mumbled to himself before covering his words with a cough. "I want to help you. My clan waits for you just ahead, but do not go to them. They are not honest. They will tie you up and offer you like dinner to the elves. But I can help, too. Oh, yes … I can be of an even *greater* help."

Tallis raised an eyebrow at Cullen. Something about him made her skin crawl, but she had little choice. Cullen had killed one of his former friends because they were going to hand Tallis over to the tremps. If he had wanted her dead, he'd had the opportunity, and he'd let it go. If Cullen knew the answers to her questions, then she would hear him out, but that did not mean she trusted him.

Turning to Rosslyn, she asked, "Well?"

Rosslyn shrugged and rubbed at the cut on her cheek that Tavie had given her. "He was the one that knocked out Donovan when they grabbed me. That Rory guy had wanted Donovan dead, but he said no."

Tallis nodded and jerked her head back towards their camp. "Come on, then. We've got to leave before that Freya girl comes back with the rest of your clan. I expect you to tell me everything, Cullen. Why your clan did this, as well as everything they seem to know about me."

Cullen gave her a wide smile that seemed a little too excited for their current situation. Plucking his arrow out of Rory's back, he silently followed them as they made their way back to where Donovan lay unconscious. All the while, Tallis exchanged uncertain glances with Tomas and Rosslyn over the mental stability of their newest group member.

# SEVEN

DONOVAN SAT SULLENLY as he nursed his head in his hands. The sun had just dawned over the horizon when they finally stopped moving, and Donovan was just now being caught up on what had occurred that ended with Cullen joining their group.

At Cullen's behest, they continued to follow the Elwe River as it made its way towards the very heart of Selkirk, where the Guldar Forest waited. He assured them, in his unsettling way, that he could keep his clan from following them, and that they needed to continue on as there was no time to waste.

Donovan had taken his advice because it made sense, but it still made him uneasy all the same. Without the horses, as Rory had let them go when they had captured Rosslyn, their journey was going to drag on once again, and they could not afford such delays if Cullen was to be believed.

"So, let me get this straight, these Sipsis managed to get around the traps, lure Tomas into their own trap, knock me out, and then cart Rosslyn away. This is all before Tallis kills three people, Rosslyn one, and you another, leaving one to run away in fear. All the while, your clan is *actually* plotting against us this entire time? Tell me, is this the part where I'm supposed to be surprised that our luck has actually gotten worse?"

Cullen nodded enthusiastically, failing to catch on to Donovan's sarcasm. "Oh, yes. Leaders Alexine and Durell were very specific, you see. They told Tavie to pick a crew to get you. She shouldn't have brought Freya, but Tavie always seemed to have a fondness for pretty Freya. Shouldn't have brought me, either, but I made her. I needed to help you because they were liars. They were going to kill you once they had the Tallis."

Cullen spoke very rapidly and in clipped sentences, his tone ranging from almost giddy to dark with anger, and all in one breath. It was dizzying to listen to him speak and it left everyone more than a little nervous about what kind of madness must plague him.

Donovan narrowed his eyes as he watched Cullen. "My first question is why? Why cart Tallis off like that? And my second is just what exactly is wrong with you?"

Cullen may have been older than Donovan, but in many ways, he acted as if he were still a child. If he was offended at Donovan's question, however, he did not show it, as he grinned in his unnerving way and mussed with his thick brown hair. "Nothing is wrong with me. I know things, lots of things. Things the clan didn't seem to like. I will explain. It all has to do with the Tallis, actually. Good story, but long. Is now a good time?" Cullen cocked his head at them like a bird.

Donovan continued to stare with a look of annoyance mingled with a heavy dose of doubt. Sighing, he took his head from his hands and vigorously rubbed his face. "It's moments like these

---

118

when I really miss the ale we had back home."

Cullen gawked at Donovan, not taking the hint that that was his cue to begin. All four of the companions stared at him, waiting while Cullen sat on the ground glancing between all of them with that same painted on grin on his face.

Eventually, Tallis cleared her throat and said, "Well? Now is as good a time as any for your story, Cullen."

"And be warned," Donovan added, "if this turns out to be another trap, we'll tie you to a tree and leave you for your clan. Understood?"

For a brief moment, something akin to rage flashed across Cullen's pale blue eyes, but it happened so quickly and so briefly that Donovan could not be sure what he saw. No one else seemed to see the quick flash, so he began to believe he had just imagined it as Cullen once again gave Donovan his painted-on grin and rocked back and forth with his hands on his knees. "If that is what the Tallis wishes."

TALLIS FOUND SHE had a hard time searching for the right questions to ask. She had dreamed of this moment for so long, and now that it was finally here, she wasn't sure what to do. She had always imagined it under different circumstances as well. That the clan would be friendlier and would help them on their journey, or that the answer would be simple, and could be whittled down to a massive misunderstanding.

Whatever she had imagined this encounter to be like, she knew this was not it.

Never once did she envision a madman sitting placidly across from her waiting to tell her everything she longed to know. Explaining why she could hear the trees and why they offered her protection in the form of wild cats and hooded crows in return, why certain parts of the forest made her physically ill, why the tremps had first hissed her name years ago, why they waited so long before decimating Kincardine, or why they even cared about her in the first place. She never thought she would be forced to kill even more people to get these answers, either. She did not feel guilty about it the way she had with the knight, but it did not make her feel any better. It was one thing to tell Tomas she had killed someone, another to have him watch as she took advantage of the unnatural speed she possessed to fell three of their would-be attackers.

Still, it did not matter now. The journey had never been what she expected, but nevertheless she was here.

Inhaling deeply, she said, "I just want to know what's wrong with me and why the elves seem to think I matter. Does it have anything to do with—" She stopped and stared at Rosslyn.

Everyone knew she had been found in the forest, except for Rosslyn. It wasn't that she wanted to purposely hide it from her and keep it a secret, but it also did not seem important, either. It wouldn't have changed anything between them. But now that Rosslyn was the only one who didn't know, Tallis felt ashamed she had not told her sooner.

Deciding it was just another thing she would have to deal with later, she continued on, "Does it have anything to do with being found in the forest as a baby?"

Rosslyn's mouth opened and her smattering of freckles across her nose darkened in surprise for a moment, and she gave Tallis an offended look, but she kept her peace. She seemed to know her feelings of betrayal were rather insignificant when it looked as if they were finally about to get what they had come for.

Cullen tilted his head from side to side for a moment. "Yes."

Tallis held her breath, only to be greeted with silence. Growing annoyed, she said tersely, "Yes, what? Tell us what this is all about, already!"

Shrugging, Cullen began picking at his filthy fingernails. "It has everything to do with you as a baby. You aren't human. No, no. The Tallis is barely human. See, the elves were losing. Losing badly in this war with you people. Tired of watching their gods felled and family lost, they prayed. They prayed and prayed and no answer came. They could talk to the trees, but the trees could not help. *Would* not help.

"But they did not stop praying. Something finally answered. Said it would help if they could free it. They had to perform a ritual that turned one of their trees into a gate. The gate would let it out and it would win the war for them.

"The elves did as they were told. Blood sacrifice was made and the tree was corrupted. And the dark one came. But it was not here for the filthy humans. It wanted the elves and it took them. The dark one let the humans win the silly war and it cut the elves off from their gods one by one. The old and the young could not handle such a loss and they died. Oh, they died in droves, those stupid elves.

"It took ten years, but the dark one got what it came for. The little minds of the elves became its playthings, but after so long they were not fun anymore. The dark one is eternal, time moves like sap for it. It got bored and it needed more. Wanted to see more of this land than the elves could show it. The dark one commanded its children to do another ritual. One that would make a vessel so the dark one could experience the land as a human *and* elf. The elves couldn't do it. Their bodies too weak to contain the dark one.

"But humans and elves made sure there were no more half-breeds. No, no more half-breeds. So another needed to be made.

"My clan took a man. Not an important man, but a good man from Fordoun. Got him drunk. Told him a great treasure awaited. The most beautiful woman in the world was waiting for him if he would just follow us. Oh, he followed. Took him to the gate tree where the dark one was waiting in a lady elf. Kept the man drugged, he didn't know what was happening. The dark one lay with the man and ensured a child was conceived. That child became the Tallis."

Cullen stopped to stare at Tallis. Tallis could feel her mouth open in disbelief and her eyes were dry from not blinking throughout Cullen's story. It sounded too impossible to be true, and yet she knew he wasn't lying. There was too much coincidence that seemed to fall into place with his story. Tallis being found in the forest, her connection to the trees, her unnatural speed, even the way she looked a little different than everyone else. Then she considered the legend of the demon that Tomas had spoken of when they had first entered the

Brethil Forest, and suddenly Cullen's tale did not seem so outlandish.

She was struggling to come to terms with this information. Her entire life she had wanted to just feel normal and comfortable in her own skin, only to find that such a thing would always be impossible. She should have been relieved to finally have some closure, but she was not. She had wanted to be normal, but being the only half-elf in all of Selkirk was as far from that as anyone could get.

There had been half-elves in the far distant past, but both races had always treated such unions as abominations for reasons no one could remember. No one wanted the half-elves, not the humans and not the elves. It usually was a death sentence for the child, but not for Tallis. Not when it seemed like a demon had made her for the sole purpose of being its host body.

Cullen met Tallis's eyes for a moment. He almost seemed disgusted by Tallis, but the look passed all too quickly for her to be sure. Shrugging lazily, he said, "It was believed that the Tallis was needed so the dark one could truly enter the world. The Tallis can hear the trees, correct? Had the Tallis stayed where she was supposed to be, she would have been taught how to properly communicate with them. But the pesky humans came and ruined that.

"The Tallis had to be kept far, far away from the dark one. The little Tallis was too frail to be near the corruption that had birthed it. It would have killed the Tallis, and the dark one would need to wait another thirty years for the right night to perform the ritual again. Your Clearing was expected, but it came too soon, too soon.

"My parents helped look after the baby Tallis. They were supposed to warn the elves when the knights came. Bad information meant that everyone was killed. Even my parents. The dark one thought it lost the Tallis and became very cross at my clan for trusting such incompetent people. The Tallis was lost.

"The dark one was going to wait the thirty years, for what are thirty years to the eternal? But the Tallis was found, so its plans moved forward once again. See, it needs the Tallis, because her connection is pure. She can connect to the trees like an elf, but has a mind like a human. Through the trees, it can infect the humans like the elves. Then the dark one will have everyone and it will be complete.

"The dark one says that only the Tallis has the right body to contain it, so it can rule amongst its playthings. The dark one is desperate for the Tallis, and my clan was going to give her back. The dark one cannot be allowed to touch the Tallis. That's how it gets inside, see? One touch and the dark one will enter the Tallis and it will never leave. The Tallis would not want that. Does it?"

Tallis was taken aback by Cullen's question. It seemed so ridiculous that he asked, and yet he almost sounded hopeful that she would confirm the answer. Frowning, she said quickly, "No, I don't want some demon to take over my body. Who would want such a thing?"

"Good, good. The Tallis does not want the dark one in her. But the dark one will not stop till it has the Tallis. It will tear the world apart looking for the Tallis, oh yes. We have to get to the dark one first, and stop it, yes, yes we do."

Shaking her head, Tallis ran her fingers through her hair and rubbed her scalp. Everything Cullen said sounded ridiculous. The elves entrusting a fiend to win the war with the humans, losing their minds as the demon took over, the demon waiting three hundred years before it got the idea to take over the rest of Selkirk to begin with. None of it sounded sane or logical, and not just because it was coming from Cullen.

Tallis was having trouble absorbing everything. She was getting the information she wanted, but she felt like it was at too high of a cost. She did not know how to cope with finding out her entire life had been a lie and that a demon had already predetermined her destiny. It was by sheer dumb luck that Tallis escaped that fate, but only to find she hadn't *actually* escaped it at all, that a destiny that involved a demon and the fate of Selkirk still firmly rested on her shoulders.

"Is that the reason Tallis is getting sick?" Tomas asked. "Is getting closer to this demon, the dark one, causing Tallis to fall ill?"

Tallis could have smiled at the way Tomas seemed to ignore so much and yet miss nothing at all. He seemed unfazed at finding out Tallis was a half-elf, and yet was still concerned over her illness. She wondered how he was able to process the barrage of information while Tallis felt like she was losing her grip on reality and would drown in the madness that Cullen had brought them.

Cullen cocked his head to the side and quickly looked Tallis up and down. Nodding vigorously, he said, "Yes. The Tallis was to be introduced slowly to the dark one's power. Enough to where she could handle it, but not so much she became like the elves. The Tallis was taken before my parents could slowly take her back to where she belonged. Time, the Tallis just needs more time to get used to it."

Silence fell with each of them trying to process everything Cullen just said. None of them wanted to believe the story he told, and yet all of them felt the prickles of certainty as the puzzle pieces began to fall into place.

Suddenly, it made sense why the elves were so intent on capturing Tallis without doing her harm, and why they would hiss her name. She was the prize they were attempting to reclaim for their demon master. Her ability to understand the trees and her unnatural speed all made sense now, too; it was because she was partly an elf.

Tallis felt sick to her stomach. She wasn't sure if it was the corruption she was feeling from being closer to the demon, or her body rebelling against the truth in Cullen's words. She clutched at her stomach and doubled over as she struggled to remain strong and in control, and failing at both. She wanted to rage and throw things and scream until none of this was true anymore. But, instead, she buried her face in her knees and refused to raise her head until the world made sense once again.

DONOVAN WAS TOO stunned to speak. He had questions, but they tumbled over in his mind so furiously, he could never form the words. All he could do was stare mutely at Cullen and digest what the odd man said.

"I still don't get why your parents would agree to babysit Tallis, Cullen," Rosslyn said, after moments had passed that felt more like hours.

Cullen sneered at Rosslyn in open contempt. "You forget what the clans were. The clans were the humans and elves who were parents to the half-elves. Didn't want to end their union and kill their babies. No, they wanted to live. Made clans outside of the king and high priestess of the humans and elves and made roving groups. The Sipsi forgets her history, just like the rest of the traitors. My parents did *not* forget. Long ago we were half-elves. They will help bring that back to this land. Or they would if they lived."

Taken aback by the harshness of his tone, Rosslyn was rendered momentarily speechless as she gaped back at him. But Cullen's anger was fleeting, as moments later he was once again grinning and rocking back and forth.

Donovan watched Cullen through narrowed eyes. He was concerned about everything the man said for many reasons. Mostly, he still refused to believe that the girl he had thought of as his family the majority of his life was half tremp, half of the very monsters he was sworn to protect his town against. He looked at Tallis and saw none of the evil in her that the elves posed. She was just a young woman who seemed to be in way over her head as she fought against a destiny she never wanted.

Still, there were plenty of holes and questions left unanswered by Cullen, and Donovan was not going to leave it that way. Finding his voice at last, he said, "And what is it that you get out of all this? Why agree to help us stop the demon taking over Tallis if that was what your parents had died trying to make happen?"

At his question, everyone's heads turned to look at Cullen, as he still sat cross-legged in the center of the group. He seemed surprised and confused by Donovan's question, as if he had never expected to have been asked, and now that he had, he didn't know what to say.

His face contorted as he took his time answering. "My parents died for it. Doesn't mean I want to. The clan kept me as a *slave* my whole life. They want to make themselves servants to the dark one. I don't. Not me. I won't be the servant again."

Donovan continued to watch Cullen warily. He had no doubt that Cullen had little desire to help his former clan, and it made sense for him to not want to completely follow in his parents' footsteps. Still, it seemed like despite the wealth of information that Cullen had already shared, he still wasn't sharing everything. There was more that he was either purposely withholding, or they just hadn't asked in the right way yet.

Donovan resolved to keep a close eye on Cullen for the time being and see where things went. He had enough on his plate with trying to help Tallis through her identity crisis that he could not afford to try and puzzle over something that might turn out to be nothing, anyway.

# *EIGHT*

ᕼALLIS KNEW THEY couldn't dawdle any further, and now that they knew why the elves were so intent on her capture, they should do something about it. But she just couldn't bring herself to disregard what Cullen had said about her origins and simply plunge headfirst into more uncertain danger.

She tried to process everything as she sat there with her friends. She tried to focus on what Cullen was saying to Rosslyn about the origin of the Sipsi clans and his reasons for helping them, but her mind had already shut down. She propped her forehead against her fingers, forcing her long, wavy hair into her face, as if that would shield her from all the conflicting thoughts and emotions racing through her.

Tallis did not want to accept or believe that she was half-elf. That she was half of that vicious creature who had plunged its hands into her mother's stomach and ripped her apart.

*But that wasn't my mother. She wasn't my* real *mother.* Her real mother had been an elf possessed by a demon, forced to conceive her through a dark religious ceremony that would make her body a suitable host for a creature even more evil than the elves.

*What does that make me then?* Tallis didn't think she was a bad person, maybe not the best person, but certainly not an evil one. How could it be then, that she was supposed to be the host for this demon? And what would happen to her, the girl she thought she was, if the beast ever did get a hold of her? Would that piece of her that always felt wrong suddenly be mended and she would become whole? Or would the girl everyone knew as Tallis simply cease to exist?

The idea of her disappearing while the shell of her body was paraded around like an evil puppet to bring all of Selkirk to its knees was too much for Tallis to bear.

She would rather kill herself than allow that to happen.

She began hyperventilating, and the sudden urge to be away from Cullen and everything he had just said forced Tallis to her feet. Blindly, she ran through the forest until she collapsed a little ways off on the banks of the Elwe River.

Landing on her hands and knees, she stared at her reflection in the clear water. The gentle ripples from the river's current contorted her face until Tallis swore the woman she saw staring back was not someone she recognized. Her ears looked more pointed, her face more malicious, even her teeth seemed to be as ragged and pointed as that of the tremps. The thing Tallis saw staring back up at her was not a human, but an elf.

In fury, Tallis swatted at the water, disrupting her reflection. But no matter how much she beat the water the image would not leave. The sneering face of the elf was still peering back at Tallis as if it were mocking her.

Desperately, she beat her reflection with her fists as tears streamed from her eyes. She didn't want to be a vessel, didn't want to be half an elf; she just wanted to be herself and nothing more.

She was still hyperventilating as the voices in her head began arguing with one another, telling her that, in a way, this is what she had wanted and that she should accept it. She'd finally be someone, something worthwhile. The other part was screaming at her, telling her that she was Tallis and nothing more.

She buried her face in her cold wet hands, trying to force her tears back in her eyes. She was losing control of her mind and nothing she seemed to do would allow her to claw her way back to sanity. She wanted to yell at the sky and force it to take it back, to take away the part of her that was meant for evil and give it to one of the Sipsi clan members who seemed to want that partnership with the elves.

A scream of frustration, pain, and denial escaped from her before she knew it. She was vaguely aware of the sound erupting from her, but she still didn't register that the bone chilling sound of pain, hurt, and general rebellion against an unfair situation was actually coming from her. Tallis had always thought she was too strong to allow the darkest and most hurtful of her feelings to come out in such a primal way. But she was finding she had been wrong about a lot of things, none of which made her feel any better.

Tallis didn't know who or what she was anymore, and it made her wonder who or what Donovan, Rosslyn, and even Tomas would now see when they looked at her. The idea of them treating her differently, looking at her like she was a monster, or even leaving now that they knew what she was, was all too much for Tallis to handle. While she knew she would have to continue on to destroy the evil at its source, no matter what her friends did next, she didn't know how she was supposed to do it without any help.

As she struggled to come to terms with everything and shake the madness and denial from her mind, she heard someone approach. She turned her head, ready to spring to action if her guttural scream had attracted unwanted visitors, only to find Tomas shyly standing a little ways back, looking at Tallis with nothing but concern shining in his dark green eyes.

Tallis's eyes widened at seeing him there before she turned away in shame. Tomas was a pious man and Tallis was now an abomination. Her fleeting hopes at discovering what a normal life might be like with him were now completely crushed under the weight of her newfound lineage.

Tallis heard Tomas walk towards her and sit down next to where she kneeled in the mud, but she still could not bring herself to look at him. She felt like a pathetic child for not being able to take this news in stride. She should have been better than what Tomas was now seeing: a woman trying to run from who she was.

Tomas put his hand on her shoulder and Tallis shivered under the touch. She wanted to scream at him to get away before the elf side of her hurt him. She never wanted to hurt anyone, but that was before she knew what she was. Things were different now, and Tallis was not sure what this new side of her was capable of.

But Tomas did not leave. Instead, he stroked her

shoulder until Tallis could not take it anymore. An involuntary sob erupted from her as she said, "I'm a thing born of nightmares and evil. What if I hurt you … or the people I care about?"

Tomas was silent for a moment and Tallis fully expected him to get up and run away in fear. Instead, she heard him say, "No you won't, Tallis. What Cullen said, it doesn't change anything."

She looked at him behind the curtain of her hair for a moment. "Doesn't it, though? It changes everything! I may never have felt like I belonged back at home, but I never expected that feeling to be because I wasn't human. I just thought I was odd or something. But now … I don't even know who I am anymore. My father was right to hate me."

To her surprise, Tomas pulled her to him as he wrapped his arm around her in a hug. She could smell the light musk of his clothes, the scratch of his familiar heavy brown tunic and his initiates robe he kept on to ward off the chill in the air, and felt his arm wrapped protectively around her, but it still didn't feel real. Tomas should be running away from her as fast as he could, but, instead, he stayed.

"I know who you are," Tomas whispered against her ear, causing Tallis to shiver again. "You are the girl who slept on the library floor, the one who took the deadly arts her cousin taught her and turned them into a dance to make money to buy yourself off the Bride Block, you are the girl who survived an elf attack that killed your mother, and you are the girl that's going to stop this demon from enslaving anyone else. Just because you found out that your lineage is … well, less than ideal, it doesn't change who you are.

---

"Suddenly realizing you are half an elf doesn't take any of that away ... not unless you let it. All those things you *are*, and all the things you *will* be, are still up to you. And the woman I know would never let a little thing like this turn her into a monster. She's far too strong, brave, kind, and wonderful to ever be anything other than amazing."

Tallis turned to look at him. His gaze was steady and his face soft; he was not lying to her or just telling her what he thought she wanted to hear. Tallis could see that he meant everything he said and it rendered her completely speechless.

He seemed to understand as he brushed the tears and hair away from her face. Letting his fingers linger on her cheek, he said, "Trust me when I say that what we have been through so far, and all the things Cullen has said, changes none of that. And not just for me, for everyone. No one thinks you are any different now than you were last night when you came to our rescue. You will always be that woman, Tallis. Don't let *anything* tell you differently."

Tallis grinned as she gently leaned into his hug and wrapped her arms around his waist. Tomas returned the embrace as Tallis buried her face in his chest. "Thank you, Tomas. Thank you for believing in me and for going to Wodan's Pits and back with me. I'd say it means the world, but it means more than that. Truly. I don't know if I'm all right just yet, if I have come to terms with this sudden knowledge, but I like to believe that eventually I could be all right, with you and everyone else at my side."

Tomas hugged her a little tighter for a moment before helping Tallis back to her feet. "Come on," he said as he stood. "We should get back before the others start to worry more about you. Just remember, you aren't alone Tallis. If you ever feel like it's getting too much to handle, just remember you have us to lean on. I—" Tomas began before cutting himself off. Starting again he said, "I will always be here for you, Tallis. No matter what."

She cupped his cheek in her hand and took a step closer. They were so close that their chests caressed each other as they rose and fell with each breath they took. "Tomas…," Tallis whispered as she stood on her tiptoes and leaned forward to kiss him.

Tomas lowered his head, but just as he was about to plant his lips atop hers, they heard thrashing in the forest behind them as Rosslyn came blundering into the clearing. Tallis rocked back on her heels and stepped away from Tomas to stare at Rosslyn, who was oblivious to the moment she had just interrupted.

"Oi, there you are," Rosslyn exclaimed as she ran for Tallis and pulled her into a ferocious hug. "We were worried that Tomas wouldn't be able to find you. Was that you who screamed? Are you all right? You can't just run off like that you know, Tallis, I heard there are tremps around."

Tallis nodded. "Aye. Sorry for scaring you. I was just … I was trying to process everything. It was a lot to digest. But," she said as she turned to face Tomas, "I think I'll be all right. As long as I don't lose sight of who I was before all of this, and continue to act in a way that's worthy of your concern, friendship, and affection."

Rosslyn held Tallis at arm's length for a moment before she snorted, "Wodan's bollocks, Tallis, that sounded very philosophical of you. You sure that elf blood isn't messing with your head?" With a laugh, Rosslyn linked arms with her and began to lead her back to camp.

Before Rosslyn could leave Tomas behind, Tallis reached behind her and fumbled for his hand. Intertwining his long, firm fingers with hers, Tallis held on to Tomas and Rosslyn as they walked her back to camp and away from the cliffs of madness.

# NINE

TALLIS FOUND TRAVELING with Cullen to be strange, to say the least. Had they not needed his guidance in tracking down the demon to end the elves' pillaging once and for all, Tallis would not have wanted to be near the man. His madness was obvious, but there was something else about him that made Tallis feel uneasy in his presence.

As they continued to linger in the forest, Cullen became increasingly more nervous. He continuously glanced over his shoulder as if he expected something to be following them. Tallis asked about it once, but he only waved her off and mumbled gibberish to himself.

Despite his eccentricities, he had been nothing but helpful whenever he was asked a direct question about where they should be headed. So Tallis tried to ignore the nagging in her mind that told her something was off about him. After all, she no longer felt like she was in a position to judge anyone.

She was still struggling with not being entirely human. She had decided she did not want to talk about it, and, for the most part, her friends respected her choice. On occasion, they would stare at her for too long when they thought Tallis wasn't paying attention, but she tried not to let it bother her. It was better than having to talk to them about what it felt like to be partially an elf, anyway.

Tallis did not exactly appreciate Cullen entering her life and changing almost everything she thought she knew about herself, but it did come with some added benefits. Not only was Tallis no longer trying to find answers to fill a void in her heart, she knew the reason why she was so different from everyone else and it had nothing to do with anything she could change. She would come to terms with that eventually, and it would be easier with Tomas there for her to lean on, if need be.

She still had Donovan, and she knew that would never change, but this was different. Donovan was family, no matter who her parents actually were. He had been a fixture in her life with his unwavering support and protection. She expected it of him, and occasionally took advantage of him always being there for her. But Tomas did not need to be there. He was not her family, and yet he still offered her everything Donovan did, but with the added benefit of occasionally making her heart skip whenever she felt like she would otherwise drown under the torrent of fear and helplessness that as of late threatened to cripple her.

If Rosslyn was jealous of Tallis's changing preferences in who she spent most of her time with, she hid it well. She did not seem to care that Tallis went to Tomas more often than not when she was feeling weak from her continuing sickness or when anxiety gripped her heart like a mouse caught in a trap. Tomas would never be able to match her own sarcastic wit the same way Rosslyn could, and that seemed to be enough for her for the time being.

Cullen's presence, however, had changed the dynamic of the group. Things that may have been perceived as slights went ignored, as they all wished to keep their own private arguments a secret from the bronze-skinned stranger clad in his hodgepodge collection of mismatched clothing. His faded green tunic with its patches made of lavender-colored fabric, and his tattered deep blue vest hanging loosely on his body; he constantly had to tug up his yellow and brown striped woolen trousers as they were at least a size too large for his frame, as well. Even his long moss-colored cloak with its fraying patches of crimson fit him poorly. Cullen fit in with their group about as well as his attire.

It was as if Cullen were an imaginary friend that suddenly became real and they were all afraid to acknowledge was sitting in plain view. But if Cullen noticed, or if it bothered him, he gave no indication. He just kept grinning and offered whatever information they asked for without complaint.

He did not seem to be aggravated by anything. Though there were moments when Tallis swore she could see hatred and contempt lighting up his pale blue eyes, if only briefly. Tallis only ever seemed to see those flashes and only when she needed to stop and rest though, as no one else became nearly as apprehensive.

They were moving slowly as Tallis overcame her illness. It was not as bad as it was the first time, but it did not make it any easier. Cullen assured them the only remedy there would be for Tallis was for her to spend more time in the deeper parts of the forest. And so far he had been right, with each passing day she felt a little better. But they were still moving slowly, and a journey that should have taken three or four days started to look like it would take five or six.

Regardless of how long their journey was taking, they still had a significant amount to learn about what they would face when they finally reached the source of all their problems. Cullen may not have been interested in sharing his own troubled past with the group, but he would not stop babbling about the demon, the elves, and his old clan. At least that was the case until they started pressing him for what weaknesses the monster had.

"I take it we have a plan that's more than just showing up at this blighted beast's doorstep and asking politely for it to shove off, right?" Rosslyn asked as they stopped again for the night as Tallis's strength began to fail.

"Oh, that wouldn't work. The dark one would just laugh. If it could laugh. Probably eat you, instead. It likes soft, squishy people." Cullen laughed and took off his clunky leather boots and flexed his bare feet in the cool evening air.

Rosslyn gave him a look of distaste before rolling her eyes and spreading her hands helplessly at Tallis. Cullen had the infuriating bad habit of not understanding sarcasm, and only Tallis was able to get him to answer such questions.

Tallis sighed and clarified, "That's not what she meant, Cullen. She just wanted to know if you had any idea about how we're supposed to deal with this monster, or demon, I guess, once we find it."

Cullen's gaze darkened before the strained grin returned to his face. Rubbing his feet, he said, "The Tallis will need to kill it. It's simple. So simple. The killing is the easy part."

Donovan cocked an eyebrow, skeptical that anything could or would be that easy after everything they had been through. "Really? We just kill it? It doesn't take some sort of special weapon or something?"

Cullen's grin began to falter. "No. It's not magic. It dies like everything. It's why the dark one needs so many host bodies. The Tallis was supposed to fix that problem. You seem to be good at stabbing things. Stab the dark one, kill it, and be done with it."

Cullen hunched over and dug his toes into the soft ground, burying them in the cold dirt before wiggling his toes free. He suddenly seemed reluctant to speak of the demon, which made Tallis share concerned looks with Donovan as they watched Cullen ignore them.

He was hiding something, but they could not tell what. He had been honest about everything else so far, he had even killed someone he had considered a friend just so he could help Tallis and keep her out of the clutches of the fiend. Cullen may have been stricken with madness, but he had yet to lie to them.

After they had eaten and prepared to rest for the night, Tallis sat down next to Donovan as he idly tossed sticks into their low fire. She watched him for a moment before saying, "Do you really think it can be that easy? Just get to this demon and kill it?"

Donovan snorted. "No. Nothing that simple. I'm beginning to think that Cullen doesn't actually know how to vanquish this dark one of his. I think he's just hoping that stabbing it will work."

Tallis was silent for a moment, watching the flames dance like birds in flight. She would be lying if she, too, hadn't also been hoping that their foe would be so easily felled. "What do we do if it doesn't work? If we can't actually kill it?"

Donovan did not answer her right away. So much depended on them being able to kill the demon while keeping Tallis out of its clutches. If they allowed this fiend to touch or possess Tallis, all would be lost and all the hardships they had gone through would have been for nothing. Failure was simply not an option, but Donovan had no way of ensuring that they succeeded, either.

"We'll find a way to get rid of it one way or another, Tally. We always seem to find a way to get out of these live or die situations."

Tallis nodded as she rested her chin over her folded arms. They did not speak as they watched Rosslyn and Tomas prepare the rest of the camp for bed while Cullen looked on. For the time being, Tallis was content to watch her friends and take comfort in being close to Donovan, allowing his silent strength to bolster her resolve.

Donovan glanced at her and nudged her with his shoulder, his heavy dark leather and dented plate mail armor, which he had not taken off since escaping Fordoun, making her arm ache in the motion. "How have you been holding up, cousin?"

Slowly, Tallis slid her eyes over to look at Donovan, the word *cousin* causing her more pain than expected. She scoffed, "How can you still call me that? It was one thing to call me cousin when you thought I was just some lost babe in the forest, another when you know I'm not even the same species as you."

"Knock that off. You are, and always will be, my family. You being adopted didn't change that, this won't either."

"Doesn't it, though? You trained your entire life pretty much to protect this country against things like me. Doesn't your knight's code dictate that you kill me?"

"No," he said quickly. "The knight's code dictates I protect the innocent from evil. You are not evil; in fact, I'd still consider you one of the innocent party members in all this. It wasn't like you wanted this or anything. Not sure why those bloody clan members of Cullen's didn't just use one of their own members. Sounds like they would have welcomed such an honor. I know Cullen said they wanted someone completely clean of the taint his clan like to believe they have, but still."

Shaking his head again, he sighed and looked down at his mud-encrusted steel-capped boots. "Look, it might make sense. You being a half-elf does certainly explain a lot. But I look at you and see my baby cousin, like always. As long as you don't get those creepy yellow eyes or start clicking like the elves do, then I don't really see how you being a half-elf changes anything."

Tallis chuckled lightly. "You sound like Tomas. He said pretty much the exact same thing the day Cullen told us about my parentage."

Donovan did not answer. He smiled at Tallis and gently mussed her hair like he used to when they were just children playing in his father's dirty hovel. She missed the days where her biggest concern was getting the other children to like her, rather than having to deal with the burden of saving all of Selkirk from the destiny the demon wanted for her.

After a moment, Donovan gently pushed Tallis away so he could finish running a whetstone over his broadsword. "Go on, go get some sleep. You'll need your rest if you ever hope to beat this monster's corruption."

Tallis was too exhausted and her body ached too much to argue with Donovan as she slowly made her way to her bedroll. Before she left, she rested her hand on his armored shoulder and squeezed gently in silent thanks before attempting to get some rest.

TOMAS WATCHED AS Tallis and Donovan spoke to one another. She seemed to have aged so much in the past few days. Her aquamarine eyes were lined in dark circles from stress and lack of proper sleep. Her complexion had always been one of fresh milk, but she had never seemed as deathly pale as she did now. He knew it was not just the lingering effects of the illness brought on by the demon's corruption, either. Tallis was wrestling with so many different ideas and honorable notions that she was nearing a crippling exhaustion.

She was completely guilt-ridden over everything that had happened, even more so now because of her lineage. Tomas suspected she may even feel bound to the concept of self-sacrifice to trap and kill the demon the only way she knew how: within herself.

He swallowed the lump in his throat, forcing himself to start thinking about the very thing he had been avoiding since Cullen had joined their group. He had never truly considered what would happen if Tallis felt the need to follow that route, but he could avoid the thought no longer. He could not even bring himself to imagine what they would do if Tallis forced them to kill her.

Tomas was not sure what he would do, what any of them would do, if that happened, or what they would do to ensure the demon never had an opportunity to claim its vessel. All Tomas knew for certain was that he would rather die than to watch Tallis cease to exist if the monster won.

It was in that moment that clarity settled over him like a warm blanket. He *would* rather die than see anything happen to Tallis. He had no family that would miss him and no real future outside of the monastery. He lived for Tallis, and if that was gone then he would have nothing.

Tallis, on the other hand, had a family in Donovan that would be crushed if she were gone. She had the potential and the opportunity to change their country for the better, but that would never happen if the beast won. So if it came to it, Tomas decided he would be the one to make that sacrifice, not Tallis.

# *TEN*

ᏮALLIS DIDN'T EVEN hear them coming. So intense was her exhaustion that the crunching leaves, the falling pinecones from Tomas's traps, even the muffled screams of Rosslyn, had all melded into her fevered and demented dreams.

In her dream, she was running through a forest that had no end and never changed. She was endlessly running in place, tearing through the forest with reckless abandon. No matter how fast she ran or how hard she pushed herself, it still felt like she was running through water, and she could not pump her legs fast enough to out run the things chasing her.

She glanced behind her to see the semi-transparent faces of the people of Kincardine as they lay dead in the streets while she ran away. She saw the Dumfry elders as their eyeless faces stared at her accusingly. She saw her father's scowl filled with so much hatred for her that she began to shiver in her sleep. She saw her mother's face as the light fled from her hazel eyes and when she looked down, her hands were once again covered in blood.

When Rosslyn screamed, she thought it had come

from her own lips as she tried to flee the ghosts of her greatest regrets. When she heard the thrashing of the others as they were roughly taken from their bedrolls, she thought it was the sound of the monster she was running from catching up with her at last. And when their hands roughly grabbed her and jerked her to her feet, she thought it was the very thing she had been running from the entire time.

Her eyes fluttered open and she wasn't sure if she were still dreaming. She saw a face she swore was hers, but she was no longer a human but a full elf. Bright yellow eyes stared down at Tallis as if they recognized her, but were unsure as to why. The woman's hair was the color of pale moonlight and she might have been considered beautiful except for the gaunt way her cheeks sucked into her face and the rotten needle-like teeth filling her mouth.

Tallis swore for just the briefest of moments she was, indeed, looking into the very face of the thing she was to become. Until she saw Donovan and Tomas being brought to their knees just behind the elf that held tightly on to her arms.

Tallis tried to jerk herself free of the tremp holding her captive, but it was to no avail. Her body was weaker than she thought, and unresponsive as it still shuddered its way out from under her dream world. She began thrashing wildly as she tried to get to her friends as they were bound and dragged like dirty laundry behind the elves as they carted them away.

She tried to scream and free herself as a bald male elf in nothing but an old loin cloth helped the woman Tallis thought was a vision of her future haul her away. She could feel their fingers dig into her skin and knew she would have bruises in the shape of their hands as they dragged her from the campsite. She continued to twist and thrash despite the iron-like grip they had on her, until she saw Cullen.

Cullen was skipping around the elves, humming to himself and occasionally clicking in the groaning way the elves did when they spoke with one another. Seeing Tallis look at him, he skipped over to her, a smile spread wide across his round face.

Matching his stride with that of her captors, he said, "The dark one will need a snack after she enters the Tallis. It's a hard process, unpleasant for the dark one. Your friends will help it regain its strength. I did say the dark one liked soft, squishy people, right? Yes, yes I did."

Cullen's voice seemed too loud as he spoke to Tallis. It was as if he wanted the rest of her friends to hear what he had to say as they were being dragged through the forest by what looked to be about ten elves.

Tallis saw their heads jerk as Cullen's words washed over them. Rosslyn stared at Tallis as if she expected to see Tallis licking her lips in anticipation. Tallis scowled and resumed her thrashing against the tremps that held her in place.

She should not have been surprised at Cullen's betrayal, but it cut through her like an arrow nonetheless. It would have been too much to ask for to have an ally that knew the elves' plans. It would have been too perfect for them to finally have the upper hand on the elves for once. Despite how much Cullen had lost and his eagerness to betray his former clan, Tallis realized his true loyalties were never going to be to her, but rather the tremps and their wicked master.

Tallis helplessly looked at her friends as they were dragged by their bound hands behind the elves. Rosslyn was struggling to her feet to avoid getting a face full of debris while Tomas lurched just to Tallis's left as he stumbled along. Only Donovan seemed not to try and regain his footing.

At first glance it looked as if Donovan had given up and was allowing the tremps to drag him without complaint or struggle. But Tallis knew better. By allowing himself to become dead weight to the elves as they dragged them to their master, he was slowing them down and giving Tallis the time she needed to think of a plan to get them out of the trap Cullen had led them into.

She continued to thrash, but this time she was no longer taking stock of the elves that held on to them with unwavering strength. Instead, she looked around to see what she had to use at her disposal.

In their haste and lack of foresight, the elves had failed to disarm their prisoners. She could still see Donovan's massive broadsword strapped to his back, the little black club dangling at Rosslyn's side, and Tomas with the pack holding his crossbow, its bolts, and his explosive powders. Tallis, too, still had her trident like daggers dangling from her waist and the two knives concealed in the back of her boots. But the weapons would remain useless unless they could free their hands and arms from the elves long enough to get them.

Tallis briefly met Donovan's calculating deep brown eyes as she began puzzling out how to free herself long enough to get to her daggers. Unlike her friends, her hands were not bound, and she would actually be able to use her weapons if she could just get to them.

Donovan seemed to understand what she was attempting and gave her a brief nod. Digging the heels of his boots into the ground, he tried to slow the group of elves dragging him even more to give Tallis all the time she needed.

But all the time in the world would not have been enough.

The elves that had them now were not like the ones they had come across before. All of them seemed stronger and smarter, despite the fact they had not disarmed their prey. Tallis may have been a match for one of them had she been at her best, but her body felt sluggish and diseased from the corruption of the demon. No matter how much she tried to twist out of her captors' grasp, she could not seem to out maneuver them this time.

Tallis was still twisting wildly when the elves finally stopped marching through the forest. They tossed her friends on the ground as if they were rotting meat, and all but the elves holding Tallis took three steps back in unison. Tallis stopped jerking to watch as Rosslyn and Donovan were tossed down in front of her in a heap while Tomas managed to get his elf to drop him near enough to roll to his side and kneel beside her.

Frantically, Tallis searched his face to see what damage they had dealt him, but for once, Tomas would not look at her. His eyes were fixated on something directly in front of Tallis. By the way his pupils had dilated in fear until almost all the green had disappeared from his eyes, she knew she was not going to like what she saw.

Turning her head away from Tomas, she let her eyes concentrate on the ground in front of her while she tried to calm her heart. *Whatever happens next*, she told herself, *don't be afraid*. Swinging her feet beneath her, she slowly rose from her kneeling position, forcing the elves to straighten as she stood. Taking one last deep breath, Tallis rolled her head up to stare into the face of the demon before her.

At first glance, she looked like any other elf Tallis had seen, but … enhanced. The elf stood straight as an arrow, long legs shining in the gray light of the morning. She was delicate to the point of being almost fragile in appearance, but Tallis could see that what could be mistaken as fragility was actually a controlled strength ready to spring into explosive action at a moment's notice.

She wore a long gown with a high slit that came all the way up to her right hip made out of various pieces of dark fabric. It was as if the demon had wanted to appear regal, despite the shambles of the creatures it controlled. All the while, her hands idly twirled her long coal black hair as if she had never held such a fine thing before.

She was a creature of breathtaking and terrible beauty. It was as if the demon took every feature of its host's form and enhanced it by tenfold. But despite the beauty, elegance, and taut strength, the host's body was failing.

All over the tremp's otherwise flawless body were patches of skin that looked like popped blisters. Whatever force the demon possessed, the poor elf that she had taken control over could barely contain it.

Finally looking at the creature's face, Tallis had to squint in order to meet the demon's gaze. Much like the rest of the elves, the demon's eyes were a bright, sickly yellow, with just the smallest of black pupils. But the fiend's eyes glowed with a light that was blindingly bright.

She felt the urge to speak to the villain in front of her, but she did not know what to say. Tallis was not about to beg for mercy, and she had no desire to hear the twisted plans the demon had for her. Instead, she tried to stare at her with as much courage as she could muster.

The demon cocked its head to the side like an elegant bird. "Finally, the girl child is mine."

Her voice sounded like nothing Tallis had ever heard before, distinctly female as the demon forced its host body to speak on its behalf, but all the same, completely devoid of any gender whatsoever. For the *monster* was not a person at all, but a sexless thing of pure evil.

Jutting her chin out in defiance, Tallis said, "Only took you three hundred years to come up with this brilliant plan, and what has it been now? A month at least to catch me? It's not like you had an entire army out looking for me or anything."

Tallis had hoped the demon would rise to the bait, but was disappointed when she did not. Instead, the regal beast merely stared at her with morbid fascination, like a healer examining a disease never encountered before.

The demon continued to play with its shiny black hair as it took a slight step towards Tallis, forcing her to recoil in fear. This amused the gruesome creature. "I see the girl child knows its purpose. Good. That clan of half-wit fools has not failed completely then.

"If the girl child is worried she will turn out like this pretty thing," the demon said indicating her own body, "then fear no longer. I will make the girl child the most beautiful thing to ever exist, past, present, and future. I will live forever in her, and she will never age and never decay. It's a fair trade. The girl child need not be so fearful of me."

Tallis did not answer, she twisted and looked for Cullen. If she was to die, it would not be without a few choice words for the man who had betrayed her. But Cullen was nowhere to be found. Despite his obvious loyalty to this unholy creature, it seemed as if he did not want to be in its presence at the moment. As odd as Tallis found that to be, she had no time to puzzle over it in her current predicament.

"If the girl child is afraid it will hurt, it will. But it will be brief," the monster cooed. "This body seemed to think it felt like being consumed by liquid fire for a fraction of a moment before, well, before nothing. Then the girl child will feel nothing ever again. It is not so bad. Especially when the girl child considers the pain she has been through. Oh, it doesn't need to look so surprised; I know what my creatures did to its fake mother. I know what the girl child thinks I cost her. I can take all that away, the pain will be gone forever. That is something the girl child wants now, isn't it?"

Gritting her teeth, Tallis tried to ignore everything the demon was saying, and asked, "Why now? It's been over three centuries of you controlling the elves, and doing nothing with them but hiding here in the forest and occasionally getting driven out by the humans. What's changed to make you act now rather than when you first entered this world?" She could have sworn she saw amusement crease the demon's face as she considered what Tallis said.

After a moment, the creature responded, "Boredom. I am eternal, girl child. Time has little meaning for a thing such as me. I was having fun flitting between the elves, wearing their skins like the girl child wears pretty things. I enjoyed tormenting their souls as they called out for their ancient connection to my siblings. I enjoyed seeing this world through their eyes. Then I saw all there was to see and I wanted something new. But I could not have it; I could not take the form of the girl child's race and keep my pretty little elves at the same time, at least, not as effectively as I want."

The demon turned its attention to Tomas as he finally got his feet underneath him. She seemed mildly amused and disinterested in him at the same time. Watching him, she said, "These human things are fascinating. Clunky, clumsy, and yet so strong. Their will does not crack and shatter like the elves. It would seem that your Wodan is a fearsome thing, if but a silent master."

Turning her attention away from Tomas, she addressed Tallis once again, "I needed a bridge. I needed the girl child. A vessel of both elven and human ancestry that would allow me to cross completely into this world and keep my pretty elves, and while adding the humans to my collection. It took time, too much time to get the elves to perform the rituals I needed, to find the right priestess host for me to take while you were conceived. But it was done, and done so perfectly, there was no need to try again."

Sneering, she glared at the male elf holding Tallis, and said, "But the elves had grown stupid, so stupid, and the humans I trusted were no brighter. They lost my vessel. I punished them, and their fear tasted delicious as I took my time devouring those who failed me. And yet, the girl child still lived unbeknownst to me. When these slow-witted creatures finally found your trail again and brought me this news, oh, how I wore their skins with joy.

"What the girl child assumes is a failure is false. I needed all the humans clustered together rather than spread across all their disgusting little dwellings. I always knew where the girl child was, except briefly when she was with her human kind once again. I *let* the girl child go about her quest. I needed the girl child to get used to my presence and become connected to my ancient siblings. I *needed* the girl child to do just that, and she did just as I wanted.

"Now everything is in place. The humans are tucked behind their silly walls, and the girl child standing before me has been made stronger for surviving my corruption and connecting herself to my trapped brethren. I will savor this moment as I bring every one of the inhabitants of this place under my control." The demon gurgled a cackle that sounded more like falling rocks than it did laughter.

As the demon spoke, all her companions managed to get to their feet. But the elves surrounding them seemed to only care about Donovan and Tallis. They recognized Donovan as one of the humans responsible for carrying out the Clearing, and knew better than to let him stand without being restrained. And while they glanced at Rosslyn and Tomas from time to time, they did not see them as a threat warranting their immediate attention.

The demon licked its perfect pink lips as it looked at the elves holding Tallis firmly between them. It did not speak to them, instead making eye contact as it mentally gave them instructions. The elves kicked Tallis behind her knees, forcing her to the ground once again. Then they pulled her hair back so she was forced to look at nothing but the demon as it gracefully made its way to her.

Tallis tried to struggle, but she could barely move her head and arms with how tightly she was being held. She watched as the female elf that the demon inhabited began to shudder and convulse as the beautiful beast slowly made its way to Tallis. It reminded Tallis of a snake trying to shed its skin, and she suddenly knew with sickening dread that the demon was preparing to leave its current host to take its true and final form within her.

That was when something moved at the corner of her vision and she saw Tomas awkwardly run as fast as he could with his hands still bound to come between her and the demon. Her eyes widened and time seemed to slow as she realized what Tomas was about to do. If the demon required but a touch to enter Tallis's body, then Tomas would intercept it before that could happen.

# *ELEVEN*

𝕿OMAS LURCHED TO his feet, and to his credit, did not tremble or waver as he put himself between the demon and Tallis, ready to sacrifice himself so that Tallis could flee to live another day.

The elves did not expect such a thing from a human they did not consider a threat. As the elves rushed for Tomas, they momentarily relinquished their grasp on Donovan.

The demon raised its elegant hand just as Tomas managed to toss himself over Tallis to shield her from its touch.

In that moment, Donovan saw Tomas succeed in saving Tallis only to lose her forever as the demon squelched the life right out of him. He saw Tallis's heart break a million times over as she was forced to slay the only man who had seen the ugly side of her being, and despite it all, never once left her side. He watched the brilliant fire of Tallis's spirit be extinguished, never to be rekindled. In its wake, Selkirk would be lost as the humans and the tremps continued to war with one another even without the demon's guiding hand.

Tomas's intentions were pure and noble, but poorly thought out. Tomas had no armor, too much skin was exposed, he could be touched by the monster and then immediately touch Tallis and pass the taint. Donovan did not know if that would be possible, but he also would not, *could* not risk it.

The fragments of a heartbeat it took for Donovan to reach the demon seemed like an eternity. He finally got close enough to dive sideways at it, forcing the creature to fall away from Tomas as he landed squarely on top of it, his heavy platemail driving the air from their foe.

For a moment, Donovan believed he was fortunate enough to land correctly on his armor and the demon's tattered black gown, avoiding any skin contact. He was about to send a silent prayer to Wodan when he felt a fire consume him from the inside out.

ROSSLYN HAD NOT been idle while Tallis spoke to the ghoulish monster as she covertly began to free her hands from the bonds that held her. Her pop would never have let her forgive herself if she could not manage to free her hands from the fraying ropes without being detected. As the ropes fell off her wrists like massive spider webs, Rosslyn scrambled to her feet just in time to see Donovan land on the demon with a loud thud that plunged the whole forest into silence.

The hush was short-lived as Tallis's bloodcurdling scream pierced the chill morning air like a hot poker. Rosslyn shut her eyes, as if that would shield her from the gut-wrenching sound that came from the depths of her friend's soul. When she finally managed to open her eyes once again, she saw Donovan writhing on the ground as if he were engulfed in flames and Tomas shielding Tallis as the elves relinquished their hold on her.

She managed to get a glimpse of Donovan's face as he convulsed on the ground and the sight brought tears to her eyes. His skin was beginning to form blister-like pustules, just like the now discarded form of the demon. He blinked rapidly and one moment his eyes would be their normal steady brown and the next the glowing yellow of the elves.

She knew that Donovan was struggling to keep the demon from overtaking him, all the while trying to keep it from escaping. But despite his heroic efforts he was losing the battle.

A sob erupted from Rosslyn as she shakily got to her feet and took the crossbow out of Tomas's discarded pack. With a wobbly hand, she brought the crossbow up, aimed, and released the bolt.

Rosslyn dropped the crossbow to the ground with a *thunk* as Donovan ceased his struggles, and she could see that her aim had been true. She felled the demon within Donovan with a bolt to the head. As he lay still on the ground, she watched as a sigh like a fleeing wind escaped Donovan's lips and his now yellow eyes fixated on the sky above.

It all seemed too surreal; it did not feel as if a true battle had ever occurred. Tomas had tried to sacrifice

161

himself for Tallis only to have Donovan sacrifice himself, instead. And now that Donovan lay dead on the ground, the elves did nothing about it. They collapsed to the forest floor as if the invisible strings holding them up had been cut, and stared up into the gray sky completely unconscious.

If it hadn't been for Tallis's screams, Rosslyn would never have known what had happened or what she had done. She would have simply thought she was dreaming when she killed Donovan, and she would wake at any moment to see the big knight scowling back at her.

But this was no dream.

The agonizing screams of her best friend told the truth of the matter, that while she may have destroyed the demon, she had also just slain the only family Tallis had left.

## OF LOSS, LOVE, AND DUTY

## TWELVE

TALLIS TRIED TO toss Tomas off of her as he kept himself between her and Donovan. But by the time she was able to dart around the ex-initiate, it was too late, and Donovan lay dead on the ground with a bolt protruding from his forehead.

Tallis saw the bloodied wound in Donovan's head, saw the way his eyes gleamed with a yellow light even in death, and she saw the beginnings of boils litter his body as it fought against the monster within him for the mere moments that he had been possessed.

While part of Tallis knew that Donovan was dead the moment the demon took hold of his soul, none of it seemed real. It felt too anticlimactic of a death for such a strong a man.

"No, no, *no*!" Tallis moaned as she rushed for her fallen cousin.

She reached out to hold him only to feel Rosslyn grab her hands and whisper, "Don't touch him; we don't know what that might do to you."

Pushing Rosslyn away, her hands quivered as they

hovered over Donovan's face, instead. Rosslyn might have had a point, but that did not make it any easier for Tallis to not want to cradle her cousin's body like he used to do for her when they were growing up, whenever Tallis had a bad dream or when she needed solace after her mother died. It had always been Donovan that she ran to when she was scared, overwhelmed, or needed help. Who was going to protect her now?

"You can't leave me like this, you can't! I can't do this without you, Donovan, please. *Please* let this be a dream … just a bad dream. Come on, you big oaf, get up, this isn't … this isn't funny. Donovan please wake up, please."

As her tears landed on Donovan's pale cheeks, Tallis swore she could hear them hissing with steam. And no matter how much her heart begged her to turn away, to stop staring at the blood pouring from Donovan's wounds, she couldn't look away.

"I don't know what to do … please don't leave me to figure this out on my own. I can't do this without your help. I would just curl up in a corner and cry without you, remember? Donovan?"

She could feel hands gently holding her, pulling her ever so slightly away from Donovan. Her heart plummeted to the bottom of her stomach at the very idea of leaving him behind, and she roughly pushed the hands off of her.

"I can't … I won't just leave him here!" she cried as she fought against the memories of her mother's death as they bubbled to the surface once again.

Without her mother or Donovan's guiding hand, Tallis didn't know what to do. She felt the pressures of life and responsibility weighing her down and crushing her under the uncertainty of what to do without the pillars of support that had propped her up her entire life.

She felt the tightening in her chest as heartbreak and soul crushing anxiety robbed her of any hope she had of being able to walk away from this journey unscathed. She felt the panic rise in her throat like bile as she struggled with trying to keep from being overwhelmed. But it was too late for that now.

Tallis stared at the pale and mildly disfigured face of her cousin. She marveled at how death could change someone's appearance so drastically. Donovan had been so full of life and strength that he looked almost like a stranger in death. The demon's yellow eyes certainly didn't help, but Tallis felt like she could have seen past that if it weren't for the long wooden shaft of the crossbow quarrel sticking out of his forehead.

And in that moment as her eyes fixated on her cousin's face, she wanted to be overwhelmed by the panic, the fear, the hurt, and the despair raging away inside of her. She wanted to give up and lie down next to Donovan and never move again.

Life had never been simple for Tallis, but part of her always thought it would at least be manageable with Donovan there to look out for her. Now that he wasn't, Tallis simply did not know what to do or where to go for comfort or reassurance.

She felt hands on her again as they tried to pull her away. This time she did not have the strength or the will to stop them.

Pulling her into a hug was Tomas as he tried to shield her from the image that was already permanently scarred onto her heart, never to fade away. She was aware of how he stroked her hair and mumbled unintelligible things into her ear that were meant to be comforting. But Tallis was beyond being comforted now.

Tallis was not even aware she was still sobbing uncontrollably. Vaguely, she could feel the hot tears streak down her face and could feel her entire body shudder with each sob, but she was too numb from the shock of Donovan's death to really register what her body was doing. It was as if she were a dark shadow hovering over the grisly scene all around her; she was aware of it all, and yet still trying to believe she was watching the scene rather than being a part of it.

Somewhere amidst the sorrow, she registered they had killed the demon and ended its reign of terror. Soon the elves would wake up and they would not be feral anymore. Soon their two races could work together to find a way to live with one another once again.

But despite the good they had accomplished with destroying the twisted creature, she still did not want to live anymore. She felt like her whole body had been made of glass armor and it had been shattered by the same bolt that had taken Donovan's life.

She had lost her mother, her father hated her, she was a half-breed mongrel that belonged nowhere, and now she had just lost the one true tie she had that had made life worth living. Without Donovan, Tallis did not know what she had to keep living for now that Selkirk was saved.

*There is Tomas.*

The thought came to her unbidden, and once there

it refused to leave. Despite losing so much, she still had someone. Remembering he was there, holding her tightly to him as her body convulsed in wrenching sobs gave Tallis, if not the will to live, at least the will to try.

She looked up at him, and much to her surprise, there were streaks of tears rolling down his face as well. Tallis had thought she would be the only one to mourn or care about Donovan's passing, but now she saw what a lie that was. Gingerly, she touched his face and brought his forehead to hers, unable to speak.

Tomas ran his hand through her hair and cupped the back of her head. Tallis tried focusing on the reassuring pressure of his hand, anything that would take her mind off the stabbing pain in her chest where her heart had once been.

"Oh, Tallis, I'm sorry. I am so, so sorry. It should have been me. I tried … I was going to shield you from the demon, but…," his voice cracked with emotion and he could say no more.

Tallis didn't know what he wanted her to say. Tomas should not have tried to sacrifice himself for her any more than Donovan should have. The fact that they were both willing to die for her, with one of them actually succeeding, did not make her happy.

She knew she should have been touched that they both loved and cared for her so much, but it was her sacrifice to make. She did not want anyone to die on her account, and for a moment Tallis felt nothing but anger towards the both of them.

Her face began to burn with rage and she could feel a scowl begin to form on her face. She may not have wanted her destiny, but she would not have let anyone else shoulder such a burden. Yet that was precisely what had happened. And for a moment, she was overcome with fury at how selfish both Tomas and Donovan were with wanting to shield her. She did not want nor need them to protect her from the demon.

Tallis dropped her gaze, and was about to wrench herself out of Tomas's consoling embrace, when she saw the discarded crossbow lying near Rosslyn's feet.

Rosslyn was standing a short distance away, arms wrapped firmly around her stomach as she shifted uncertainly from foot to foot. Tallis could tell her friend was wrestling with wanting to comfort her just as Tomas was doing, but not being sure if she should, considering she had been the one to strike the killing blow.

All the hurt, anger, pain, and despair Tallis felt now found their outlet in Rosslyn. Pushing Tomas off of her, she stumbled to her feet and lurched over to where Rosslyn stood. She clenched her fists and glared into the bloodshot eyes of the person she had thought of like a sister for the better part of six years.

Part of Tallis wanted to look into Rosslyn's honey brown eyes and see the boisterous girl who liked to drink ale and cheat at cards. She wanted to be able to look at Rosslyn's face and see only the sprinkling of mocking freckles. But all Tallis could see now was the woman who had fired a crossbow directly at her cousin's head and did not miss.

Without really knowing what she was doing, Tallis swung her fist at Rosslyn, connecting with her jaw and sending her sprawling to the ground.

Rosslyn LANDED WITH a thud, holding her face where Tallis had struck. She was not sure what hurt more, the punch itself, or the fact that her dearest friend had struck her at all.

Tallis seemed to think she had wanted to kill Donovan, and that she had simply been waiting for the opportune moment to strike and took advantage of a bad situation in order to do so. Tallis did not seem to understand that Rosslyn did not want to kill Donovan, but that he had ceased to be the knight they all knew and loved the moment the demon had entered his soul.

Deep down, Rosslyn knew she should forgive Tallis. She was in shock, as were they all, and she needed someone to blame for Donovan being dead. She couldn't blame the tremps who still lay on the ground around them staring vacantly up into the sky, their eyes still glowing. And she could not blame the demon, for it had perished with Donovan. Therefore, she needed to blame the woman who had loosened the bolt.

The fact that Tallis was so blinded by her pain that she could not see the kindness in Rosslyn's actions, hurt more than she was willing to admit. But as Tallis's glare of anger intensified, Rosslyn, too, lost her patience.

Rosslyn darted to her feet in a most ungraceful manner and pushed Tallis hard enough to send her falling to the ground as well. Planting her hands on her hips, it was her turn to scowl down at her friend. "Oi!

Don't you dare, Tallis. Don't you dare blame this on me. It's not my fault you're too blinded by your own shock and heartbreak to see the mercy I gave. Donovan was gone, completely consumed by that demon, and was in excruciating pain. *I* ended that for him. *I* made sure the last memory you'd have of Donovan wouldn't be one tainted by a bloody monster's words. So, you can be sad all you like that he's gone, but don't you dare think that I *wanted* to kill him."

She watched Tallis's sea green eyes turn cold as she slowly got to her feet again. It was a calm anger, an anger that Rosslyn had never seen before, and it sent shivers up her spine. Tallis frightened Rosslyn sometimes, but she would never tell anyone that she was scared of a woman who looked more like a fragile, if beautiful, girl. Instead, she tried to hold Tallis's cold gaze as if it were nothing.

After a long moment, Tallis's eyes narrowed ever so slightly as she turned her back on Rosslyn. Then she said with a voice that was uncharacteristically devoid of any inflection or emotion, "There must have been another way, a better way."

Rosslyn screwed up her face in both confusion and indignation as she blurted out, "Another way for what? To destroy the blighted creature? We had no chance to free ourselves to properly fight before that thing would have taken you. A way to save Donovan? From what Cullen and that monster said, there was no coming back from being possessed. Or do you mean that you should have been the one to die? How would that have been any better? Don't be so selfish, Tallis. Donovan sacrificed himself for *you*. He gave you a chance to live your life in freedom. Don't you dare demean that by saying it should've been you instead."

Rosslyn saw her body stiffen, and she worried that Tallis would use her elf like speed to round on her and attack once again. Instead, Tallis stared a long while at Donovan once more before silently turning her back on the gruesome scene and walking away.

Rosslyn exchanged skeptical glances with Tomas for a moment. Both were not sure what to do now that everything was over. Neither of them knew what they were now supposed to do with Tallis, or where they were supposed to go. But Rosslyn did know that in Tallis's current state of mind, she should not be left alone.

Tomas and Rosslyn quickly grabbed their items, as well as anything that might be useful off the still comatose elves, before darting after their friend. Rosslyn felt her stomach lurch at the idea of leaving Donovan behind with the bolt still sticking out of his head, but there wasn't anything they could do about it. None of them wanted to risk potentially touching him, just to find out that the demon had not completely died yet. And for as hard as it was for Rosslyn to leave Donovan behind, she knew it was infinitely worse for Tallis.

# THIRTEEN

ᏟALLIS DID NOT speak again until night had fallen upon the Guldar Forest. She let her mind roam and after the first few hours, stopped trying to keep herself from crying. Eventually, the tears ceased but Tallis suspected it was because she no longer had fluid enough to cry, and not because she was coming to terms with Donovan's passing.

She could not honestly say what she thought about, just that her mind was churning like troubled water. Her friends did not try to speak to her, something she was markedly grateful for. The last thing Tallis wanted to hear was that either of them understood anything about how she felt.

Tallis wasn't even aware of where she was heading. She knew she was following the Elwe River back to where they had come from, but she could not say to what end. She did not know where she was going, nor where she would end up. All she knew was she could not be near Donovan and the overwhelming guilt she felt.

She might have even kept walking all night if it hadn't been for Tomas sneaking his hand into hers and pulling her to his side. He squeezed her hand and Tallis could tell he was struggling with wanting to do more, but was unsure if he should, or what kind of physical contact she would find comforting.

Tallis sat down on a nearby felled tree ensnared in soft green vines and watched as Tomas and Rosslyn started a fire. Tomas didn't even bother with setting up his tripwire traps this time. There was no further need, not with all the elves currently lying in their unconscious state as the demon's poison seeped out of them.

As she watched them move around each other, Tallis could see a large bruise forming on Rosslyn's jaw and a fresh pang of guilt stabbed her in the gut. She wanted to apologize to her friend for striking her, but at the same time she could not shake the image of Rosslyn firing Tomas's crossbow. Still, everything Rosslyn had said was true. While it pained Tallis to lose her cousin, he had sacrificed himself so that she could have whatever normal life she could, and she would do her best not to squander such a gift.

Instead, Tallis kept to herself and hoped that her silence would be admission enough to the others that she was sorry for her actions and did not want to speak about it any further. Unfortunately, only Rosslyn seemed to take the hint as she went about cooking them dinner and Tomas fluttered around Tallis like a bird newly free of the nest.

Eventually, Tallis could take no more of his worried glances and sorrowful grins. Rising to her feet, she ran off into the darkness to clear her mind. She heard Tomas rise to follow her only to have Rosslyn hiss at him to stay put for the moment. It only made Tallis feel all the more guilty for striking her when

Rosslyn was still looking out for her, despite everything.

She only stopped running when she could only faintly see the soft glow of the campfire. Slowly, Tallis cleared a circular space around her and unsheathed her daggers. Her heart and mind were raging, and the only thing that ever seemed to truly clear her mind and calm her down were the battle meditations that Donovan had taught her all those years ago.

It had been ages since Tallis had truly meditated, but she still remembered how to do it. Slowly, she moved like rolling sap as she envisioned parrying foes then dealing the death blow while they were off balance. She twisted her body into impossible angles as she avoided assaults on all sides, only to deliver deft kicks and jabs to faces and exposed necks.

Tallis could feel the sweat begin to collect under her armor as her body twisted in familiar patterns. She felt her heart rate calm, despite the effort she was exerting to keep her body going in slow and controlled movements.

It was almost as if she could feel the oppressive weight of sadness being lifted from her shoulders, when suddenly the once faceless foes she was fending off turned into that of Donovan's blotchy face with the bright glowing eyes as the demon overtook him.

She stumbled and fell to the ground, eyes flying open, only to be greeted by even more darkness. Unbidden, the sobs returned as she knelt on the ground, the image of Donovan's twisted face burnt into the underside of her eyelids. No matter how much she shook her head and rubbed her eyes, the vision would not fade.

As she sat there, sobbing, Tomas softly came to join her as she crouched in the darkness. He did not speak; he simply sat beside her and wrapped his arm around her shoulders.

Normally, she would have taken comfort in his quiet presence, but instead, it just made her fume inside as she realized that if Tomas had succeeded, he would not have been here, either. Instead, it would have been Donovan to comfort her as she mourned Tomas's passing, and she was not sure which would have been worse.

The thought made her blood boil. No matter the outcome, Tallis's heart would have been broken, and she found that to be one of the cruelest injustices of all.

As that realization settled upon her, she said, "I know you need to believe I'll be all right. If I'm fine, then it's easier for you to move on and not worry about me. But the truth is I'm not all right. I'm madder than a soul trapped in Wodan's Pits, and hurt in a way I didn't think possible. So if you need me to smile so you can sleep at night without fear, then fine, I will. But don't think for a moment that I'm all right with any of this. You were going to let yourself be *murdered* for me, Tomas. I'm sure there are some girls out there who would find that terribly romantic, but not me."

Sighing, she continued, "I was either going to lose you or Donovan, or you two were going to lose me. You do see how unfair that whole situation is, right? How are any of us supposed to live with this knowledge, even if we did just save everyone in Selkirk? Not that they know, and even if they did, I doubt they'd be grateful."

Tallis wasn't sure what fair was anymore, but she

knew that this entire journey had been unfair and slated against her from the onset. She felt betrayed by the whole world for making her believe all she had to do was try her best and be a good person and eventually things would turn out for the better. She now realized that was just a lie parents told their children in order to get them to behave, just like any tale of monsters eating children who did not eat their vegetables.

After a long while, Tomas said, as he tightened his grip on her shoulders, "I know, Tallis. But it *will* be all right. You have to trust me on that. We'll get through this, and eventually, it will get better."

Somehow Tomas's words of comfort only made Tallis all the more angry and bitter. "You don't know that. You only feel like you need to say it because right now I'm making you uncomfortable. Me being sad and upset and angry has everyone at a loss for what to do to make it all better, and that makes you uncomfortable. But right now, I don't think I want to feel better, because if I feel better, then that makes the only true family I had left being dead somehow acceptable. So I'm sorry if that makes things awkward and uneasy, but I think I need to feel this."

"You always make me uncomfortable. I never know how to act around you, and this doesn't change that. I just ... I don't want you to be cross with me when I am only trying to be here for you." Tomas's arm quivered, as if he were debating releasing his hold on her.

"Then be here with me and acknowledge that this whole thing—" Tallis cut herself off and breathed deeply, letting the rest of what she would have said die on the cold night air.

---

Eventually she started again, and said with a slight tremor in her voice, "The world is a cruel and broken place, and I just want someone to acknowledge it and to stop pretending that this mess will eventually turn into just a dull ache in my memory. I just want you and Rosslyn to accept that this is really hard for me right now and for that to be all right."

Tomas did not answer, whether for lack of anything to say, or just not knowing the right words to not make things worse for her, she could not say. But it didn't matter that he did not speak, as Tomas firmly pulled Tallis to him and allowed her to sob her heart out into his dirty tunic as she took comfort in his now familiar embrace.

Rosslyn did not say anything as Tallis and Tomas returned to their campsite, hand in hand. She gave them a brief glance and turned her attention back to the slabs of beef and pine nuts she was roasting. Tallis sat cross-legged across from her and prodded the fire, sending pieces of ash to float into the icy air.

"I'm sorry, Rozy," Tallis mumbled just when the silence had become uncomfortable.

Rosslyn shrugged her shoulders delicately and pushed her curly black hair from her eyes. "I'm going to tell you that it's all right that you sucker punched me. I understand why you did it. But really, none of it will matter unless you believe me when I tell you that I never wanted to harm Donovan, and shooting him was a last, and desperate resort."

"I know it was. If it hadn't been for Cullen's betrayal, then we would've been able to find a better way to dispose of that monster, but … well, I do know you didn't want to kill him. You … it was a mercy killing. I understand that now."

"Then I forgive you. Besides, now we all have our various battle scars from the ordeal. Not that my bruise is nearly as impressive as the scars on your arm from where that first nasty tremp clawed you and rendered you unconscious, but I guess it will have to do."

Tallis chuckled dryly and bobbed her head, the tightening in her chest dissipating slightly with Rosslyn's forgiveness. She did not know if she would ever feel the same again with the gaping holes in her heart that had once been occupied by her mother and Donovan's constant love. But with her friends' forgiveness and acceptance, it was at least a start in the right direction.

"So, where to now? It seems like we have the whole of Selkirk in front of us. We could even revive those fishing villages, like the one at Lake Mithrim if we wanted to. Without the threat of the elves, we could go anywhere and do anything, possibly even leave Selkirk, if we really wished to. So what is next for us?" Tomas's voice wavered slightly, as if he were concerned that the answer to his inquiry would lead to a place where he could not be with Tallis.

Tallis's brow furrowed as she thought. It was true that with the elves no longer under the demon's spell that Selkirk's old trading partners would once again open their borders. They could take a ship and travel to Theda, Andor, or even try and find a new nation altogether. The possibilities seemed endless because Tallis did not know just how many options were truly available to them. But one thing was for certain, it would be something completely new.

As she considered the options, a name entered her

mind that sent a cold chill deep into her bones. *Nessa. I have to tell Nessa.* The realization caused Tallis to drop her head in her hands with a groan.

"What?" Rosslyn quickly asked.

Tallis looked at her. "We have to go to Isildor."

"No, we don't, we don't have to go there at all. Especially if all you're going to do is groan about it." Rosslyn shook her head and turned her attention to pulling the meat and the now popping pine nuts from the fire.

"Yes, we do. I have to … according to my father, Nessa and my Uncle Baird are in Isildor. I have to tell them what happened to Donovan, or they will waste the rest of their lives waiting for him to come home."

Tomas put his hand on Tallis's back and met her eyes, the firelight making them twinkle like emeralds. "Then that is where we will go."

Tallis smiled sadly and nodded, worried that if she tried to express her gratitude it would only come out as a hoarse croak.

Rosslyn started passing out their supper with a frown. "Fine, but then I get to do some shopping while you deliver your news. Isildor is the only place to get decent pale ale in all of Selkirk, and my mum would never forgive me if I didn't get her a bottle while we were there."

Tallis would forever be grateful to Rosslyn's unwavering conviction that she would somehow always be able to find her family again. It did not matter to Rosslyn that she did not know where they would be after Kincardine fell, let alone where they would go if the town they fled to also fell victim to an elven raid.

# FOURTEEN

ᗰORNING CAME WITH a bone piercing coldness and a gray fog that settled in the air like a wet shawl. Normally, the chill would have aggravated Tallis who never liked being cold, but today the chill and grayness of the morning seemed to perfectly suit her mood. The first of her friends to rise, Tallis decided to take advantage of the few moments she would have alone before they continued on their trek to Isildor.

After rekindling their fire to chase away the icy air, Tallis crept through the forest with all the grace of a doe avoiding hunters. She could feel the reassuring power of the ancient trees pulsating through her boots, and she wanted to take advantage of their strength before she had to look into the sweet face of Nessa as she broke her heart, or meet her uncle's eyes as she told him that his only child was forever beyond his reach. She was also curious if the communication with the ancient trees would be different now that she knew what she was and the demon was gone.

She stopped at the foot of a tall juniper tree with needle-like leaves and fat blue berries hanging just out of reach. The juniper's berries were aromatic and had a sweet calming effect on Tallis's raw nerves. Smiling softly, Tallis placed her hand on the tree's ash gray bark and waited.

Tallis had envisioned this encounter being different, with the tree not hesitating to meld with her mind, or with the juniper being relieved to learn that Tallis now knew she was a half-elf and, indeed, one of the voices it had been missing. At the very least, she had expected the tree to thank her or rejoice at being once again connected with all the elves after centuries of being disconnected.

But that was not what happened.

It took a while for the juniper tree to realize a half-child of the forest was even touching its rough bark, and when it finally shook the slowness from its consciousness, it offered no gratitude and no comfort for Tallis. Instead, all Tallis felt was the pleading feeling as the tree once again asked her in a wordless deep tenor melody to return the songs of its children. She could feel the sadness emanating from the tree as it begged Tallis to hurry, and she was once again shown the fleeting image of the ancient yew tree.

Tallis dropped her hand in confusion and slowly blinked open her eyes. She took a few steps back and stared up into the green needles of the tree as if she were searching for a face to address.

She had freed the tremps; surely the trees must know that? Surely the elves must be coming to their senses and rediscovering what it truly meant to be an elf rather than a thrall to a demon?

She left the juniper tree feeling no better, but instead, more confused and vaguely concerned. She had watched the beast die and had seen the elves collapse with the demon's passing. Why had that not been enough to cauterize whatever wound had been caused by the demon's foul corruption?

She wanted to believe that it would simply take time for the elves to come out of their stupor and be reconnected with their ancient ways; after all, it would take time to free their minds completely after being a thrall for three hundred years. But there was a nagging in the depths of her heart telling her that something was not right. If she could find this ancient yew, she should, if only to reassure the trees she had, indeed, returned the elves back to what they had been like prior to the demon's enslavement.

By the time she had returned to her friends, they were no longer sleeping. Both Tomas and Rosslyn were lazily lounging around the fire, allowing its comforting warmth to chase the chill from their bones and the sleep from their faces.

Tomas smiled hesitantly at Tallis as she returned. She could tell he wanted to ask her where she had been, but was unsure if she were hunting out a quiet spot to be alone and cry in privacy, or if she had snuck away for a different purpose. Tallis sat down next to him and silently took the warm brown bread stuffed with dried fish from Rosslyn. She nibbled as she thought over her encounter with the juniper and what it could mean.

She wanted to tell her friends what had occurred, but she was not sure if it was relevant. None of them understood her connection to the ancient trees in the forest, and she doubted they would know why the trees could not feel the elves now that the demon was gone. Still, given everything that happened, Tallis was simply not interested in keeping anything to herself anymore.

"So this tree doesn't know that the demon is dead yet? Fantastic." Rosslyn said. "But from what you said, it doesn't sound like the trees even knew about the demon from the beginning. So why would they know when it died? Maybe the elves have to do something, some ritual or rain dance, or … something to reestablish whatever the demon cut off from them?"

"I don't know, maybe? I just thought that something would've been different now that things have been fixed. But you're probably right. I'm sure that whenever the elves actually wake up they'll need to do something to reestablish themselves with the trees, or, I guess, their gods? Whatever they are."

Tomas remained silent as he considered what Tallis said. She knew that he mostly found what she had to say curious and fascinating from an academic standpoint more than anything else. Tallis wished he would say something that would help push the doubt from her mind that something was still amiss in Selkirk but was hardly surprised when he didn't.

They ate their breakfast and only begrudgingly packed up their camp and continued along the Elwe River for a while longer. Eventually, they would no longer be able to follow the river, not if they wished to get to Isildor. They would need to cut back through the Uldor Forest and cross the Maglor River before they would even come within a day's walk of the city. Still, Tallis was in no great hurry to get to her Uncle Baird and Nessa to deliver her sad news.

They had just cut away from the Elwe River when they had encountered their first elf since the demon's demise. It was a young mother with an infant held tightly in her pale and stringy arms. The mother's feathery chestnut-brown curls fell over her wide and staring yellow eyes as she lay perfectly still on the forest floor.

She was a lovely woman with a delicate button nose, high cheekbones, and a heart-shaped face. If it weren't for the faint yellow glow in her eyes and the way she unnervingly stared up into the afternoon sky, she would have been utterly captivating.

The same could not be said of the infant clutched in her arms. The slight baby boy no longer had eyes with which to stare. Instead, he had two charred holes where his eyes should have been, as if they had been burnt form the inside out. His toothless mouth was open as if he had died mid-scream from whatever had burned out his little eyes. Tallis thought the saddest thing of all was not that this child had died, but that its mother had no knowledge that the babe she held in her arms had perished more than a day ago.

The sight made Tallis's stomach lurch, and it was all she could do not to hurl up her breakfast right then and there. Rosslyn was not as fortunate, as she darted behind the nearest tree to vomit as the gruesome scene overpowered her. Tomas's fascination was the one thing that saved him from following Rosslyn's lead. His curiosity at what could have caused such a thing to occur momentarily outweighed his disgust.

Tallis watched him kneel down next to the comatose mother and check her pulse. Dropping her hand, he puzzled over the dead baby for a moment longer before rising and turning his back on the scene. "The mother is still alive. If I had to guess, I'd say that the process of disconnecting from the demon was too much for the youngest members of the elven race to withstand. A pity really, the young ones would have had the easiest time forgiving and forgetting the Clearing." He wiped his hands on his trousers as if he could brush off the smell of death.

Tallis spared one more glance for the young mother and her eyeless infant before walking away. Her stomach may have churned at the sight of the dead child, but she was still having difficulty feeling remorse over any calamity the elves might've had to face. "You may be right, and if that's the case, I don't want to be near her when she wakes to find her child dead."

As they left the river farther and farther behind, they came across more tremps. Those that appeared young and healthy were all staring vacantly up into the sky, never once blinking. The old, frail, or the very young, however, all had gaping holes where their eyes had been burnt from the inside out as their connection to the demon was instantly and brutally severed upon Donovan's death.

Despite Tallis's ire at the elves for taking the lives of the people she loved the most, even she could only handle seeing so many eyeless carcasses before she could take no more. Tallis cut sharply into the Uldor Forest in hopes that if she deviated from their current course, they would get away from the trail of misery and death.

They had been idly walking for the majority of the day when a shiver ran the length of Tallis's spine. It was unlike anything she had ever felt before; it was not an unpleasant feeling, but she could not say she enjoyed the sensation, either. It was not a shiver of cold or fear; it almost felt electric in nature. It was as if she had been struck by a small bolt of lightning directly on the spine sending a shock to tingle throughout her body.

Tallis stopped dead in her tracks as the electric shiver ran its course, feeling her body tremble and shake as it went. When she turned to her friends, they were both watching her strangely, as if all of a sudden, they expected her to give in to the evil elven side of her nature.

"Well that was vaguely unpleasant." Tallis shook out her hands to be rid of the last tingles tickling her fingertips.

"What was that all about?" Rosslyn asked.

Tallis shrugged. "I don't know. I just … it was a shiver of sorts." Tallis lost her trail of thought as something in the distance caught her eye. Through the tree line, Tallis could vaguely see a meadow-like clearing in the middle of the forest.

Meadows themselves were not odd, Selkirk was known to have quite a few of them, and all were rumored to be very lovely. But for one to be located in the middle of an otherwise dense forest peaked Tallis's curiosity.

Without a word, she made for the small clearing of soft bright green grass. She could hear Tomas and Rosslyn protest behind her, followed by their clatter as they hurried to catch up with her all the same. By the time they had, Tallis had already stopped dead in her tracks.

In front of Tallis was none other than the ancient yew she had been shown when she had tried speaking

187

to the other trees. It stood alone in the middle of the clearing like a yawning monster. But despite the appearance of a gaping mouth and bushy green leaves that made it appear to have hair, Tallis did not get the impression she should fear this old little yew.

Tallis swore she could feel the pulse of a heartbeat all around her. This area was overflowing with life, energy, love, and it made her want to do nothing but curl up at the base of the tree and let its overwhelming power wash over her until all the pain and bad memories fell away like snow at the end of winter.

Glancing at Tomas and Rosslyn, she couldn't help but smile. By the mixture of fear, awe, and happiness flitting over their faces, Tallis knew they could feel *something* as well; it may have just been wonder at such a blemish free meadow in the middle of a dense forest, but Tallis liked to believe that they felt some of the same things she was feeling, even if they didn't understand why.

*Tallis.*

She grabbed her daggers and sprang into an offensive position as she heard her name. It seemed to come from all around her at the same time, giving her the impression she was surrounded, but it didn't sound like a snake, like the way the elves said her name. Instead, it was a slow contralto like drawl, as if it had come from very far away.

As she looked for the source of whatever said her name, she noticed that both Tomas and Rosslyn were giving her fearful looks; they had not heard a thing.

Dropping her daggers to her side, she opened her mouth to explain when she heard her name again. Nothing was in the area, though, no elves, no people and, despite some ravens and crows being able to mimic names, she knew it was no bird or animal. And despite how mad it seemed, it left only one possibility as to what could have said her name in such a way that only she could hear it.

"You can't hear that, can you?" she asked, hoping she was wrong and the tree was not speaking directly in her mind. But when she got nothing but blank stares in return, she had her answer.

"The tree is, well, speaking," Tallis said with a shrug, hoping that would be enough of an explanation to ease their worry over the state of her sanity. When it did not, she rolled her eyes. "It's hardly the most surprising thing to happen, if you think about it."

Turning to the old yew, Tallis trotted over, and just as she was about to place her hand on its oddly smooth bark, she hesitated. Before, she always needed to have physical contact with the tree in order to sense what it was thinking or feeling. But the yew tree was already speaking in her mind without any physical contact. She was not sure if she should then answer the tree normally, or try and direct her thoughts to it. She also wondered which would make her appear less insane to her friends as they now crowded around her. After a moment longer of hesitating, she firmly planted her hand on the tree and shut her eyes.

*It is good you have found me,* the tree sang, its contralto voice oozing through her mind like overly wet dough, thick, slow, and sticking to every crevice it could find.

"Yes, but finding you was completely by accident. Your brethren seemed intent on making sure I knew that I should locate you, but couldn't tell me where you were, or why I should find you in the first place. I'm still rather new to all of this, and I couldn't understand what they were trying to say." Even if talking aloud was not necessary, she wanted to make sure the others at least knew half of the conversation.

*It has been a very long time since we have needed to speak with these clunky words your kind use. Even when our children still sang with us, we hardly needed to speak in this manner. Many of my kind never learned how to begin with. Now most have forgotten and have lost the way to speak with anything beyond the most basic of our language, let alone yours. Without the children of the forest, they have forgotten much, and yet, there is still so much more to forget.*

"Was it you then that gave me that dream? The one that warned me about the owls and twites watching our progress?"

*No, but it was one like me.*

"We killed the one responsible for turning the elves and animals against everyone. It was a demon the elves had summoned, so they could win the war they raged against the humans. Or something like that, I don't know, it's all rather confusing. Either way, the elves lost in every sense of the word, and they paid for it dearly. Surely the elves will return to you now and everything will go back to how it was before all of this, right?"

Tallis couldn't hide the hint of anger and sadness in her voice. If slaying the demon was not going to fix the elves, then she wasn't sure why she even bothered tracking the beast down in the first place, especially with the price she had to pay.

*A demon you say? Our children must have been*

*desperate to resort to such dark measures. Had they spoken to a Second or Third about it, we would have discouraged such a course. Promises from a tainted First are never without their price.*

"A First? What?" Tallis said, obviously confused. But before the tree could respond, she pressed on, "So wait, you didn't know? You had no idea that there was a demon controlling the mind of every elf for hundreds of years?"

*When you can live for thousands of years, young one, a few hundred does not seem so long. We felt our children be severed from our hearts, the wound never to be cauterized. We did not know why, and we could not speak with them to find out. We had lost our eyes, Tallis, and could not see what had become of them.*

"But how is that possible? How can you know I was here if you can't see me?"

*I did not need to see you to know you were there. I feel you much as you feel me. When we were connected to our children, we could see through their eyes. Now we can only share what has already been seen.*

"How could the demon have done all of this?"

*The creature is not a demon. But was once one such as I. One of the ancient beings that our children consider to be gods. A First.*

"You aren't the elves' god?"

*I cannot say for certain, for I do not know. I know I tend to this land, and have for more years than I can recall. I was the Second to find our children. I prefer to be a parent, not a god. But that is not important now. Each of my kind is an individual. Our children managed to find one of us who was not content to live as it was meant to. It wanted to see and experience your world for itself.*

"So, in order to literally see Selkirk, it had to trick the elves into believing it was a creature capable of winning the war. That's why they had to find a way to bring it out of the tree itself? That doesn't even sound possible."

*Possible or not, it does not matter. All that matters is that it happened. A creature that should have never left its realm has, and taken away the one thing that made our long and slow years meaningful.*

"So, it's just a tree spirit like you then? Or it was. It wasn't even a demon at all? I don't understand."

*It was and it was not. When it no longer was content to be what it was, it became the thing you know as a demon. A creature meant to destroy and corrupt, rather than protect and nourish. And it is still corrupting our children, even now.*

"No, that's not true. I told you already, we killed it. We killed it before it could take over my body and enslave both the elves and the humans of this land. It's over now."

*I am sorry, young one. But the sacrifice that was made was not the end of this evil creature.*

"No, this Sipsi traitor, Cullen, he said that we had to just kill it while it was inside a body. The body's death would send it back to wherever it came from."

*I do not know of the one you speak, but he has told you falsely, little one.*

"Don't call me that, only my mother calls me that, and you are not her! I have lost my entire family to return these bloody tremps to you. Creatures so twisted that we have to purge them every four years so they won't plague our towns and steal our children. I have given *everything* to fix a problem that should've never been mine to fix. And now you're telling me that I lost the one real family member I had left for nothing?"

Tallis's voice was cracking with emotion. As it was, she was having a hard-enough time comprehending the wealth of knowledge the tree was imparting to her, let alone the further heartbreak that her cousin's sacrifice had been in vain.

She felt Tomas plant his hand on her shoulder and give her a squeeze, as if he could give her strength to better shoulder the weight of what the tree was telling her without knowing what it was. It helped a little as Tallis blinked away her tears and focused back on the old yew tree, trying to make sense of its slow words.

"What did we do then if we didn't actually kill it?"

*By destroying the mortal vessel the creature inhabited, you have greatly weakened it. It would have needed to return to the gate where it came from. It is there you will find it once again.*

"The gate? You mean the tree the elves summoned it from?"

*Precisely. Our children cannot return to us until the gate has been shut.*

"And how do I do that? I assume there isn't really a door for me to close, is there?"

*I am unsure. I can, however, show you the gate and how to reach it. But that is all I can do, young one. The rest will be up to you. I can offer some aid, if you should need it. Our children will remain alone and lost to all unless the creature manages to capture another vessel with which to animate them. I would ask you to hurry, young one. The longer our children remain as they are, the more will be forever lost to us.*

---

"So, if I do this, close this gate or whatever it actually is, then it's over? You won't need me anymore?"

*I do not know when the need for you will end, young one, if it ever will. But if you manage this, you will have done us the greatest service one could have ever done.*

Tallis gritted her teeth before speaking. She was not relishing the idea of plunging back into the forest to do more errands on behalf of the tremps. In fact, it made her stomach churn into angry knots over the mere idea of doing anything to help the elves after what they had not only done to her, but to Kincardine, and her country as a whole. She did not feel like they deserved any further help, and that they deserved to lay comatose on the ground until their bodies decayed naturally.

She wanted nothing more than to leave right now and continue on her way to Isildor. She knew what awaited her there would not be pleasant, but she knew she would get closure from it, and that it would allow her to one day be able to move on with the rest of her life.

The citizens of Selkirk would eventually forget that the tremps had risen up and hissed her name as they pillaged and burned everything to the ground in the same way that they had forgotten so much else. Everything from their own humble origins before the monarchy and what the other nations across the sea were like. They would be able to go back into the forest once again without fear, and there would never need to be another Clearing ever again, for the elves would finally be eradicated once and for all. She may never be hailed as a hero by the king and queen, but at least she would be free to live a life of her choosing.

Tallis was not sure what there was to gain by returning the elves back to the way they were, now that she was being given the choice. The tremps had been warring with the humans even before the demon's influence. Returning them to their own minds would not fix that. Who was to say they would not continue fighting once they woke up? Who was to say they would not turn to a twisted deity once again just to have the cycle begin anew?

The yew tree sensed the thoughts racing through her mind as it softly interjected, *We will ensure our children do not make the same mistakes of the past. We will instill peace in their minds and hearts, and no creature will ever again take them from us. I promise you, Tallis.*

Tallis dropped her head and stared down at her muddy boots. With all her heart, she did not want to help the elves. She did not want to save them. But she knew it was what her mother would have wanted. It was what Donovan would have encouraged, despite the fact he had been on more than one Clearing during his time as a knight. And with the way Tomas was watching her now, she knew he would disapprove if she allowed the elves to now wither and die.

She could almost hear them telling her it was wrong to condemn a whole race for one mistake. She could hear her cousin tell her if there was a demon responsible, that it changed everything he believed about the elves. The memory was not an old one, he had said as much when they had first reached Lake Mithrim, but it felt like a lifetime ago. Tallis knew her family would ask her to try and forgive the elves. That it was the right thing to do.

She sighed and shut her eyes, forcing the tears, caused by her memories and shame for wanting to let all the elves die, roll down her cheeks. After another moment, she whispered, "Very well, tell me where this demon's gate is."

The yew tree did not speak; instead, it implanted a type of map into Tallis's mind. She was being shown the path to take that would lead her back into the Guldar Forest and just across the murky green water of the Osse River. There, in the center of a circle much like the one the yew tree was in, was the tree that was the demon's gate.

*It will be different now, young one. The path is the same, but my sister will not look the way she did before she left her true form behind. The corruption used to bring the First into the world would have destroyed the land, and I cannot see the damage that has been done. But that should not matter; you will know the gate when you find it.*

Tallis was still walking the path the tree had just shown her in her mind's eye, digesting and committing it to memory, when she asked, "You said you would offer us assistance?"

*The creature has lost its hold; the animals that attacked you before will aid you now, if trouble should arise. They will keep you safe from all harm as you travel down this path. You will not be alone, Tallis.*

She could feel the tree withdraw from her mind, causing a warmth to bloom in her chest and spread throughout her body. It would have been comforting if her heart hadn't already been sick with the idea of helping the very creatures that had murdered her mother and caused the violent death of her cousin. As her mind once again became completely her own, she brushed away her tears with the back of her hand and turned to face her still shocked friends.

"It would seem we have more work to do it," Tallis said as she quickly went through what the ancient yew had told her, and ending with where it had said the tree the monster had come through would be waiting for them.

Rosslyn looked unconvinced. "We have to close a gate that is also a tree?"

"Something like that, yes. The tree wasn't particularly helpful in telling me how to accomplish that, but it shouldn't be too difficult now that we don't have to worry about the elves. At worst, we spend a few days trying to burn the tree down with some of Tomas's special powders." Without knowing what else there was to do or explain, Tallis shrugged and started back the way they had come.

Tomas began rubbing the back of his neck. "I've never tried to actually start a fire with my explosive powders before, Tallis. I would need to find more ingredients before that would even be possible."

She glanced at him and could not help but grin a little as his eyes twinkled with the prospect of solving a challenge. Despite the sickening feeling Tallis had at the idea of doing the elves any favors, she couldn't help but find Tomas's quiet enthusiasm endearing.

"I'm sure you'll think of something brilliant, Tomas, you always do," Tallis told him as she continued to plunge into the forest, hoping to get to the demon gate as quickly as she could in order to be done with this quest. As it was, it was going to take three to four days of brisk walking before they could reach the place the yew tree had showed her, even without having to worry about being attacked along the way.

"So what did it look like?" Rosslyn asked as she skipped alongside Tallis.

Normally, Rosslyn's unabashed curiosity and playful demeanor would have lifted her spirits. But for various reasons, Tallis only found it aggravating. "What did *what* look like?"

"The demon tree, or whatever you want to call it. I'd think it's got to look pretty scary, considering what came out of it. Was it yellow and glowing like all the tremps's eyes? And did it have a hole in it that looks like a face, sort of like the yew tree? That tree you were talking to looked pretty frightening, and it was one of the good guys. I can only imagine what the bad guy would look like."

Tallis wasn't sure if her friend was excited or nervous, with how quickly she was speaking. It wasn't like Rosslyn to really care one way or another, and it made part of her wonder what could really be on Rosslyn's mind. But mostly, she did not want to be bothered with it right now.

Tallis shrugged. "It looked like a normal tree, really. Wasn't anything special or notable about it, other than it was in a clearing just like the yew. It did look a bit stooped, though, like it was in the process of bending over to pick something up. Beyond that, nothing all that scary about it, though the tree did mention it may look different now. Why does it matter?"

Rosslyn balked at Tallis as if she were not

expecting such a question. She scratched the back of her head, avoiding Tallis's eyes. "No reason. I just ... I was curious, is that a crime now?"

Tallis cocked an eyebrow, but did not question Rosslyn any further. Tallis was tired and not in the mood to force anyone to tell her what was bothering them. If there was something on Rosslyn's mind, she figured Rosslyn would volunteer the information when she was ready.

She was so lost in her own thoughts afterwards, that Tallis almost completely forgot Rosslyn's strange behavior until Tomas said as he matched his gait with hers, "I think she just wants things to go back to how they were before she, you know, shot the demon when it was in Donovan."

Tallis looked at Tomas oddly for a moment as it took her a while to realize what he was talking about. Her eyes widened and mouth dropped open as understanding washed over her.

"I know it must be hard. Well, no, I don't really know what it must be like, but I hope you don't ... blame Rosslyn. I know you say you don't, after you two had that fight, but still. I think she's worried that once we actually finish this and we burn down this ... gate, that we will go to Isildor, and you will conveniently lose her when you go to see Nessa. I know that's what I'd be worried about if I were her, anyway."

Tallis had never really stopped to consider what Rosslyn must be going through. She never considered that perhaps it had been hard for her to shoot Donovan, regardless of knowing that it was the right and merciful thing to do. She was not sure if Rosslyn felt guilty or upset about what she had done. But either way, Tallis knew that despite Rosslyn's nonchalant personality, she must be conflicted about what she had done, no matter how justified she might have felt.

Tallis's shoulders sagged and she deflated a little. "I never really thought about what Rosslyn must be going through. I know I ... I still need time. I don't necessarily blame her, but Donovan's dead, and I'm just having a hard time trying to process everything. At this point, to say it's a lot to handle is a little bit of an understatement. But no, I don't blame her or hate her. But I can't really pretend nothing happened, either."

Tomas nodded and she saw his fingers twitch, as if he were about to take her hand, but thought better of it.

"That makes sense," he said, finally. "I don't think you should act as if nothing happened. But I do know your friendship with Rosslyn is important, especially now that ... well, now that she's all you really have. I just ... I just think it would be a shame if you two could not go back to how you were before all of this, that's all."

Tallis nodded and gave Tomas a sad half-smile. Taking his hand and squeezing it briefly, she said, "You're right, Tomas. I just need a little more time, I promise."

Tomas blushed and nodded his head as Tallis continued to hold his hand. She wondered if she should let go, but the rough warmth of his hands helped keep her bad mood at bay. So despite his blushing and bashful glances, she continued to hold his hand as dusk began to fall around them.

# FIFTEEN

ᏛHE NEXT MORNING, Rosslyn found Tallis sitting on the ground with her knees pulled up under her chin and her face buried in her arms. She tried to sneak up quietly so as to not frighten Tallis, but she needn't have bothered as Tallis said without raising her head, "It's all right; you don't need to creep through the forest on my account, Roz."

Tallis using her pet name made Rosslyn grin a little and hope that perhaps things were not as strained as she believed. But when Tallis raised her head as she approached, Rosslyn's hope started to slightly ebb. She did not see any warmth or friendliness in Tallis's red rimmed eyes. Instead, Rosslyn saw how Tallis's shoulder's stiffened and her jaw clenched as she approached, and it reminded Rosslyn once again that Tallis had yet to truly forgive her.

Frowning at Tallis, Rosslyn sat down on the ground across from her and crossed her arms. They stared at each other in silence for a time, as if waiting for the other to break the spell that hung over them.

Rosslyn could see the heavy circles under her eyes from the lack of sleep, crying, and the sorrow that was following Tallis like a pack of starving dogs, ready to rip her to shreds if she stumbled. It was hard for Rosslyn to stay mad at her when the cracks in Tallis's resolve were so obvious.

She kept forgetting that Donovan had only been dead barely two days. Given everything that had happened, his death felt long ago, but still so fresh that Rosslyn swore she could still feel the cold weight of Tomas's crossbow in her hands.

"We need to stop this, Tallis. I … I need you to forgive me."

"I already told you I forgave you. And I also said sorry for hitting you. We've been over this already."

Rosslyn furrowed her brow and clenched her fists. "This, *this* is what we need to stop. You say you forgive me and all that, but you really haven't. Oi, I know it's still fresh, but I can't—"

Rosslyn cut herself off and hung her head, a single tear rolling from her cheek to land in her lap. After a moment, she continued, "I can't stay with you if this is all our friendship is going to be. It's too painful. I followed you halfway across Selkirk because this sounded like the adventure of a lifetime with my best friend, and I wasn't about to miss it. But now…."

Rosslyn stared off into the distance, letting her sentence hang in the air like heavy mist. Eventually, she said, "I miss him, too, Tally. I know it never seemed like we got along, and I know it's not nearly close to what you feel, but I have to live with knowing I killed my best friend's only true family member. I can't be here with you if you won't ever let that go, if we can't be like how we were before."

Rosslyn could feel Tallis's stare, and all she

wanted was for Tallis to relent, for her bitter anger to deflate. But as the silence stretched, Rosslyn knew that was not going to happen.

"Roz, I don't know what you want me to say. As much as I say that it's all right, that I understand, part of me wants to blame someone for this. I know it isn't you I should blame, that it shouldn't be. But I wish I could help it. And I'm trying. I really am. But I'm afraid to close my eyes, because all I see is the bolt sticking out of Donovan's head and I think of who put it there. I told Tomas that I just needed time and things would be fine, and I do think that's true."

It would have been easier if Tallis had been irrational about it. If she had exploded and outright said she blamed Rosslyn and could not forgive her. Then Rosslyn could have gotten angry, and it would have been easier to leave. But with Tallis being rational and extending the promise of one day things returning to normal, it made things so much harder.

She wanted everything to be better now; she *needed* everything to go back to the way it was before Donovan died, so that her own guilt would not consume her. Guilt was an unfamiliar feeling to Rosslyn, one she did not like at all. If this was the feeling Tallis had carried ever since Lana had died, Rosslyn wasn't sure how she had survived all these years, and especially when she was having trouble dealing with it for just a few days.

"Tallis, I—" Rosslyn started only to have Tallis shake her head and cut her off.

"Roz, don't. I know this is hard for you, believe me. It's a weird feeling to take a life, even when you know you have to. I can't imagine what it's like to take the life of a friend, even if … even if they had died before you actually pulled the trigger. I want to help you; I want to make this easier for you. I just don't know how to right now. I'm not that decent of a person, apparently. I'm sure it would disappoint my mother to know that."

Rosslyn opened her mouth to speak, but found she had nothing to say. She wasn't sure if she had been selfish to want Tallis to completely forgive her, but she was no longer as bitter and desperate as she had been. She understood that Tallis's forgiveness was coming in the near future, and that needed to be enough for now, or she would, indeed, completely push her friend out of her life.

"You'll let me know then, when things are good between us?" Rosslyn asked as she got to her feet.

Tallis awarded her with a soft smile. "You'll be the first."

𝕿HE EERIE SILENCE that had nestled over the forest with the demon's passing still lingered, making the hairs on the back of Tallis's neck stand on end. Something felt wrong and she could not say necessarily what it was. For the moment, she chalked it up to the idea of the fiend not completely being gone mixed in with her own bone-crushing sorrow making her believe a storm was about to erupt.

"You feel that, too, don't you?" Tallis asked as they carefully crossed one of the many rivers between them and their destination.

Rosslyn's nose twitched as she struggled with trying to pinpoint the source of her unease. "Something just feels *wrong*. It's almost as if my body knows something my mind doesn't." Rosslyn laughed sardonically. "Now I sound as mad as you, Tallis. Fantastic."

Tallis rolled her eyes and considered what Rosslyn was actually saying. Tallis did not feel as strongly as Rosslyn did; while she felt that something was wrong, it was not with the same strength that both Tomas and Rosslyn seemed to be experiencing. At most, Tallis felt uncomfortable and a little paranoid. From the sounds and looks of things, Tomas and Rosslyn were on the verge of becoming ill with the intensity of their unease.

With the slightly green pallor that was beginning to spread across Tomas's face, it began to remind Tallis of her sickness when they had crossed Lake Mithrim and again after leaving Fordoun, and the unexplainable discomfort it had brought with it. She wasn't sure what was causing it or why it seemed to affect her friends more than it did her, but it made Tallis hurry all the more on their way, as if they could outrun whatever it was causing them to feel so wrong in their own skin.

Unfortunately, they could not move as quickly as Tallis would have liked, as whatever it was that was plaguing her friends began to worsen and slow them down. Before long, it was becoming dusk once again and Tallis hadn't nearly covered all the ground she had wanted to.

As they paused to catch their breath, Tallis heard clumsy crashing coming through the forest. She pushed her friends against a fat oak and motioned for them to be silent as she peered around the trunk. Walking through the forest as if they were intoxicated and could not see where they were going, were a whistle of elves.

Tallis's mouth dropped open at the scene. It was completely different from what the elves had been like under the demon's influence, but it was still obvious they were being organized, even if it was not under the same level of control as they had once been. Still, the elves seemed completely disinterested in Tallis and her friends, as a few went right past them without a second glance.

Cursing, Tallis turned away from the horde and asked, "Do you think that demon, or god First-thing is back?"

With great difficulty, as Tomas fought to stay alert and appear as if he were doing better, he said, "That seems awfully fast for the demon to recover, but ... I don't have another explanation for the elves suddenly waking up, either. All the more reason for us to keep going."

Tallis knew with a sinking certainty that her friends could not accompany her where she was headed this time. She remembered all too well what it felt like to be afflicted by the demon's corruption, and how it almost completely incapacitated her. She would never be able to do what needed to be done if she was also distracted by trying to keep her friends safe.

"Not this time, Tomas," she said. "I have to do this alone the rest of the way."

Both Rosslyn and Tomas made to protest and follow her, but with a heavy heart and tears in her eyes, she put her hands on their shoulders and stopped them. "You know I have to do this. I won't let Donovan's death be in vain and, with your illness, you'll both be easy targets for the tremps. Trust me, I know what you're going through. But if I wait for you both to recover ... who's to say what will happen or what body the demon will take next? I either do this now, or ... or all of this, everything we've done, survived and lost, will be for nothing."

"You're being overly dramatic," Rosslyn spat. "You don't have to go bloody tramping through the forest by yourself to do this, you just think you do because that's what heroes are supposed to do and say."

Tallis shook her head to argue, but Tomas cut her off. "She's right, Tallis. We have a better chance of succeeding if we stick together and face this demon as a group. There's no need for us to split up."

"I'd agree, except that the longer we wait the stronger the beast gets. We barely escaped last time, and the cost ... I can't risk losing either of you. I won't. Especially when this is my destiny. I was literally born to face off with this creature. I won't ask anyone else to put themselves in danger on my account. No, I have to go the rest of the way by myself." Tallis squared her shoulders and met their eyes, her tone brooking no argument.

Rosslyn placed her hand over Tallis's and nodded. Even though it was obvious Rosslyn still wanted to go with her, she relented to Tallis's argument.

Tomas was still not having as easy of a time with the idea, though, as his face contorted with pain and longing. "I can't let you do this alone. What if ...

Tallis, please. Don't do this."

Rosslyn gave Tallis one last squeeze of the hand. "Be safe, my mum would be very sore with me if I didn't bring you home. And trust me, she isn't one you want to cross." Tallis gave Rosslyn a soft smile and nodded her head as her friend slowly waddled away.

Tallis watched her go, her stomach tying into knots. There was so much Tallis still wanted to say and do with Rosslyn. Despite still being unable to completely forget her role in Donovan's death, she knew it was not her fault and she longed for her heart to completely accept that.

She could still remember chasing her through the streets of Kincardine as she attempted to get the money Rosslyn had pilfered from her. If someone would have told her that the same girl who had stolen from her on their first meeting would eventually become her best friend, Tallis would have laughed right in their face. Life was strangely glorious like that sometimes; just as it could be cruel and unforgiving, so could it be a mysterious wonderland of unexpected joy and chance encounters.

As Rosslyn settled herself at the base of a tree, Tallis turned back to the man in front of her. She didn't know how it happened, but she had grown to care for Tomas in a way that she could not understand. Often, Tallis had envisioned the kind of man she would have been all right settling down with, and she would have never guessed that it would have been a bashful and brilliant young man raised in a monastery.

The constant and reassuring presence of Tomas had planted a seed in her heart that had begun to grow and bloom before she was aware it was even happening. The way he always listened to her and never judged or questioned her after he found her sleeping on the monastery floor, were moments she had come to treasure as much as her mother's wedding ring. The way he had always wanted to impress her with his intellect more than his brawn had been something Tallis had been completely unprepared for. It was something she had never expected of any man, and it had allowed the tall, chiseled, ex-initiate to plant himself in her heart when no other man could.

Tallis touched her forehead to Tomas's and cupped his head in her hands. She could feel him tremble at her touch and she knew it was not his illness sending shivers through his body. The realization sent a thrill through her core and made her heart ache at the same time. For as much as it hurt to wake up every morning knowing her mother and now Donovan wouldn't be there, she knew for a certainty that she did not want to die and leave Tomas behind.

She felt his hands rest tentatively on her waist, and, when she didn't wriggle out of his grasp, become more confident as he found the space between her leather and chainmail where his fingers could lightly brush her skin. She felt her skin prickle under his touch, his calloused fingers leaving her skin warm wherever they touched her. She marveled at how a man who had lived such a sheltered life could have such a strong and sturdy grip.

"Let me come with you. You will need help. If there are elves or, Wodan forbid, the demon *is* back, you'll need help burning this gate while simultaneously dealing with any resistance. The illness … it's not that bad. I can help you," Tomas mumbled, his lips a mere breathe from hers. She could feel the air move over her mouth as he spoke, and it made her want to inhale and taste his words as her heart began thumping all the faster.

"Tomas—" she began only to be cut off as Tomas gripped her hips harder and pulled her closer to him.

"I can't lose you now. I just ... it seems like we finally found each other. I can't ... Tallis, please don't go where I cannot follow."

Running her thumbs over his cheeks and the stubble growing there, she found her resolve crumbling, and all she wanted to do was take his hand and lead him and Rosslyn out of the forest and let someone else deal with this problem. She wanted to be selfish and have a normal life, where her biggest concern would be trying to decide what she would make them for dinner.

And there it was: *them.* She wanted to have that life with Rosslyn and especially Tomas; she wanted to know what it would be like to truly live for someone else's happiness.

Before she had always envisioned that she and Donovan would be neighbors all their days, and if she never married, at least she could live vicariously through Donovan and Nessa, and be the best aunt she could be to whatever children they had. Even before that no longer became a possibility, she had begun entertaining the idea of perhaps not living vicariously through her cousin, but experiencing it for herself.

"I don't want to leave you, Tomas," Tallis whispered.

"Then don't. Let's just ... let's just go home. We'll tell King Ailbeart what has happened and he will bring his armies and we can end this that way. As long as the creature never gets you, we can end this. We'll find another way."

"We can't, Tomas. We'd never forgive ourselves if we turned and ran away now. It would poison whatever we created afterwards."

"Then let me come with you, you don't have to do this alone. I can help you."

"Oh, Tomas, you know you can't, not like this. You have already tried to sacrifice yourself once for me, let me return the favor."

"But you haven't thought this through, Tallis," Tomas countered. "If you insist that Rosslyn and I are too ill to assist you, at least wait before you plunge headlong into this. Come up with a better strategy, gather supplies, something. And, Wodan willing, Rosslyn and I will have recovered enough by then to be of assistance."

"The longer I wait, even if it was for what you suggest, is another hour, another day, that allows the demon to find another vessel. We can't risk that, under any circumstance."

For a moment, Tomas looked like he was going to argue further, but Tallis's firm stare, and a cramp that nearly toppled Tomas with its sudden intensity, silenced whatever retort he was about to say. His chin jutted out stubbornly for a moment before Tomas crushed her to him in a fierce embrace.

Unbidden tears rolled down her cheeks, and she pressed her body against his, as if she hoped to meld into him. His hands gripped her with a hungry desire as his breathing became labored and she could feel the thrashing of his heart.

211

She could feel his lips lightly brush against her with every breath he took and Tallis could take it no more. She kissed him with all the passion and longing she had and hoped it would be enough for them both. For as shy as Tomas normally was with her gentle touches and caresses, he returned her kiss with as much fervor as she gave, as if it had been the most natural thing he had ever done.

For the first time in a long time, Tallis felt *right*. Everything about this moment felt so natural and right, she couldn't help but hate herself a little for not seeing it sooner and allowing to lose herself in what she hoped was love.

Reluctantly, Tallis broke off the kiss. She didn't step out of his grasp, though, as they panted against each other, their noses rubbing against one another. While she knew what she had to do, she wanted to savor this moment as long as she could.

Tallis could not say if she would return from what she had to do next, and if she did, if she would be entirely in one piece. She did know, however, that she wanted to come back.

Since Donovan had died, she had woken every morning thinking it might not be so bad to cease existing altogether. But now that it was an actual possibility, she could not bear the thought of leaving Tomas and Rosslyn behind. They were a fixture in her life, and she knew she would want it no other way for the rest of her days.

Tallis took her hands away from Tomas's face and gently took off her mother's wedding ring. She ran it over her fingers as she kept her forehead pressed against his. After a moment, she slipped the ring into his coat pocket and pressed it firmly against him, as she said, "Wait for me, Tomas. I will come back for you. I'll always come back for you and Rosslyn. And if … if I don't, keep my mother's ring safe and out of the hands of that demon. And try to remember me as that little girl who would sleep on the library floor and the woman who climbed up a tower to return your coat and rescue you from the monastery."

"How will I know if you're all right or if you're…? I can save you if you just let me, Tallis."

"Your illness will abate if I succeed. It won't if I fail. If that happens, then you'll have your chance to save me. I'll count on you to end it so that I can't hurt anyone else."

"That's not what I—"

"I won't blame you for what you have to do. It won't be yours or anyone else's fault. And even though you'll have no need of it, know that I would forgive you and would thank you for saving me."

"That's not what I meant by saving you, Tallis."

"I know. But it's the way it has to be. I'm just sorry we couldn't … that we never really got a chance to be together."

"I'm begging you, Tallis. Stay with me."

Tallis could take no more, her heart was already broken enough without it aching further for her to give in and listen to Tomas's words. With one last hungry kiss, she stepped out of Tomas's embrace and led him by the hand to where Rosslyn was waiting.

Pressing his hand into Rosslyn's, Tallis said, "Take care of each other while I'm gone, no matter how long I'm gone for. I'm sorry for whatever pain I have or may cause, and just know that … well, you know. If I'm able, I'll return to you. And if not … well, just know that despite everything that's happened, I wouldn't have wanted to save Selkirk with anyone other than you two. And If I don't come back … I'll tell Donovan you both said hello."

She gave their hands a firm squeeze, and before they could protest or stop her further, Tallis turned her back and ran away.

She could hear Tomas behind her, and it took all her resolve not to stop and fall back into his embrace. Tallis wasn't sure what love was, but she was beginning to understand what it *could* be. It seemed only fitting that as soon as she thought she had found it, that Wodan would force her to give it up in order to save Selkirk from the sins of its past.

ᏮOMAS HELPLESSLY WATCHED as Tallis ran away. With her speed and the illness spreading throughout his body, he had no hope of catching her. Instead, he watched her and focused on the shattering feeling he had in his chest as she disappeared from view.

With a great effort, he turned away and tried to keep his composure. He may not have been raised by a traditional father, but the brothers had taught him enough for Tomas to know that men were not supposed to cry, especially over women, and such trivial things as a broken heart.

He was beginning to understand that the brothers

who had taught him that had clearly never loved a woman, let alone a woman like Tallis, who had snuck into his heart from the moment he first saw her.

Just when he thought he would be able to see what it felt like to run his hands through her long, pale, and shimmering blonde hair every day, just when he thought he would know what it was like to court a woman free from the scrutiny of his order, Tallis was out of his grasp once again. It was the ongoing story of his adulthood really, to have Tallis, only to see her slip away from him for one reason or another.

Tomas was so wrapped up in his own pain and heartache that he failed to notice that Rosslyn was gathering their belongings as if she made to follow Tallis. He watched her for a moment, his mind too sluggish to fully comprehend what he was seeing.

"What are you doing?" he asked once Rosslyn had finished packing their gear.

"Getting ready to go, what does it look like I'm doing?"

He continued to watch for a moment, understanding coming painstakingly slowly to his mind. Finally, with a hoarse chuckle, he said, "We aren't going to stay put, are we?"

"Not a chance," Rosslyn said with a hint of amusement in her husky voice.

"We're going after Tallis?"

"Of course we are. Just because she says to stay here so she can play hero doesn't mean I'm actually going to let her. Now come on, we may not move as quickly as she does right now, but that's no reason to let her get even further ahead of us." Rosslyn winked at him and shouldered her pack.

---

215

Tomas couldn't help but smile through the tears that would not fall. Sometimes he really did love Rosslyn's complete disregard for doing what she was told.

# SIXTEEN

THE SUNLIGHT FROM the early morning dawn gently woke Tallis, but only for her to be greeted with the sight of a half dozen elves surrounding the tree she had slept in. They were evenly split between men and women; all were disheveled and gaunt-looking, as if they had not eaten in days. And while their eyes still gleamed yellow with the demon's light, Tallis could see the red veins prominently etched into their eyes from not blinking for days on end.

They all stared up at Tallis, but made no move to grab and wrestle her from the tree like they would have previously. Instead, they just stared at her as if they could not quite understand what they saw.

They seemed to know she was what they were looking for, but they did not appear to have any recognition as to why. It concerned Tallis as she watched them with growing trepidation from the safety of her tree branch.

Much like the owls and twites of before, the elves only moved when she did, and none possessed the uncanny speed and grace they were known for. They maneuvered with jerky movements that often left them crashing into one another, almost as if they were not fully aware they were not alone and had no spatial relation as to where nearby objects were.

Tallis watched curiously, wondering what had changed to make the tremps behave as such. She assumed that when Donovan died, he had so damaged and weakened the demon that this was all it could manage now in terms of controlling the elves. The elves' odd behavior, however, coupled with Rosslyn and Tomas's illness told the depths of her being that something was different and very wrong this time around.

Carefully, Tallis climbed down as far as she dared before jumping the rest of the way and landing a short distance from the elves. It took the elves a long time to register that Tallis had completely left the tree, long enough for Tallis to get a running head start on her would-be captors.

In unison, the elves turned their heads at awkward angles to look at Tallis before lurching after her, their skill and grace all gone as they stumbled and tripped through the forest like large lumbering animals, instead of the petite and graceful creatures they were.

Tallis listened as they crashed behind her as she darted ahead. She would have to dispatch them if she hoped to reach her destination without drawing too much unwanted attention, but part of her was curious as to why the elves were acting so strangely.

There were times when Tallis thought she saw one of the tremps break free of whatever was caging their minds as they collapsed to their hands and knees. It was short-lived, though, as an invisible string tugged them up from their chests and forced them onward once again.

The scene was almost enough to make her take pity on the elves that pursued her. But it was a fleeting feeling; no sooner had she begun to feel pity than it was cauterized from her heart as if by a red-hot poker. No matter how pitiful and sad it was that the tremps were being so obviously manipulated against their will, they were still the monster's that had brutally taken her family from her.

Unsheathing her daggers, Tallis stopped running to face the mob behind her. She regarded them with a stone coldness that she was unaccustomed to and which would have frightened her if her heart hadn't been so fragmented with pain and loss.

Part of her did not like harboring such bitter hatred for these creatures, but she could not forgive them, either. All she could see were their long and dirty talons ripping into her mother, their gleaming yellow eyes as they snatched her from her sleep, the way they had presented her to their master like a delicacy to be savored. She wanted them to suffer the way she suffered; she wanted them to experience her pain.

Twirling her daggers, she rushed at the elves. They still moved in unison, as if their master could no longer control them as individuals. Even if she was engaged with one of the tremps, the rest could not seem to comprehend that she was not currently fighting them, and that it was the opportune moment to flank her or take her from behind.

It made cutting down the elves and ending their lives too easy. If Tallis had hoped killing them would bring her some satisfaction or closure, she was sorely disappointed.

Panting, she circled the last of the elves that had pursued her. Despite being overwhelmed by Tallis's fury, the elf did not turn and flee. Instead, the lanky male elf with filthy hair the color of carrots in spring limply stood his ground.

She wanted him to fight back; she wanted him to show the animalistic wrath that had been all she knew of the elves. She wanted him to gnash his pointed teeth at her and try to take a bite of her flesh, like she knew the tremps were accustomed to doing. But, instead, he stood there as if he were already dead, not fleeing nor fighting back, but accepting that he would die here and now and there was no point in trying to flee such a fate.

With a primal scream, Tallis launched herself at the elf and tackled him to the ground. Instead of stabbing him, though, as she had the rest of his kind, she pummeled his face and body with her clenched fists over and over again. The elf did not resist, nor did he try to stop her as she punished his person.

"Why?" she screamed over and over again as her own hands became bruised and bloodied with the force of her punches. She did not expect the tremp to answer, but it was the question that she had been burning to ask ever since she found out just what she was.

Stopping the beating before she killed the elf, Tallis stumbled away only to fall at the banks of the Osse River. She fell to her hands and knees into the icy green water and stared at the reflection of the young woman she saw there.

Her eyes were encased in dark circles, her mouth sagged with sorrow, and there were new wrinkles from exhaustion that had not been there a month ago. Tallis saw a woman who had aged years in the span of days.

She missed the innocent girl who had snuck into the monastery to read the night away, the girl who considered a bad day to be one where she was being pawed at by drunks at the Lonely Tavern while avoiding Raghnall. A girl whose greatest fear was to be auctioned off like a prized cow on the Bride Block. Tallis was not sure when that girl had perished to be replaced by the woman she saw now, but there was no going back to the person she once was.

"Why me?" she mumbled to her reflection. "Why did it have to be me? I didn't want this. I don't want this to be my destiny, my only legacy. Why did you have to take them away?"

Tallis couldn't say who she was talking to, if she was speaking to her bloodied reflection or to Wodan Himself. And while she knew she would get no answers, she still yearned for them.

Despite everything she had learned and everything she had been told, she still understood so little. She wanted an explanation for her loss and her pain, but knew that no matter what the reason was, if there, indeed, was one, it would never be adequate enough to justify what she had gone through.

She just wanted to understand why. She thought that if she just knew, if she just understood why the elves had made her through their dark religious ritual, and why they didn't just simply try to make another vessel rather than pursue her across Selkirk, burning its towns to the ground, she might not hurt the way she did.

Even if Tallis did manage to win the day and accomplish what she set out to do, she would never again be accepted by her country. Even if they could forget her, and forget she was the one the elves had hissed as their loved ones fell all around them, they would not let her live, if for no other reason than she was a half-breed mongrel.

She could feel her paralyzing panic well in her once again as she desperately tried to figure out where she was supposed to go and what she was supposed to do if she could not remain in Selkirk. It was one thing to idly muse about getting on a ship and setting sail for the unknown, but that had been when Donovan was still alive. Tallis was a different person now, and her fear was threatening to overtake her.

*Worry about that when it comes. It doesn't matter now,* she told herself as she got her breathing under control once again and her panic began to ebb away.

She could not say how long she sat in the freezing water, only that when she finally roused herself from her kneeling position her leather and chainmail seemed to be stiff as if with ice and her knees numb with cold. She was aware that the chill from the water was settling into her bones, and that if she did not dry her clothes she would regret it later, but she also did not care. The only thing that forced Tallis to build a fire once she had crossed the river was the voice of her mother in her mind chastising her for caring so little for her health.

For the moment, she was content to watch the flames dance as they consumed the dry kindling she was feeding it. She wanted to focus and think about nothing other than the violent and graceful shapes the flames made as they turned the wood to ash, anything that would keep her from seeing the dead faces of her loved ones every time she closed her eyes.

TOMAS DIDN'T BOTHER checking the pulse on the elves they found scattered across the forest as they made their way to the Osse River. He knew they were dead, and knew just how they had died.

He could feel an anchor crashing into his stomach as he scanned over Tallis's handiwork: slashed throats, punctured hearts, and severed arteries. She had not been overly cruel to the elves; none had suffered nor lingered long in this world once Tallis had done her work. Still, there was a brutality to the way they were littered across the forest floor that made Tomas worry.

There were two very different sides to Tallis that Tomas could never reconcile. There was the girl he had fallen for as she cradled a book like a pillow on the floor of the monastery library as her iridescent pale hair covered her like a blanket. The girl with eyes as deep and wonderful as an ocean after a storm, and nearly as endless, with an insatiable curiosity and yearning to find meaning to life outside of Kincardine.

Then there was the woman who was going to save Selkirk, whether they knew it or not. She was a woman who had sacrificed much and lost even more to a battle where she was the unwilling hero. A woman whose special elf-like talents made everything she did as graceful as a skilled dancer, but also as brutal and cold as an assassin in the dead of night.

Tomas loved the girl he had grown up with when he was still an initiate in the monastery, and he owed his life to the woman who had embarked on a journey to clear her name and save Selkirk, but he was not sure how he felt about her.

He knew it was still Tallis, and that she was doing what was necessary, but a lifetime of study and prayer to Wodan had instilled a strong belief that every life was worth something, and that belief was constantly being tested the longer he followed Tallis. That was not to say he believed she should be sparing the lives of these evil creatures, it just made him question what he had thought he knew every step of the way. He wondered which side of Tallis would win out if they all survived their final encounter with the demon.

He did not expect Tallis to pity or show mercy to the elves, but he also knew she did not necessarily need to kill them, either. With how erratically they had been running, and the disjointed way they seemed to be processing the world around them, Tomas knew it would have been altogether easy for Tallis to avoid or lose the elves.

However, he was not sure what he would have done if he were in Tallis's place. Would he be a big enough man to spare their lives if they had brutally taken his family while he was powerless to stop them?

Tomas knew he could never fully or truly understand her pain and loss, as he had no family to speak of, but this seemed a bit excessive. He wasn't sure if this changed anything within Tallis's core being, or if she needed to vent her anger and agony before it blackened her heart forever. He just hoped she would get whatever it was she needed to out of her system, for if she didn't, he wasn't sure he would like the person she would turn out to be.

As he looked from one lifeless elf to the next, he

caught movement from the corner of his eye. Slowly, he turned his head to avoid another dizzy spell, and saw a badly battered male elf with hair the color of carrots.

The elf paid them no mind as he sat a short distance away looking vacantly ahead. He did not seem to be pained by his wounds, though Tomas knew he must be. His nose and jaw were clearly broken, and his eyes were so puffy with bruises that it was a wonder he could see at all.

Despite the state he was in, Tomas could tell that there was something different about this tremp. While his eyes were still a sickly yellow, they did not seem as bright as they once were. It gave him a faint glimmer of hope that not only were the elves not beyond saving, neither was Tallis.

His musings were soon interrupted by Rosslyn. "Well, at least we know we're on the right trail."

Tomas went to her side and helped her cross the river before they both collapsed in exhaustion from the mysterious illnesses taking its toll on their bodies. Tomas cradled his head in his hands as the throbbing in his head began to match the painful pangs piercing his stomach.

"Tallis must have a gut made of steel if she was able to endure this. Wodan's bloody backside if this isn't the worst I've felt in … well, ever. It feels like my worst hangover's hangover after a night of too much of Selene's strongest ale back at the Lonely Tavern."

Tomas wanted to smile and banter the way Rosslyn was able to, even through her pain, but every time he tried, it only came out as a painful grimace. Giving up, he pushed himself to his feet with a groan and stumbled onwards.

He did not make it very far before he stumbled again only to vomit behind a tree. He had hoped that by not eating he could avoid situations just like this, but apparently, he had been wrong. As he wiped his mouth and covered his sick with debris from the forest, he noticed an abandoned campfire.

Calling out to Rosslyn, he carefully made his way over to the discarded embers and tentatively put his hand over the few remaining pieces of wood. As Rosslyn came to stand at his side, he said, "It's not warm anymore, so it's hard to say when Tallis came this way. But at least we know she managed to get away from those elves."

"As if there was any doubt about that."

Tomas shrugged as he went about carefully rebuilding the fire Tallis had left behind. "You never know. One of those elves could have scratched her like that one back in the Brethil Forest."

Rosslyn sat down next to him and groaned as she clutched her head. "So, you have no idea how far behind Tallis we are?"

"If I had to wager a guess, I'd say a day at most, considering how fast she can go. We've been making decent time, but Tallis does have the advantage of not being ill." He shrugged as the flames began to dance to life once again.

"So for all we know, it's already over? Tallis could be the big hero and we'd have missed it all by now?"

"I doubt that. If Tallis had killed the demon, then we would not be sick. If she had failed, then the elves would already be back to their normal evil ways once again. Neither has happened. I figure she hasn't succeeded or failed just yet."

"Yes, but *why* are we the sick one's this time?" Rosslyn asked. "Shouldn't we *not* be affected, or, at the very least, shouldn't Tallis be sick alongside us?"

"Well, I suppose it's like Cullen said, Tallis's body has been accustomed to the taint and ours haven't. I assume that whatever happened when the demon entered Donovan before he was … before he died, had some sort of lingering affect. The spoils of which we are now experiencing."

Rosslyn was silent for a moment as she reclined against a tree, closing her eyes, as if that would ward against her unshakable illness. Just when Tomas had thought she had fallen asleep, she mumbled, "Think we'll get to her in time?"

It was a question Tomas had been dreading the moment he and Rosslyn had set off after Tallis. He wasn't sure what would be worse, either, getting to her only to find she did not need their assistance, or getting to her and being too late to save her. Tomas didn't need or necessarily want to be a hero, but that did not mean he could bear the idea of not being there if Tallis needed him.

He wasn't sure what good he would do, even if he did get to Tallis and she needed his help. As it was, he was almost too weak to carry his own pack, let alone pull the crank on his crossbow enough to be able to fire one of his explosive powders. That didn't keep him from wanting to believe that if he managed to get to Tallis and she needed his help, he would be able to rise to the occasion, sickness or no.

But Tomas was ever the realist, and unless there was something that seriously detained Tallis, they would never be able to catch up to her. He was not sure what Rosslyn wanted to hear, if she wanted hope they would be able to catch up, or if she simply wanted to hear the truth as her illness robbed her of her patience.

After a moment, Tomas swallowed the bile rising in his throat, and said, "Perhaps. If Tallis runs into any more of these elves, we may just get to her in time. It's hard to say, but I do hope we manage to get to her before the end."

ᏉOMAS ONLY MANAGED a few hours of sleep at most that night, and by the way Rosslyn tossed and turned, he knew it was much the same for her. For as much as Tomas wanted to sleep, in hopes that it would banish his lingering illness, he knew from what happened to Tallis that the insomnia would only get worse from here on out.

Rekindling the fire once again to ward off the frosty night air, Tomas began boiling water with the pine needles and thyme that he'd managed to collect along the way. It wasn't tea, but he hoped the soothing flavor would help ease their stomachs.

It wasn't long before Rosslyn opened her eyes to watch him, and she took the steaming cup when he offered it to her without complaint. Tentatively, he sipped the hot liquid and waited in silence for the last tendrils of sleep and grogginess to fade from both of their minds, before he said, "If we can't sleep, we should make the most of the time and try to catch up with Tallis. It's the best chance we have of closing the distance between us."

Rosslyn didn't speak as she sipped her makeshift tea. After a while, she nodded and lit the lantern they had taken from the Sipsis and got to her feet. Slowly, they packed their things and set off in near total darkness and followed Tallis's trail as best as they could.

Tallis was making it easy on them to follow her, whether she intended to or not. She was not hiding her tracks, and more often than not, they would come across either a dead elf, or obvious signs that she had done her best to lose whatever elves came after her.

In a way, it made Tomas glad to see that she had either lost her interest in killing every tremp that she came upon, or she simply thought it was no longer worth the effort. Whatever the reason, it made his heart lighter to think that sorrow and bitterness had not darkened the woman with whom he had fallen deeply in love.

Even with walking whenever they could not sleep, Tomas knew they were not making up for lost time. The closer they got to wherever the demon was, the sicker both he and Rosslyn became. It made them constantly stop to rest or vomit, which negated any time they would have otherwise made up for by moving forward even in the dead of night.

Tomas was not the only one to notice they had not managed to catch up with Tallis yet, as Rosslyn's patience continued to wane. She had stopped speaking to Tomas altogether, and would even occasionally kick at a dead body if it happened to be in her way. No matter how much he tried to reassure her that they were, indeed, getting closer and that they were not too late just yet, Rosslyn still would not speak to him.

He knew she didn't believe him each time he tried to reassure her that they were getting closer to Tallis; he was having a hard time believing it himself. But the mere fact that their illness persisted and got worse while the elves did not improve one way or another, told Tomas that Tallis had yet to succeed or fail. He just hoped that something else tragic had not befallen her which, given their current luck, was all too real of a possibility.

# *SEVENTEEN*

SHE COULDN'T KEEP going at this pace, not if she wanted to reach the demon or its gate with any strength left to fight with. The elves were never hard to get rid of or get away from, but the sheer number of them was starting to take its toll. For as much as she was beginning to hate to admit it, Tallis needed help if she wanted any hope of surviving.

Part of her was starting to wish she had allowed Tomas and Rosslyn to come with her. But as soon as the thought flitted through her mind, she squashed it like an insect. She knew it would be suicide if they were to join her.

Even without being ill, Tallis was barely making it through the Guldar Forest. It would be near impossible for them to move as quickly as they needed to with Tallis constantly stopping to defend Tomas and Rosslyn from all the tremps she was encountering.

Panting after just having lost another two female elves as they clumsily chased after her, Tallis went in search of any tree that could connect her to the animals of the forests. The old yew had told her if she needed help, she would, indeed, have it. If there ever was a time when she could use all the help she could get, this was it.

Tallis crept through the forest as silently as she could to avoid alerting the elves that were still looking for her. She simply wanted a respite from the onslaught to catch her breath, something she did not think was all that much to ask for.

It took her longer than she would have liked before she finally found a congregation of old oak trees. She could feel the familiar warmth of their power emanating from their roots to tingle up from her toes to the top of her head. Grinning as the familiar sensation eased the aches in her tired limbs, Tallis almost threw herself at the tree, as if it were an old friend she had not seen in years.

She did not have to wait long before the familiar rush of warmth and tenderness began to pulse through her hands to warm and soothe her troubled soul like hot, spiced mulled ale on a snowy night. This particular cluster of oaks reminded Tallis of an elderly grandmother who always had fresh cookies waiting: kind, gentle, and a little oblivious to what was happening, but always glad to see her loved ones no matter how long they might have been away.

Tallis tried to keep from completely losing herself to the oak's comforting embrace, but she was finding it hard to want to do anything but let the oak console her, and relay how glad it was that she had come back in its soft wordless mezzo-soprano melodies. But she knew that if she lingered too long where she was, the elves would eventually find her. But after what she had been through, and the never dulling longing in her heart for Donovan's presence, Tallis couldn't help but allow herself to get caught up in the tree's comfort.

With a chest-rattling sigh, Tallis finally brought herself back to the present enough to try to communicate with the tree. She tried speaking to it and when that did not work she, instead, tried showing the tree what the yew had shown her. She recalled the images of the animals that would help, and the portal tree from which the demon had escaped from, and hoped that the tree could see them as well.

Just as Tallis was about to give up, the bright feeling of clarity and understanding erupted from the oak as it further gave the impression it would relay her message. All she needed to do was stay and rest while it was being delivered.

Tallis placed her forehead against the tree as a single tear rolled down her cheek. A great weight was lifted from her as she finally found a way to speak to her would-be guardians. So much had gone so wrong, that she could have sworn she was dreaming when the oak began passing her message from tree to tree through the labyrinth of roots hidden beneath her feet.

The sound of a snapping branch finally forced Tallis to open her eyes and scamper up the tree before the elves found her. She may not understand why they were acting like drunks as they crashed through the forest, but she knew it had something to do with whatever had happened to the demon after Donovan died.

Tallis watched a group of three elves stumble beneath her as she sat like a bird high above them. For the first time their presence did not frighten her or send pangs of red hot loathing coursing through her veins as the ancient presence within the tree replaced such feelings with soothing comfort.

She could feel the gentle prod of pity as the oak beseeched her to show mercy and forgiveness to its lost children. And while Tallis tried to reassure the oak that she would not kill the trio below, she still did not pity them.

She watched them sniff around the tree like ineffective bloodhounds, never once looking up to see if she were above them. It was like it had never occurred to them that Tallis could be anywhere but on the ground. She found the thought rather amusing for reasons she did not fully understand, nor did she care to. And it was with a faint smile on her face and her body warmed by the ancient oak that sleep finally claimed her.

TALLIS WAS BACK in Dumfry surrounded by the elders who had looked at her so scornfully when she had come to their rescue. Except this time their looks of hatred and resentment melted like fresh snow into the gentle smiles of spring. They welcomed her with open arms and led her through cheering streets packed full of the people who had perished in the elven uprisings.

Tallis was reunited with Tomas and Rosslyn, who strode proudly beside her. They meandered their way through the crowd only to come to a stop at the cold gray stone monastery at the center of the thriving town. Atop the steep stone steps that were polished to a bright white gleam, waited her mother and Donovan with open arms.

Tallis fell into their embrace and sobbed as the pressure from their hug told her this was more than just a dream. She could feel her mother smooth her wavy hair and Donovan pat her back like he had used to when she was small and could not stop crying. Gently, they pulled her away from them and said as one, "You are almost there, little one."

Tallis blinked slowly as she understood this was not a real dream. What she was experiencing was akin to what she had dreamt the night the trees had infiltrated her mind to warn her of the danger that lurked in the trees above her.

Tallis shook her head, willing what she saw to just be a pleasant dream where she was finally being forgiven for what she considered to be her greatest mistakes, rather than a message from a benevolent spirit in an old tree. But no matter how much she yearned to have her mother look at her with forgiveness and to have Donovan smirk at her tear-streaked face, it was never to be.

"No, I don't care about that. Just tell me you love me, tell me it'll be all right, and that you forgive me. That's all I need, that's all I want. Please."

The faces of her loved ones remained jovial, as if they could not empathize with her greatest desires. Instead, in a voice that was not just Donovan and her mother's tones, but that of a thousand other echoes as well, said, "Soon you will find our misguided sister. Be merciful to her, dissatisfaction has always been her greatest sin. Our children were desperate, forced into a corner by your father's kind. We ask that you spare

---

235

them, that you help them find their place in this land when it is done."

Tallis tried to free herself from the firm grasp of the shades of her loved ones. Sneering, she shouted, "How dare you! How dare you ask me to help those creatures even more? Is it not enough that I'm returning them to you? You can't ask me to forgive them, to forget what they did to me."

"Oh, but you must, little one. They would never have done that without our twisted sister's guidance. They will need a link to this land again, an ambassador. We would ask that you be their voice, their champion in the days to come."

"No, no, you can't ask me to do that. I can't … I can't do that. Please, let me just send the demon back to where it came from and be done with this. I just want a normal life, I want to mourn my cousin and never see another tremp again."

She could see a faint glimmer of confusion and disapproval flit across Donovan and her mother's face. It was as if they could not understand why Tallis could not, and would not, forgive and forget the injustices the elves had perpetrated against her and in her name all over Selkirk.

"But you must," her mother and Donovan said again, their tone persistent and laced with confusion.

Tallis began to thrash as she tried to free herself from their grasp and the dream as a whole. "No. I can't, I won't!"

It was only when Tallis nearly fell out of the tree she was sleeping in that the faces of her loved ones began to fade from her mind. She stopped her struggling to watch her dream world begin to crumble and fade into nothingness around her.

At first it was just the monastery that blinked out of existence. But it was soon followed by the smiling faces of the elders, and as they faded from her mind, Tallis swore their grinning faces were once again replaced by the scowls of hatred that they had bestowed upon her as they fled the fires of their burning town.

She turned wildly around her as Dumfry fell away piece by piece. The last thing to disappear was Donovan and her mother. As they began to fade, Tallis suddenly did not want them to go.

Despite the fact that she knew the oak she was sleeping in was only manipulating the images in her head, she did not want to lose their smiling faces. All she saw as of late was their bitterness and their accusing glares as her guilt plagued her mind. With all her heart, she wanted to hold on to their approval, even if it was not real.

Tallis ran for them, hoping to embrace them once more before they, too, vanished with the rest of her dream. She reached out for them, and just as her fingers gently caressed their pale clothing, they vanished.

She woke with a muffled scream forcing its way out of her lungs. Blinking in the darkness, Tallis could feel the hot tears of frustration roll down her cheeks once again.

Jabbing her palms into her eyes, Tallis began berating herself for once again crying over her family, for once again being too weak to combat these kinds of dreams and to fend off the jagged pangs of guilt that stabbed at her heart every time she thought of her mother and cousin.

Biting her lip, Tallis forced the rest of her sobs back down into her throat and stared up into the night sky. She could not fault the trees for being so desperate to want her to spare more of their children. Between the clearings, those killed by the demon, and Tallis's last few days in the forest, she knew their numbers must finally be dwindling. But she could not forgive them, nor could she show mercy to the beast that commanded them.

The thought left her feeling numb as she watched the cold stars twinkle above her through the tree branches. She had never really thought about it before, but now that she did, she saw the truth of the tree's words.

The elves, indeed, were going to need an advocate when this was over. Someone who could explain what had happened and help broker a type of peace between them and the humans. Tallis was an obvious choice, as she was the only true half-elf left, but there was no forgiveness in her heart for the creatures she was supposed to be kin to.

If the elves wished to repair the fragile relationship they once had with the humans, they would need to do it alone. The scars on Tallis's heart were too fresh to allow her to do any more than free them from the demon that controlled them.

# EIGHTEEN

ROSSLYN HAD NOT spoken for what seemed like days, and not because she was particularly cross with Tomas, either. For once in her life, she simply had nothing to say, and therefore said nothing.

She knew it wasn't nearly as long ago that she said something to Tomas as she imagined, but with walking through the night when neither of them could sleep, it completely skewed her sense of time.

As she tried to remember the last time her and Tomas actually had a conversation, it struck Rosslyn that she also was not sure when she had last eaten. She knew it hadn't been for lack of trying, but each time she had attempted to eat anything, it came back up almost faster than she could swallow.

The lack of food and proper sleep was making her hear and see things that weren't really there. When she first realized she was imagining things, it had been nothing substantial. Sometimes she thought she heard voices in the trees whenever the wintery breezes tickled their branches, or Tallis calling her name, and sometimes she thought she saw movement in the underbrush when there was none. It wasn't until she had begun to lose track of time that her hallucinations became more severe.

Now, she sometimes thought she saw rabbits dance around her as she stumbled forward, and even thought she saw a pair of owls perch on Tomas's head as they traveled in the moonlit night. At first, when these fantastic sights had appeared, she was not only shocked by what she saw, but frightened, as she initially thought it was more of the demon's handiwork.

It wasn't until Tomas accidently walked through a garden snake that Rosslyn realized she was just imagining such visions. However, knowing she was hallucinating never seemed to be enough to banish the false images from the scenery around her.

Rosslyn knew better than to tell Tomas what she was seeing for fear that she was actually losing her mind. She also knew that if she told him, they would waste even more precious time as either his kindhearted nature or his inquisitive side got the better of him.

If his inquisitive side won out, then he would want to stop and examine her so he could make nonsensical notes in his journal before pressing on again. If he decided to be a gentleman, then he would demand they stop until she was better. If that happened, they would have no hope at all of ever catching up with Tallis and could potentially never see her again.

So when Tallis fell from the sky to land in front of her, Rosslyn did not even stop walking. She blinked slowly as she and the shade of Tallis made eye contact before Rosslyn gently sidestepped out of the way and ignored the surprised and confused look her hallucination was giving her. *Tallis is still a good day's march ahead of us,* Rosslyn rationalized in hopes that her mind would stop playing tricks on her.

Just as Rosslyn left Tallis behind, she was pulled into a vicious hug. It took Rosslyn a moment longer to fully understand that her imaginings never actually touched anyone. Anytime she had tried, the image had dissolved under her touch. Once she remembered that, it became clear as polished crystal that this particular Tallis was no illusion.

Laughing at her own thick headedness, Rosslyn held Tallis at arm's length before cupping her face in her hands and turning it every which way. Still laughing, she said, "It really is you! Wodan's Garden, aren't you a welcomed vision."

Once she started laughing she couldn't stop. Rosslyn knew her laughter was beginning to sound manic, and she couldn't say what was so funny or what had so tickled her other than the idea of almost believing that Tallis wasn't real. But all the laughter was beginning to leave her lightheaded and dizzy as she struggled to regain control over herself. Tallis's smiling face was the last thing she saw as the world seemed to pitch under her feet, causing her to lose her balance and tumble head over heels into the darkness of unconsciousness.

She was not sure how long she had been out, but by the time she finally came to, Tallis had started a fire and was fussing over Tomas as he feebly tried to bat her away. Rosslyn watched them silently, letting their tenderness warm her sore body and settle her swimming head.

It was such a touching sight to watch Tallis fret over the boy she had begun to fall for, and for him to stare at her in wonder, that Rosslyn was almost nauseous with its sweetness.

As Rosslyn shifted her body so she was no longer watching her friends fall in love, Tallis finally noticed that Rosslyn had woken. Rushing to her side, Tallis gently touched her clammy forehead and shook her head. "What in the name of Wodan were you two doing following me like that? You could have gotten yourselves killed in your condition."

"But we didn't. Besides, you can't have all the fun." Normally that would have made Tallis smile, but this time she just looked down at her with concern and annoyance. Rosslyn could tell that she was conflicted about whether to be glad they were all right, or annoyed by the fact that they had ignored what she had asked when she had run off to face the demon alone.

Waving her off, Rosslyn said, "Oi, be mad if you want, but we're here now, and we're going to help whether you like it or not."

"Aye, whether I like it or not, is right. Really, Roz, what do you and Tomas think you're going to do in your condition? Get sick on the demon and hope it's so disgusted it will just leave? I didn't ask you not to follow me because I wanted all the glory for myself, I asked you not to follow me because I didn't want you to be easy prey for whatever's waiting for me."

"Oh, sure. But admit it, you're glad we're here."

For as angry as Tallis was, she couldn't help but chuckle at her as she helped Rosslyn up into a sitting position. "I really do hate you sometimes, Rozy."

Rosslyn could only manage a faint smile before she

doubled over in pain as her stomach twisted into painful cramps. Tallis helped as best as she could, and when the pain had finally subsided, her frown of both concern and annoyance had returned in full force.

Shrugging, Rosslyn said, "It doesn't matter. We're both here now, so why not just tell us how we can help rather than giving that pretty face of yours even more wrinkles from all the scowling you're doing?"

Tallis didn't answer, nor did she stop frowning. Instead, she slowly rose to her feet and tossed a few more branches into the fire before tucking Tomas's coat back under his chin. After a moment more of fussing over Tomas and Rosslyn, Tallis sat back down with a thud and stared sullenly into the fire.

Rosslyn was about to ask the question again when Tallis mumbled, "That's just it; I don't know how you could help now that you're here. I don't know what will be at this gate. Regardless, you two are barely able to stand, let alone do anything else. I'll admit that I'm glad to see you both, and more than a little touched that you came after me, but it would've been easier, and safer, if you had just stayed where you were."

"We can figure out what we should do later, once we've all had a chance to rest a bit," Tomas said. "For now, why not tell us how much farther it is before we get to this gate?"

Tallis shrugged. "From what the yew showed me it's not much farther, maybe half a day's march at a decent speed, a day if we take it slowly. I could have gotten there a day or so ago if I hadn't stopped here to wait."

"Why did you stop here?" Rosslyn asked. "You aren't getting sick again, are you?"

C. E. Clayton

Tallis shook her head. "No, nothing like that, fortunately. It's because of the trees. They promised to send me help, and that help hasn't arrived yet."

"How do you know we aren't that help?"

Tallis gave her a hard stare. "Because you're not."

Rosslyn's face fell at Tallis's sharp words. She had hoped with how Tallis had been tending to her that she had finally let go of the hurt and anger at her for shooting Donovan after the demon had taken him. Clearly that wound would take even more time to heal and Rosslyn wasn't convinced they would get the time they needed.

Because of her sickness, Rosslyn was unable to hide her hurt and surprise at the coldness in Tallis's tone. Almost instantly Tallis hung her head and sighed before saying more softly, "It's the animals. Remember the mad deer and elk that attacked us outside of Kincardine? Well, the yew said that it would send me that kind of help, but it's been over a day and nothing's come yet. I'm not sure how much longer I can or should wait for help that may not actually arrive."

Rosslyn couldn't help but smile at the ridiculousness of Tallis's words. Despite her cramping stomach and pounding head, the image of Tallis running into battle at the head of an animal army was too fantastic to be real. Had someone told Rosslyn she would one day be remembered for helping Tallis save the elves from the clutches of a demon as the forest animals came to their aid, she would have asked for a pint of whatever they were drinking and laughed the rest of it off.

But all too well, Rosslyn remembered the massive

elk as it charged at Tallis and forced her up a tree before Donovan managed to kill it. She could still see the red deer's frothing mouth as it pawed at the banks of the river, its eyes fixated on them with hatred unknown to such creatures. Suddenly, the idea of those same creatures turning that hatred and ire for being unwilling soldiers back onto their former masters was not such an absurd story any longer.

"Well, surely we can wait here the rest of the day, and if nothing else, set out come the morning," Tomas said eventually as his illness began to get the better of him. "It'll take us a little longer to get there as it is; it may be enough time for these animal helpers of yours to catch up with us."

Tallis looked wearily at the fire and did not answer. Rosslyn wasn't sure what thoughts plagued Tallis's mind, but she knew they weighed heavily on her.

Tallis's sea-green eyes darkened with worry even with the reflection of the firelight. But if Rosslyn hoped that Tallis would share her burden with them, she was sorely disappointed as Tallis continued to keep her silence and stare sullenly into the fire.

As the silence continued to stretch between them, with only the crackling of the fire to penetrate the stillness, Rosslyn began to worry about Tallis's morale. Tallis always seemed so strong and unshakable that Rosslyn never truly thought she could ever have her spirit broken. But after Donovan's passing, she was beginning to have her doubts.

Tomas shared Rosslyn's worry as he fished something out of his pocket and gingerly forced it into Tallis's balled fist. Tallis looked down at the tiny object in her hand before shaking her head as she tried to give it back to Tomas. When he would not take it, tears began forming in her eyes and she croaked, "Please, just hold on to it until this is all over. Just in … just in case."

"What is it?" Rosslyn asked, curious as to what Tomas could have possibly given her that would cause Tallis to cry and plead in such a way.

Tallis didn't have a chance to answer as Tomas responded tenderly, "No, you take it. It will help give you strength to have something of hers with you."

"Something of whose?" Rosslyn prodded, getting annoyed they were treating her as if she were not even there.

"My mother's wedding ring. I gave it to Tomas to hold on to until I got back, or to remember me by if I didn't return."

Rosslyn mouthed, "Oh," and turned away as Tallis and Tomas shared tender glances with one another.

For reasons Rosslyn did not completely understand, she was a little upset that Tallis had not given her Lana's ring to keep safe. In her mind, it made perfect sense for Tallis to give it to Tomas for safekeeping, but her heart was thumping with a twinge of bitterness that she was finding hard to ignore.

Slowly she lowered herself to the ground and hid her face beneath her coat. Rosslyn doubted she could sleep, but she needed to try and do something to banish the strange jealous feelings that were churning in her mind.

"If you two are going to get up to any funny business with all those looks you're giving each other, do me a favor and keep it down, some of us are going to try and sleep."

# NINETEEN

𝕿HE MORNING CAME with the crisp chill that signaled fall in Selkirk was finally coming to an end and winter would soon be upon them. Tallis had always found winter in Selkirk to be mildly insufferable, because it left her perpetually feeling cold, something she always hated.

Huddling underneath her cloak did little to warm her. Its thick, fur-lined leather should have been more than enough to ward off any chill, but she had been wearing it so often with little break, that her body had grown accustomed to it to the point of rendering it almost useless.

The chainmail tunic with its thick metal rings at her sides did not help, either. They only absorbed the chill and it took sitting by the fire to the point of making Tallis's face burn before the cold was banished from it. The way Tallis shivered beneath her hood with her hands buried in the leather armor beneath the chainmail, one would think it was the dead of winter rather than the end of fall.

Her mother used to tease her about how grumpy she got when she was cold. "You clearly are not meant for Selkirk, little one," she would say with a twinkle of amusement in her hazel eyes. But no matter how much grief her mother gave her about not being able to handle the cold, she would still hand Tallis the gloves she had been warming for her near the kitchen fire.

The memory made Tallis smile as she turned her mother's ring around her thumb. There had been a time when such memories would have sent violent spasms of tears raging over her body. Now, she was at least resigned to them, whereas the same could not be said of her memories with Donovan.

Thinking of such things made her sigh and give up trying to get warm. Sitting up, she glanced at her still sleeping companions and couldn't help but blush with how close Tomas had been to her as they slept. Had he moved but a fraction of a hair closer, he would have been cuddling with her throughout the chilly night.

The idea of Tomas holding her as she slumbered did more to warm her from the inside out than the fire ever could, as she went about making them a hot porridge made out of the last bits of rabbit, bread, and grain that they had. She knew Rosslyn's mother would have scolded her for how poor the fare was, but this was the best she could do with the few remaining provisions. If this was to be their last good morning together, Tallis at least wanted to pretend they were eating a real meal.

It smelled more tantalizing than it tasted, but Tallis didn't mind, as the aroma slowly brought her friends back to consciousness. She grinned as they rubbed the sleep from their eyes, and was glad to see that a little color had returned to their cheeks.

She knew their bodies were finally getting

accustomed to the corruption that emanated from the demon. While Tallis knew it would make it easier to travel, she worried about what the long-term side effects could be if their bodies began accepting the sick evil that the demon was forcing upon them.

She kept those thoughts to herself as she handed them each a bowl of her hodgepodge porridge and watched them hesitantly nibble on small spoonfuls in hopes of being able to keep it down. Once they realized their stomachs were strong enough to hold some food, their ravenous hunger took hold, and they unceremoniously scarfed down the porridge as if it were the most decadent thing they had ever tasted.

As they began to dismantle their camp and make to leave, a wave of crippling dread and jittery nervousness in the oak's mezzo-soprano tone momentarily kept Tallis from leaving the confines of the old tree they had been camping beneath. So strong was the wave of apprehension that Tallis fell to her knees panting as she struggled to loosen the paralyzing hold the trees feelings had upon her.

Gritting her teeth and squeezing her eyes shut, Tallis shook her head and forced herself back to her feet. She tried to soothe the tree, to show it where they were going, and to have the animals go there, but the tree was far too agitated to be able to comprehend what Tallis was trying to tell it, and she could not even begin to understand the warning it was trying to give her.

"What's the matter now?" Rosslyn asked as she cocked her head to the side to watch Tallis.

"Nothing. It's nothing. Let's just … let's get a move on," she said hurriedly, not wanting to worry her friends any further by explaining the sudden fear that gripped the tree with such a force that it actually made her knees quiver.

Tomas and Rosslyn exchanged hesitant looks with one another, clearly not believing Tallis. With a shrug, they turned away and once again began gathering their things in silence, leaving Tallis to shake herself free of the last tendrils of desperation holding her in place before she could leave the tree behind.

Tallis couldn't understand why the tree suddenly seemed so desperate for her to stay and fearful for her if she left. She had known the trees to be needy before, when they thought she would never return and they would have no one to talk to, but this had been wildly different than anything she had experienced so far. It left her with a numb chill that went all the way to the bone, one she could not shake even after they had left the campsite and Tallis could no longer see the tree.

"So, is there a plan?" Rosslyn said timidly as the uncomfortable silence stretched following the odd incident. "I'm assuming there's a plan."

Tallis had been concentrating on what had happened and listening for tremps too much to really consider what they should do. She had never really had a plan, not even before Tomas and Rosslyn had joined her.

Without knowing what she was going to actually be facing, she didn't even know what to plan for. Her strategy had always been to just figure it out as she went, but clearly that was not going to be enough.

"I don't rightfully know. A lot of it depends on what we find when we get there. What form the demon is in, if the animals show up to help, how many tremps are waiting for us … I know I have to burn the tree down, but beyond that I have no specific strategy in mind," Tallis whispered, too nervous and frightened to banter the way she knew would put Rosslyn at ease.

"And what if the demon is back and has another elf enslaved? You'd have to avoid getting touched, but as long as it's focused on you, we should be all right, right? You'd just have to, you know … dance around the demon thing like you do so well, and me and Tomas will fire one of his exploding powders at the gate it came through and destroy it."

Tallis shrugged as she thought about it. Theoretically it could work, but she wasn't certain. Killing the vessel the monster inhabited had done wonders to weaken it, and it would give them time to destroy whatever it was they needed to without fear of the elves. Something told her that it would not be enough, though.

"Like I said, I don't really know, Roz. I guess that may work, but there's no way to be certain if that's all we'll need to do. I'm just the brawn in this operation. I'm relying on Tomas to be the brains and to come up with something brilliant."

Tomas stammered, "I think … based on everything you've told us of the yew's instructions, we'll need to do both to ensure that the … monster is dead and gone. I can make one of my powders into something … much more powerful as we go, and hopefully that will be enough to speed along the destruction of whatever this tree is that the demon came from."

Tallis nodded. "Sounds like a better plan than what I was originally going to do."

Blushing under her compliment, Tomas busied himself with once again modifying his explosive powders as safely and quickly as his lingering illness would allow. If nothing else, it gave him something to do and focus on rather than the idea that these could be their last moments together. Now Tallis just had to do the same for Rosslyn and she wouldn't have to worry about them anymore.

Tallis was beginning to feel sluggish, though, too sluggish to focus on helping Rosslyn calm down. *It must be a side effect of the fear from the tree.*

Regardless of what had caused it, it was becoming harder for her to think about much beyond putting one foot in front of the other. If Rosslyn and Tomas were feeling the same, or even if they noticed the strange way she was acting, neither gave any indication of it as they plowed forward as if they had not just been devastatingly ill the day before.

As the cold midday sun beat down through the thick tree boughs, Tallis's sluggishness only got worse. More and more it felt like a great pressure was building on her forehead and the bridge of her nose, forcing her thoughts back down into the pits of her mind. So profound was the pressure, that Tallis thought it was even beginning to affect her hearing as everything seemed to sound a little more hollow and far away.

She began trying to force air through her ears to pop them in hopes it would help alleviate the pressure, but it was to no avail. The heaviness continued for what felt like the rest of the day, but in fact had only been a few moments as the sun had yet to begin its descent.

Tallis wondered if she were beginning to feel the sickness of the demon again as the forest around her began to brighten ever so slightly. The debris of the forest floor took on a barely noticeable orange hue to its normal warm earthy brown, the leaves in the trees carried a slightly crisper green, despite the chill, and even the bark on the trees themselves seemed to brighten a little like drying red clay.

It was such a subtle change that Tallis wasn't entirely convinced she was not just imagining it. When Tomas and Rosslyn didn't appear to notice anything different about this part of the forest, Tallis decided it must all be in her mind. She tried to pass it off as an effect of getting closer to where they needed to be and tried to ignore the nagging feeling she had that something had changed.

As the sun continued to hang above them, Tallis began to wonder if they were heading in the right direction. They had been walking without pause for what felt like a very long time and were getting nowhere.

She felt like the time for them to be able to stop the demon from regaining its full strength was coming to an end, and they were getting no closer to where they actually needed to be. But Tallis knew that couldn't be true, either, as her feet had begun to ache with the constant walking over uneven surfaces. Her body knew she was moving, but her mind was stuck at a time that had already come to pass.

Tallis could take the pings of her nagging conscience no longer, and was about to stop, when a violent rustle just a little ways ahead, distracted her. The disturbance seemed to shift the oppressive fog settling on her mind as her senses became alert and her curiosity took hold. She motioned for Rosslyn and Tomas to keep quiet as she unsheathed her daggers and slowly crept forward.

If she had observed how eerily silent everything was even with her walking over mulch that had not been disturbed in possibly centuries, she didn't care. So intent on discovering what had caused the disturbance, Tallis didn't even notice that her trident daggers didn't make their customary soft rustling sound as they left their leather sheaths.

Before Tallis could pounce upon the collection of beech ferns the color of a praying mantis and overgrown laurel green scaly ferns, two red foxes and a juvenile reindeer with a hooded crow perched on its budding velvet-covered antlers emerged from the foliage. Tallis stopped dead in her tracks and stared at the animals as they calmly stared back.

She gaped at the animals, unsure of what to make of these woodland creatures that patiently stood before her. She knew she should be expecting such help, but somehow seeing it for herself was far different than anything she could have ever envisioned. The way they watched her seemed almost human as they regarded her thoughtfully, sending a subtle shiver up Tallis's spine.

Without knowing what else she should do, Tallis said, "Um, hello there. I'm Tallis, and this is Tomas and Rosslyn. We're, uh, we're the friends the trees maybe told you about? Can you … can you even understand me?"

*This is stupid. The yew told you that help would be available and this is it. Of everything that's happened, you shouldn't be so surprised or skeptical when things like this happen anymore,* a voice said in her mind.

Tallis had never really talked to herself before, but

the voice in her head was right. She should not be so surprised when these kinds of things happened anymore, no matter how ridiculous it all seemed.

She nodded, deciding to listen to her conscience and to trust what she saw in front of her. Putting her daggers away, she waved at the animals, and said, "All right then, I guess we'll just follow you?"

The foxes, hooded crow, and reindeer momentarily exchanged glances before slowly turning and disappearing in the overgrown ferns once again. Tallis indicated to her companions to follow her and tried to ignore the unsettling blank stares she thought they had given her.

*You are asking them a lot in trusting a bunch of animals,* she said to herself. *It's natural for them to be a little leery. Pay it no mind.*

Unsure what to say to her friends, Tallis followed the animals as Rosslyn and Tomas trailed behind. The silence left Tallis alone with her own thoughts, which ended up causing her only to brood further and focus on a stony panic feeling she had not experienced even in the direst of circumstances. Even when it looked as if the demon would take over her body and have the vessel it so desired, even when Donovan died, she had never experienced this kind of fear before.

It was a sharp, cold pang deep within her soul that caused her heart to thump erratically in her chest, as if it would burst free and run away. It was a fear full of self-doubt and questions as to why she was even doing this, why was she going to face such a terrible monster with nothing but a handful of forest animals and two sick companions at her side?

*Isn't this something someone like Donovan should*

*take care of? Someone with training and with an army to command? You will only get more people killed,* she thought as she now reluctantly followed behind the young reindeer.

If she failed, more people would die, and she would have saved no one. As it was, she had not actually saved anyone but the sad handful of Dumfry elders, and all of them, save Athdara, seemed to hate her just as much as the elves that were devastating their town. At her best, and with Donovan at her side, that was all she was able to accomplish. Now her chances seemed so slim, that Tallis was beginning to wonder if it would not simply be better for her to turn around and leave.

*If Donovan couldn't survive this, what hope do you have?* the voice nagged. Tallis rubbed her eye with the palm of her hand, trying to force the distressing voice out of her mind. No matter how hard she tried, it was right.

Donovan fell so easily to the demon and he was a trained knight nearly twice her size, what hope did Tallis have? So many people had already died as the tremps took the country by surprise that Tallis would be a fool to think she, of all people, could do what the king's trained knights could not.

Tallis could feel the cold fear and dread spreading over her body causing her to break out in an icy sweat. She could feel her chest tightening, forcing the feeling of her thumping heart to go all the way down into the churning pit of her stomach.

She could feel her nerve slipping, as she couldn't stop herself from thinking about what would happen when she undoubtedly failed. All she could hope for was to die before the fiend could use her as the weapon it so craved. Otherwise, there would be no stopping the creature as it ravaged all of Selkirk.

The more she thought about it, the more she could see it play out before her eyes. So clear was the vision, that Tallis swore she was getting a true glimpse of the future.

She could see all of Selkirk burning as she wasted all the cities and towns while the people succumbed to her corruption. She could feel the desire for their pain, and the twisted sick curiosity to cut one open to see what made a human so different from the elves. She wanted to uproot all of the ancient trees that had stood in her way and throw them from the cliffs into the raging sea below. She watched herself feasting on her friends and relishing the taste of their love for her as their dead eyes stared up at her as she nibbled on their insides.

Gasping in horror, Tallis stopped and forced her fingers into her temples, focusing on the pressure there rather than the visions that had been dancing in front of her eyes.

She turned to look at Rosslyn and Tomas and felt her blood run cold for a brief moment when she thought she saw the unmistakable sneer of disgust cross their faces. It was as if they knew the kind of monster she was to become and weren't just disappointed in her, but hated her for failing.

Tallis firmly shut her eyes, and by the time she opened them again, Tomas and Rosslyn were merely looking at her impassively. They didn't seem surprised or worried about her odd behavior. *You have acted more strangely than this, they are simply getting accustomed to it.*

---

257

Tallis shook out her hands and tried to get her breathing under control, but the fear persisted. "I can do this," she mumbled to herself as she tried to regain her courage. All the while their animal guides patiently waited for her, as if they were in no great hurry.

"Can you?" Tomas asked as he appeared at Tallis's side.

"Can I what?"

"Kill the demon, destroy the gate, save Selkirk. Can you do it?" he asked patiently. He wasn't asking it in an accusing way, but stating the question matter-of-factly. Still, it seemed odd coming from Tomas, especially now of all times.

"I-I think … I mean, I'm going to try, yes."

Tomas awarded her with a blank stare before turning his back on her to fiddle more with his powders. It was so unlike Tomas that Tallis found herself gaping at the back of his head as she wrestled with believing what she was hearing and seeing from a man who supposedly wanted her to succeed.

*He is scared. If you cannot do this, he will die. Wouldn't it be better to stop now before more people died?*

She felt her nerve slipping even further as she wrestled with the possibility of losing Tomas and Rosslyn. She would mourn them both if they died, but something seemed so bitter and unfair about having Tomas ripped from her now when she had only newly discovered her affection for him.

Then there was Rosslyn. She had promised Akira and Tyree that she would bring her home safe and sound. How could she bring Rosslyn home if either one of them were dead? How could she look Rosslyn's parents in the eye and explain that she had failed once again to save the people she loved and cherished the most?

Tallis began pacing in circles as she shook out her hands and forced air deep into her lungs and expelled it in deep ragged breaths, as if that would banish her rising panic. She could feel herself becoming overwhelmed, just like she had when she first held her mother's lifeless body in her arms, just as she was when she was forced to leave Donovan behind. She couldn't afford to be overwhelmed, not now, not when they were so close to ending this once and for all.

*You can't do that again. You can't leave anyone else behind. If you fail again, they will be the ones to suffer.*

For as much as she believed she was too strong to be felled by her own fears, she knew it was true. She could not bear to have that happen again, it would destroy her.

Even worse would be if she failed and then became personally responsible for their deaths. She knew she would cease to exist as soon as the demon entered her body and that she wouldn't literally be killing them, but even that realization failed to give her even the coldest of comforts.

*What have you accomplished in your life? This will just be another notch on your list of failures. Jon was right to hate you.*

She looked to Rosslyn and Tomas for support, but neither seemed to notice or be interested in her panic attack. Even the animal guides didn't care that Tallis was in distress. Everyone and everything she turned to for support was currently either ignoring her or completely oblivious to what was happening.

Forcing herself to believe the latter, Tallis darted for Rosslyn and gripped her hand. "You believe in me, right? I can stop this demon, I can … I can keep anyone else from dying. You trust that I won't fail, right?"

Tallis expected Rosslyn to laugh in her face and tell her how absurd she was being for even thinking she couldn't do this. She wanted Rosslyn's jokes and sarcastic eye rolls, but, instead, she got a subtle sneer as she took her hand slowly and deliberately back from Tallis.

"If you can't, then what's the point? Why are we even here on some suicide mission if you don't believe you'll win?"

Tallis stumbled backwards as she once again struggled with what she was hearing. It was so unlike her friends to give her the cold shoulder when she needed their support and reassurance. In fact, it was so out of character for both of them that Tallis started to doubt, if but ever so slightly, that any of this was actually happening.

*You haven't exactly been the best friend to either of them. All you have done is put them in danger, spurned Tomas and his feelings for you, punched Rosslyn, and blamed her for Donovan's death. It's no wonder they are turning on you now,* she heard the voice in her head say, almost as soon as she began to doubt the reality of what she was seeing.

Her conscience was right; she had been a terrible friend, as of late. She constantly spurned or put her friends in danger, and that was on top of the confusion that surrounded her feelings for Tomas and the coldness she felt towards Rosslyn after she had shot her cousin.

There was now a strain in their friendships, when before there had been none. The thought of losing these relationships sent her spiraling out of control as she descended further into her pitying self-doubt.

Pulling at her hair, Tallis continued to stumble backwards as she struggled against what her mind was telling her. She was desperately trying to grasp at anything in her memories that would keep her from believing she had failed her friends, or that she would falter and more people would die as a result of her weakness. She didn't want to believe the only thing her father and uncle would remember of her was their disappointment and contempt for the monster she would become if she continued down her current road.

It was beginning to be too much for Tallis as she slid to the forest floor, her back scraping over the rough bark of a juniper tree. Continuing to tug at her hair, she gritted her teeth to keep from screaming as her panic attack began to overwhelm her.

"I can't do this ... I can't do this ... I-I don't want anyone else to die. I'm not ... I don't want this mess to be my fault. I can't ... I just can't," she said in a low groan as she began to believe that perhaps it would be better if she did not go to face the demon. That perhaps if she stayed where she was, then fewer people would come to harm, for there would be no chance for the demon to possess her and slaughter her friends, or any innocents who stood in the way.

"It should never have been up to me to save everyone; I'm nobody, and certainly not anything special," she moaned as she tried to fully convince herself that by not going to confront the demon, she was actually saving their lives.

Without her, the demon would have to create another vessel, and if that happened, Tallis could help *that* person end this once and for all. She would no longer have the fate of all of Selkirk on her shoulders, and she wouldn't be responsible for any more deaths. Even if the monster never created another vessel and simply continued to control the elves, the Clearing had done a decent job so far of keeping the elves in check.

Except....

"Except I saw what the tremps can do if they really tried. They've already brought Selkirk to its knees, despite three hundred years of clearings," Tallis said groggily as if a fog had begun to shift from over her eyes.

*Perhaps if Donovan were alive, the clearings would work once again. Perhaps the demon can be bargained with. Maybe it will bring Donovan back in exchange for you,* her conscience said as Tallis tried to focus on just what was making her head feel so heavy.

More than anything Tallis wanted Donovan back at her side. "Donovan would know what to do, he always knows what to do."

He had always been so strong, confident, and so selfless that Tallis doubted a better person would ever be found in all of Selkirk. That was the kind of hero they needed now, not a young woman who was losing her nerve. "Donovan would never be this scared."

She wanted to believe that if there was anything that could return her cousin to her, it would be the very thing that had caused his death in the first place. *Surely the demon could bring back Donovan's soul from wherever it had banished it to when it had possessed him,* her conscience said, as if it were trying to convince her of an idea that wasn't wholly her own.

And in her grogginess, it seemed like a fair enough exchange. All she would have to do is go to the demon alone and she would have her cousin back at her side once again.

The thought was more than a little tempting. If she made a deal with the demon to take her in exchange for bringing Donovan back, then Selkirk would have a true hero. It would have a hero it deserved rather than a half-breed mongrel in its stead.

All she would have to do is go to the gate and offer herself to the demon within. And Tallis wanted Donovan back so desperately, that it seemed like a good idea. That was until she really thought about it. Bringing Donovan back in exchange for her undermined his sacrifice, and ultimately would force Donovan to then slay *her.*

"Donovan wouldn't want that. He wouldn't want to be brought back if it meant such evil was allowed to live. It goes against everything he stands for ... stood for," Tallis whispered as she continued to puzzle over the strange thoughts entering her mind at her conscience's behest.

For as much as Tallis wanted Donovan to be alive, she knew in the very core of her being that bringing him back was the wrong thing to do. The more she forced herself to actually consider the thoughts popping into her mind, the more aware she became that these thoughts were not entirely hers to begin with.

While there was a grain of truth and genuine desire to everything the voice in her head was suggesting, something had begun to tell her that this wasn't right, this was not *her*.

In her haze, Tallis forced herself to her feet once again. As she stood, the animals that had been guiding them stood as well and exchanged uncertain looks with one another.

For as much as Tallis was trying to remind herself that these were no normal animals, their mannerisms were so unnatural and subtly so human that it stopped Tallis dead in her tracks as she began to puzzle over the things she was seeing all around her.

*They are grateful to be free of the demon's grasp and are simply worrying over you. That is all.*

Frowning at the foxes and reindeer, Tallis shook her head to free her mind of the oppressive fog that had settled over it once more. But her conscience did have a point, the animals had been enslaved for Wodan knew how long; perhaps it was only natural that they act even more oddly than anything Tallis could have imagined.

*They just want to be free of all imposing forces. Just like your foe in a way. Is that really such a terrible thing? To want to be free of its tree-shaped prison?*

Tallis couldn't imagine what it would be like to be imprisoned, either within a tree, where you could never experience the richness and wonder of the world around you, or to have your mind entrapped within your own body. She imagined that living a life where you were completely devoid of any personal freedom to be a fate worse than death.

*You could watch the world pass you by and never experience those changes for yourself. You'd be a slave to your gilded cage, not even the master of your own destiny,* the voice in her mind chimed as her heart began beating erratically with the idea of forever being trapped.

But....

"But is it worth it? To get that freedom, it cost so many innocent lives, and the enslavement of an entire race. The demon wanted freedom, but that wasn't all it wanted."

The demon didn't just want freedom. It wanted to conquer and control every single life on Selkirk, not just the elves and the animals, but all the humans as well.

Being free of a cage, no matter how gilded, was a wonderful thing, but the cost at which the demon was enacting for its own personal desires was too high. After everything the demon had done to her country, its people, and to Tallis personally, she knew she would never actually believe that the demon was just a misunderstood entity in this entire ordeal.

"What's happening to me?" she groaned as she forced her palms into her eyes and rubbed them so hard she began to see spots.

She could feel the oppressive fog shift in her mind once again as she forced herself to concentrate on the strange thoughts that had entered her mind under the guise of her conscience. All of them formed from a fragment of truth that was born from her deepest fears and desires. And each time she had gotten close to seeing through the fog of her own terror and self-doubt, her conscience would force another idea into her head to distract her.

"This isn't me. I would never believe or want any of this," she murmured as she continued to rub her eyes, forcing herself to think through all the strange things that had happened after she had been reunited with Tomas and Rosslyn.

The more she forced herself to think about it, the more the oppressive heaviness that had been sitting on her mind fought back. Opening her eyes, she saw the world around her begin to shift, the subtly brighter hues of the forest darkened to their natural tones, the silence began to lift, and the sounds of the forest began to return. Even the animals seemed to shiver and twist as they transformed from the foxes, reindeer, and the hooded crow into the forms of elves.

So strange and fantastic was the whole experience, that it took Tallis longer than it should have to understand what had just happened. When she finally did, a bone chilling shiver ran up her spine.

"That monster was in my head," she said in both fear and awe of the demon's abilities.

Once she realized that, everything else suddenly became so clear. The reason the tree seemed so desperate to keep her from leaving, Tomas and Rosslyn's strange behavior towards her, even the human like mannerisms of the animals she had been following. All of it had been a ruse planted in her mind by the demon.

*This must be what the elves experience on a daily basis,* she thought as her mind became her own again and she unsheathed her daggers.

As she readied herself to deal with the group of elves standing dumbly in front of her, she wondered what the demon hoped to accomplish by breaking her spirit. It seemed so intent on her not continuing onward that she could not help but wonder if perhaps the demon was still too weak to face her, it didn't need her anymore, or it simply did not want her finding the tree it had originally emerged from.

But before she could ponder it further, the elves lunged at her with vicious snarls and outstretched talons as they finally realized that Tallis had broken the spell she was under. Sparing a glance for her friends before countering the elves' onslaught, Tallis could tell from their glassy stares and the gentle way their lips moved, as if they were speaking to ghosts, that they were under a similar spell and would remain so unless Tallis could free them.

# TWENTY

TOMAS FURROWED HIS brow at Tallis as she shook his shoulders, his mind reluctantly emerging from the thick and oppressive fog it had been under. His heart still raced and he wasn't entirely sure he could trust his senses just yet. But the way Tallis's eyes darkened to a stormy sea-green with concern told him this was the real Tallis, not the temptress from before.

Frowning at her as his mind focused once more on reality, he glanced from Tallis to the dead elves strewn about her, to Rosslyn as she vomited behind a tree, before resting on Tallis once again. Clearing his throat in a vain attempt to free it of the terrified squeak he worried would be there, he asked, "What is going on? At first I thought you … well, never mind that for now. I take it we were being fooled by that unholy beast?"

He watched her face relax and soften with relief, and he wondered if she, too, had been under the same spell as he was. If she had been, then he wondered what terrible visions she had seen, and if he was a prominent part in them like she was for him. He wanted to ask her, to reassure her if necessary, that whatever he had done or said wasn't real, but Tallis didn't give him the chance to ask.

Squeezing his hands, she nodded. "Yes, I wasn't sure I could get you out from underneath its power, that I wouldn't be able to bring you back to the here and now. Now that you're, well, you again, we need to get moving. We aren't safe here. The demon is close, and if it's all the same to you, I'd rather not give it the chance to do that again, or send more tremps after us."

Tomas swallowed the lump in his throat as she let his hands drop to his sides once more, and he wished he could have just held her a moment longer. If the red circles around her eyes were any indication, whatever Tallis had just gone through was just as overwhelming of an ordeal as his own. He knew a touch from her would be enough to calm his fluttering heart, he just hoped he could offer her the same.

He watched Tallis trot over to Rosslyn and help her to her feet once again and his heart ached for her. There would never be any respite for Tallis until the demon was dead and gone, and yet she still took her time to make sure her friends were recovered, instead of barreling ahead to deal with the beast and put her own mind at ease. Tallis might always believe that it was Donovan who had the will of steel and heart of gold, but Tomas knew otherwise.

Just as Tomas decided that he would tell Tallis as much, an icy rain began to fall from the sky. Despite the biting winter chill that came with the rain, it washed the last tendrils of the demon's corruption from his mind, and Tomas found that he did not mind the teeth-chattering shivers as the visions the demon had forced into his head began to fade with each cold drop.

The rain had the same effect on the others as they

closed their eyes and let the rain fall on their upturned faces. As Rosslyn heaved a great sigh of relief, Tallis opened her arms and turned her palms upwards, allowing the rain to pool into her hands. It was as if she were allowing the pureness of the rain to cleanse her soul and wipe away whatever the unholy creature had done to her.

Tomas watched Tallis inhale deeply, as if the earthy aroma of the wet ground around her could mask the metallic smell of the elven blood pooling all around them. And, with the way she was acting, Tomas could swear that Tallis was trying to repair whatever the demon had broken with the shower that was falling on them now.

If it had been up to Tomas, he would have let Tallis recover for the rest of the day and they would track down the demon tomorrow. But Tallis was not asking their opinions as she finally lowered her arms, opened her eyes, and turned away from the sky.

She glanced between him and Rosslyn for a moment, clearly struggling with what to say. He could see the curiosity burning in her eyes of wanting to know what he and Rosslyn went through, and he would tell her if she but asked. But, instead, she asked, "Are you two well enough to keep going?"

Tomas was still a little shaky and he could tell from the pallor of Rosslyn's face that she was still trying to erase everything she had seen as well. For as much as he would like to rest and recover his courage, he knew that Tallis needed this to be over, and he was not going to be the one to delay her any further.

Nodding his head, Tomas straightened his back, and with as much strength as he could muster, said,

271

"Lead the way, Tallis."

He wasn't sure if his façade of bravery really fooled Tallis or not, but regardless, she awarded him with a soft and sincere smile. Her smiles would always do more to chase the demon's influence from his mind than any cleansing rain ever could, and it gave him the courage to follow Tallis to the ends of the world and beyond, if need be. The same could not be said of Rosslyn, who was glaring at the both of them in annoyance.

Whatever Rosslyn had gone through, it was not to be forgotten through soft smiles. Still, Rosslyn was never one to be left behind, and with an exasperated sigh and a dramatic tossing of her hands into the air, she said, "Fine, let's kill this bloody beast and be done with it."

Tallis gave her a sardonic grin before rotating her daggers in a quick circle and jogging away. Tomas wasn't sure if his stomach could handle all the jostling of trying to keep up with Tallis, but he would try if it meant they would be leaving the carcasses of the elves and the demon's mind games behind.

IT FELT LIKE she had been running for days when Tallis finally came to a slow stop. Rosslyn couldn't help but pant as she rested her hands on her knees and struggled to match Tallis's strides. She knew she was not out of shape, especially after all this time on the road running from elves and people alike. But given her sickness and the still nagging fears over her family left behind by the demon, she could not help but be exhausted.

She still was unclear as to what exactly she would do to help once they got to where they were going. *A bad time not to think things through if there ever was one,* she thought as she recovered her breath. At least Tomas could shoot his crafty crossbow with his exploding powders at the demon; all she had was her club and she did not want to be in a situation where she was close enough to use it.

All Rosslyn had ever wanted was to follow her Galon Sipsiwn and go on an adventure, to live a life of pure freedom where the only master she had to abide by was herself. Now that she had that, she found that she suddenly no longer had the stomach for such things. The thought of not being the master of her own destiny and in charge of her own freedom still made her stomach twist into anxious knots, but at least if she were back home she would not be in constant fear of being disemboweled.

So engrossed was Rosslyn in her own thoughts, she failed to truly appreciate her surroundings until Tallis had come to a complete stop and crouched in the shadows of a nearly dead knotted willow tree surrounded by reddish green glittering wood-moss. Crouching beside her, Rosslyn finally took stock of the devastation around them.

This particular circle of the Guldar Forest looked like it had been dead for centuries. All the grass, trees, ferns, shrubbery, and even the moss within the circle had all shriveled, as if they had all the water squeezed out of them. If Rosslyn did not know where she was, she would swear that she was in a dead land somewhere far away from Selkirk. Despite the icy rain that still fell, nothing seemed capable of reviving this patch of forest.

Rosslyn followed the ring of gray and brown decayed grass and trees to its epicenter, where a solitary tree stood. Unlike the yew that had spoken to Tallis and given her directions, this tree was not particularly frightening in appearance, but looking at it still made Rosslyn involuntarily shiver.

The tree was doubled over like an old man without the aid of a cane. Its bark was ashen white and its branches were twisted like fingers crippled by age, with not a single leaf or piece of green foliage to be had anywhere. The tree was so devoid of any life, that it exuded the chilling feeling of something so cursed that it was responsible for the desecration around it.

Rosslyn could feel the hairs on her arms and the back of her neck stand on end the longer she stared at the tree, and she struggled to keep herself from, once again, being overrun with terror. Even without knowing what the yew had actually shown Tallis, Rosslyn knew that this was the very thing they sought.

Without realizing what she was doing, Rosslyn found herself gripping Tallis's hand and squeezing tightly. Tallis squeezed in return and allowed Rosslyn to hold on to her like a lifeline. It made her feel better to know that Tallis's hands were so steady in the face of such wickedness; it gave Rosslyn hope that good would triumph over evil, just as all the fables Rosslyn's parents had her read when she was first learning her words upon leaving their clan said it should.

She was not sure what Tallis was waiting for as

they stayed crouched in the shadows. There was no sign of the demon or of any elves guarding the tree. It seemed like the perfect opportunity to Rosslyn to rush forward and take care of the gate while they could. Just as she opened her mouth to say as much, she heard a sound that made her blood turn to icy sludge in her veins: the demon's voice echoing all around them.

"You can come out now, girl child. I know you have come for me," the demon said as it materialized from the very tree they had come to destroy.

Rosslyn clamped her free hand over her mouth to keep from screaming as she laid eyes upon the monster and its new host body. Instead of inhabiting an elf like it had done in the past, the demon was none other than Cullen, if but barely.

Even in its weakened state, the demon's life force was too much for Cullen's body to handle, as large chunks of his skin had fallen away, revealing the muscle beneath. Clumps of his jet-black hair fell out with each step he took and his shockingly pale blue eyes were no more. His eyes had completely burned out, just like the countless dead elves they had come across, only his eyes still dripped blood that was liquid fire itself.

She could feel her stomach churn and the bile rise in the back of her throat with the mere sight of the creature. It suddenly made sense why she and Tomas had become just as ill as Tallis had. With the demon in a human host, its corruption was beginning to affect any human that happened to be nearby.

Swallowing the sick in her mouth, Rosslyn turned to Tallis. She didn't know what to expect looking at her, if she expected Tallis to glow with a holy light or if she expected her to burst into flames, but part of her expected to see something other than her best friend crouching beside her. But it was still the same old Tallis that Rosslyn knew and loved.

Except now the fate of Selkirk rested in her hands.

# TWENTY-ONE

*BREATHE, REMEMBER TO breathe,* Tallis told herself as she emerged from the shadows and took a single step into the cursed ring surrounding the demon's tree. Griping her daggers, she forced herself to look at nothing but the eyeless body of Cullen.

She strained her ears as she stared at the creature before her, listening for the sounds of the elves she knew must be lingering just out of sight. The demon had fought too hard for too long to keep her away, only to now leave the tree unguarded.

As she squared off with the demon, her suspicions were confirmed as a whistle of crazed elves emerged from the shadows. Their skin was cracked and rough like that of the many oaks within the Guldar Forest, which explained why Tallis had not seen them before.

Despite the cold, they only wore bits and pieces of rags that were held together by nothing but leaves and vines. Each elf had a gaunt and vacant look to their bark-like faces, the likes of which Tallis had never seen before. If it had not been for their gnashing knife-like teeth, and the dull mustard glow of their eyes, Tallis would have sworn that these particular elves were more tree than anything truly alive.

She did not look at the elves long enough to see that their yellow eyes lacked the intensity that they once held. She could not afford to be distracted by anything now that the demon had a new host body. Cullen was the only real threat to Tallis, not the tree-like tremps.

Focusing her attention back to the fearsome creature before her, Tallis saw that Cullen still held onto his bow, an arrow already cocked and ready to set loose at a moment's notice. It made her glad to know that Tomas was ready and waiting in the shadows with his own bolt ready to fire as well, though she would much prefer for him to be readying one of his fiery powders to send at the tree rather than a bolt to fell Cullen.

"Feeling unsure of yourself, monster? You would actually risk killing your supposed vessel just to have a chance at catching me?" she said, sounding more confident than she felt as she attempted to buy more time for the animals to find her.

A slow rumbling laughter emerged from Cullen as he stood lazily in front of his dead and petrified tree. "The girl child gives herself too much credit," he said. "I would much rather kill the girl child and start again than lose my true form. The girl child is replaceable, she has always been replaceable. She would be wise to remember that."

Something about the dismissive way he said it made Tallis's heart sputter within her chest. Believing that the demon wanted her alive had made Tallis bold, almost to the point of being reckless. If the corrupted spirit truly only saw her as one possible option, like tunics in a chest, then Tallis was about to lose whatever advantage she once believed she had.

"If that were true you would've had your precious little elves kill me already," Tallis said, calling what she hoped was the demon's bluff.

Cullen shifted slightly, as if he no longer cared about trying to convince Tallis that this was her destiny. She had become no more than a biting gnat, an irritant that needed to be crushed. Even without eyes, Tallis could read the impatience and contempt Cullen had for her plainly on his dissolving and blistered face.

Cullen hissed in disgust. "This body cannot command the humans or elves as I would wish. I did not want this body, but it forced me to take it. He had such delicious evil little thoughts, that at first I did not mind wearing him. But it cannot contain me, and the girl child already knows the ordeal it takes to change one meat suit for another. I would rather be the girl child, but if I cannot then I will kill her and wait until I can take a priestess once again. The process will resume, and this time I will not lose the child."

"Cullen forced you to possess him?" Tallis asked as her curiosity got the better of her.

"The boy child knew what I was. He had come to worship me, the poor, filthy, little thing. But he knew my secrets, my weaknesses. He trapped me, believing he would be different since he was so devoted. I made sure the boy child suffered for such arrogance."

"Sounds like a funny way to repay someone who seemed to love you."

"The boy child was a fool. But he did have some interesting little wicked thoughts on what kind of torment the girl child deserved. Oh, he did not like her at all."

"So that's why you forced those visions in my head? Because Cullen was jealous he wasn't your chosen puppet, you took his twisted ideas for revenge and plagued my mind with your poison? Instead of dealing with me directly, you hoped to break my spirit from afar so I'd be what? Compliant? And you could take my body without my knowledge?"

"Did the girl child enjoy that? This body may not have been what I wanted, but he had some amusing tricks that I would not have considered otherwise," the fiend said as it gently caressed Cullen's cheek. The action made it seem as if the demon did not truly consider itself to be in Cullen, but rather Cullen was just a pet whose only purpose was to amuse the demonic spirit within.

"I will not lie; it was amusing to see the girl child's dark little secrets. I wonder if she knows of its companions' secret fears. Especially the boy child it travels with? Oh, he had some wonderfully naughty little secrets about the girl child, he did. I'm sure his silent Wodan would be ever so displeased with the thoughts his boy child had. So tantalizingly impure for one so pious." Cullen cooed before a malicious giggle erupted from deep within him.

Tallis could feel her cheeks redden at the mention of Tomas. She did not know what he had seen when he was under the demon's influence, and she had not truly wanted to, but now that the thought was in her mind she could not stop herself from wondering just what Tomas had seen. She knew that was what Cullen wanted as well, to make her angry, or to distract her so she would make a mistake.

Gritting her teeth, she focused once again on the enormous task before her. She needed more time to figure out how to attack the demon without being touched, and to avoid the elves. She needed to buy Tomas enough time to get into a position where he could set the tree ablaze before the demon knew what was happening. So the longer she could stall the demon the better. This meant she needed to keep him talking.

Ignoring the demon's attempt to rile her further, Tallis asked, instead, "What am I supposed to call you, anyway? You aren't Cullen, and I am getting really tired of just calling you *demon*. I'd know the name of my foe before I end its cursed existence."

Cullen chuckled once again, his laughter floating on the air like a melody played at a funeral: soft and haunting, a song that would have been lovely except for the circumstances in which it was created.

"The girl child's bravado is admirable. It will be such a waste to have to eat her heart, but I must say, I am looking forward to it. Such courage must make it … delectable." The demon grinned, showing rotting teeth before licking its lips.

Forcing herself not to cringe, Tallis gripped her daggers so tightly her knuckles turned white. Through clenched teeth, she said, "You didn't answer my question."

"What it calls me doesn't matter. Call me *mother* if it suits the girl child, for that is what I am. I am the spirit that bore her to life, or did she forget?" Cullen said dismissively as he idly played with the bowstring, trying to hide the shudder that ran the course of his body.

281

Refusing to even entertain the idea that this creature was her mother, Tallis shouted to hide the sound of Tomas and Rosslyn flanking the demon, "Was that fear I saw making you quiver, monster?"

Sneering, Cullen said as more of the liquid fire like blood dripped from his eye sockets, "I have no time for the girl child's mindless banter. It's as if she thinks I do not know her boy child and dark-skinned girl child companions are skittering like roaches through the underbrush. I do not need eyes to see what she is doing."

The demon had grown so accustomed to the speed and agility of its previous elven hosts that each of Cullen's movements became spasmodic and sluggish. So when the demon raised Cullen's bow and aimed it at the spot where Tomas was hiding, Tallis had ample time to react.

Tallis flung herself to the side as the shaft left the bowstring. The arrow buried itself deep within her hip, forcing a blood curdling scream of pain to escape her lips. Her scream was so loud it nearly drowned out Tomas as he yelled her name and the demon's own involuntary scream as if it, too, could feel the pain radiating out from her hip.

Panting as she snapped the shaft off the arrow, Tallis croaked mockingly, "Now look what you've done. You've damaged your supposedly flawless vessel."

"I would have given the girl child everything! I could have given her revenge over those humans who caused her pain. I could have made her false father suffer for the pain he caused her. I could have punished the children who teased her and the boy children who pawed after her. I could have brought them all under her heel and given her an eternity of nothing but ecstasy where she would never die and would stay forever lovely. Yet she spurns my gifts and dares to ruin *my* vessel. The girl child is not damaged beyond repair. I *will* have her!"

At Cullen's silent command, the elves sprang into action. Half of the horde encased Tallis in a circle as the elves tried to catch her and pin her to the ground. The other half of the tremps clumsily lunged for where Tomas and Rosslyn hid just a short distance away. All the while Cullen stood stiffly between Tallis and the dead tree it had come from, the effort of controlling the elves making it impossible for him to do anything else.

Yelling at her friends to run, Tallis attempted to force her way through the elves. But with every move and twist of her body, the piercing pain in her hip made it impossible for her move quickly enough to duck beneath their flailing arms.

Screaming in frustration, Tallis maladroitly struck out at the elves with her daggers, praying she could enact enough damage to slip through and get her friends to safety.

Just as the elves closed the distance between the fleeing Tomas and Rosslyn, a crashing sound drowned out the patter of the rain and Tallis's cries of desperation. So unexpected was the noise that even the elves stopped to gawk at what sounded like thousands of trees all being felled throughout the forest.

With a thunderous roar, dozens of massive bull elks, stocky reindeer with velvet antlers, dainty red deer, scurrying red foxes, and agile gray wild cats burst forth from the forest. Even the sky above filled with dozens upon dozens of hooded crows and yellow twites as they dove towards the elves and even forced Tallis to the ground as she tried to avoid their sharp beaks and outstretched claws.

Tallis had never been this happy to almost be trampled in her life as the help the yew tree had promised finally arrived. It still seemed completely ridiculous to her that forest animals were coming to her rescue, and she knew that no one would ever believe her if she told them, anyway.

She had never seen such gentle creatures act so viciously. The reindeer and elk trampled the tremps under their massive hooves and flung them about like dolls with their antlers. The red deer were no better as they kicked about like horses, forcing the elves to scatter, allowing Tallis a chance to crawl out of the circle they had trapped her in. Even Tomas and Rosslyn seemed taken aback as they stumbled towards Tallis and away from the hooded crows and twites as they harried the elves from above, while the foxes and wild cats gnawed at their ankles.

As Tallis rolled away from the flailing elves, a loud shriek pierced the sky. So intense was the sound, that it forced her to drop her daggers and cover her ears to keep her eardrums from erupting. The shriek seemed endless as Cullen began to lose his elves and resorted to desperate measures in an attempt to stop the animals attacking them from all sides.

The tactic worked, as one by one the animals began tossing their heads in distress as the high-pitched screech ravaged their sensitive hearing. Fearing their brief advantage was about to be lost, Tallis exchanged a long glance with Tomas, hoping he would know to strike now at the tree, while he could. Lowering her hands from her ears with renewed determination, she gripped her trident daggers once more and lunged for Cullen.

Forcing herself to push through the dizzying pain as Cullen's cry vibrated louder and louder in her skull, Tallis slowly but surely made her way closer to ending the chaos the demon had wrought one way or another. She knew it was risky to get closer to Cullen, but this was her battle to win or lose. Tallis would never again allow someone to sacrifice their life for her.

Regardless of the nobility in their actions in wanting to save her, Tallis did not want to be rescued when she was more than capable of fending for herself and deciding what her life was, and was not, worth. And she decided it was not worth letting another soul perish at the demon's hands.

As the distance became ever more miniscule, Tallis bolstered her confidence by reminding herself this was the best chance she would have to take the demon in a one-on-one fight. Whatever Cullen had done to force the malevolent tree spirit to possess him, it seemed to affect the demon's ability to command the elves, as it struggled to move in a body it was unaccustomed to. When the beast had been an elf, Tallis had no hope of out maneuvering it, at least now that wasn't necessarily the case.

Vaguely, as she pumped her legs faster, Tallis heard the familiar *swoosh* as Tomas fired one of his fiery powders from his crossbow. But the powder did not ignite the way she had hoped.

The tree did not go up in flames as instantaneously as she had imagined it would in her mind. She could feel her gut plummet to her feet with the realization that Tomas would not be able to get the tree to catch fire before she reached Cullen.

Tomas was still fixing another of his incendiary powders to his crossbow when Tallis dove for Cullen, her daggers outstretched and her body ready to twist away from his blistered and pustule covered hands at a moment's notice. Just before she was about to plunge her dagger into Cullen's heart, the world slowed, just as it had seemed to when Donovan had first tackled the demon to keep it away from her.

She watched Cullen's body shudder like a snake shedding its skin as he sidestepped away from Tallis's death blow. As she tried to twist her body to at least wound Cullen if she could not kill him, her heart stopped as she felt the gentle caress of Cullen's hand upon her cheek.

Despite the blisters and missing skin on his hands, his touch was light and soft, as if it were a feather fluttering over her cheek in a summer's breeze.

In that brief instant when his hand touched her cheek, she swore she could see the monster within him grin as it left Cullen's empty body behind in a dead and crumpled heap and fled into her own. Before she even knew what had happened, it was over. After fighting and fleeing from the demon at every turn, it finally had what it had wanted for the past nineteen years.

It had her.

Tallis had but a moment before the monster's fire consumed her soul and she ceased to exist. She didn't have enough time to warn Rosslyn and Tomas to run, she didn't have enough time to say goodbye, nor did she have enough time to beg for Wodan's forgiveness in hopes that wherever her soul went next, be it the Pits or Garden, Wodan would take pity on her and shield her in His benevolent embrace.

All she had the time for was the realization she was as good as dead, and the last choice she would have would be in how she wished to die.

She could either give up now and allow the demon to consume her soul in the fire that raged within its wrath-filled spirit, or she could destroy the demon's vessel. She could kill herself before the demon ever had the chance to do anyone any harm and force it to retreat once more back into the tree from which it had come.

The choice was simple.

Raising her dagger over her left breast, she plunged the sharp blade as hard as she could into her own heart just as the fire of the demon began to plume throughout her body.

Instantly, she felt the spirit of the demon recede from her body as if a cold ocean tide swept it away only to have it replaced with the agonizing pain of the blade searing through her tender flesh. She felt her heart shudder and suddenly she could no longer breathe.

Gasping for breath, the last thing she felt was the demon as it shrieked and raged within her as it was forced to quickly leave her body and retreat back to its petrified tree. And the last thing she saw was Tomas's second attempt succeed at getting the tree to ignite, as the gnarled and petrified tree was rapidly engulfed in flames.

The raging inferno lit up the gray sky with its bright yellow and orange flames, brighter and hotter than anything Tallis had ever seen or felt before. It was such an intense and instant heat that Tallis could feel it singe her eyebrows even as her life rapidly fled from her.

*At least I can die knowing that we stopped it*, was her last thought as the ancient tree disintegrated into ash that floated away in the soft and chilly breeze left behind by the rain.

Tallis felt more than saw a dark shadow explode out from the tree like a shockwave that flung her backwards to land on the icy ground with a loud thud. With Tallis nearly dead and the demon's original body gone, the evil spirit had finally been destroyed.

A plaintive wail filled the air as the demon dissolved into nothingness and its twisted tree fell away into nonexistence in the cleansing fire that Tomas's powders had caused. It was then that the entire forest seemed to sigh with relief as the demon's taint became no more.

Even though the moment between Cullen touching Tallis, the tree disintegrating, and the demon being vanquished had occurred over the span of heartbeats, it felt like an eternity to Tallis as her heart continued to sputter and her life's blood spilled out on the frigid ground around her. So it was, with one last gurgling gasp, that her eyes fluttered closed and she saw no more.

# TWENTY-TWO

𝕲HE ELVES COLLAPSED to the forest floor as the demon's hold over them was once again severed. They were lying comatose on the ground just as they had before, but this time their eyes were not forced to stay open. One by one, each elf's eyes softly fluttered closed.

At the same moment that the elves fell to the ground, the animals ceased their thrashing and regained their composure as the demon's shriek cleared from their sensitive hearing. Free of their duty to help, most of the animals casually left the area. There were only a few of the elk and some of the foxes to linger in the circle of decay after the demon's ordeal had ended.

As happy as the survivors should have been to know they had freed Selkirk of the demon's taint, there was no happy ending for Tomas.

He felt the sound of Tallis hitting the ground reverberate deep in his bones. Without knowing what had truly happened, as his attention had been on firing his crossbow, Tomas knew something terrible had just occurred.

All he could see was Tallis lying in a pool of her own blood, her dagger buried deep in her chest as she shuddered and ceased breathing. Even though he saw her, and knew that what he was seeing was Tallis's life ebbing away, he could not comprehend what he was witnessing. When the sight finally registered in his mind, an involuntary groan of despair escaped from deep in his chest.

As heroic and selfless as her actions were, in that moment Tomas hated her. If she had but waited a moment more before barreling ahead to attack Cullen alone, the tree would have been destroyed and they could have regrouped to deal with the demon appropriately.

Instead, Tallis had forgotten the one lesson that Donovan had struggled to teach her his whole life: that she did not have to fight her battles alone.

Before he knew he had even moved in the first place, he fell to his knees at Tallis's side. He felt Rosslyn collapse next to him as if she were physically incapable of supporting herself as she gazed down at the limp body of her best friend. He couldn't stop his hands from fluttering over Tallis like helpless birds, just as hers had done when Donovan had died, a parallel that was not lost on him.

Wrenching his hands in despair, Tomas forced himself to look past the deathly pale visage of the woman he loved and took stock of what had actually occurred. As he forced himself to stare at the dagger in her chest, hope bloomed over his face.

With a renewed sense of urgency and excitement, Tomas sprang into action. Gripping Rosslyn's shoulders he said, "Get my pack, Rosslyn. Now!"

Blinking through her stupor, Rosslyn did as she was bid, if for no other reason than she had never heard Tomas speak with such urgency before. Turning his attention back to Tallis, his hands hovered for a moment over the dagger protruding from her breast.

The demon had entered Tallis just as it had with Donovan. He was fairly positive the demon was no more, but he was not entirely sure that the life he'd be saving would be Tallis's.

*It's worth the risk,* he heard his heart say while his mind urged him to be cautious and to think this through.

But he could not do that. Tallis was losing too much blood, and if he did not act now, he knew he'd never forgive himself if he did not try to save her, even if there was nothing left of Tallis to save. He could not spend the rest of his life wondering if he had lost the one chance he had of saving the woman he had fallen for from the very first moment he saw her.

With his jaw set in a firm line of determination, Tomas gripped the dagger and carefully freed it of Tallis's chest just as Rosslyn returned with his pack. He ignored her wild-eyed stare as she stared at the gaping wound and, instead, focused on cleaning his hands as best he could and digging in his pack for his book.

His heart sank; he had traded his book for Tallis's ring.

He had memorized all the pages, but with Tallis's life in the balance, he suddenly could not remember what his notes had said to do. In his panic, he could not even envision what page the medical information would have been located on.

At the time, it had seemed so important to get Tallis her mother's ring back. At the time, saving her from her own guilty heart had been more important to him than any of the contents within his trusty tome. He was paying for his short sightedness now.

*Calm yourself, man. Tallis needs you. You know how to do this.* He ripped his pack apart looking for any quill he could find.

"What are you doing?" Rosslyn asked as Tomas snatched one of his bolts and meticulously cut off the tips of the quill on either end and then rid it of the last of its feathers.

"Tallis can't breathe. She's punctured her lung, not her heart and she can't get enough air. If I can give her a way to breathe, then we have a chance to get her to a healer to take care of the rest of the damage. I need you to strip the area around the wound and clean it with the gauze I use for my powders as best as you can. Hurry and be careful!"

Tallis was a wonder of a woman in her own right, but there were moments when her lack of a proper education showed and this was one of those moments. She had aimed for where she *thought* her heart was and not where it actually was.

Both of their hands flew over their respective tasks as they rushed to save Tallis's ebbing life. Tomas, for his part, did his best to try and not think about the woman lying motionless before him, her blood beginning to stain his clothes as he knelt at her side.

He tried to only focus on carefully and firmly forcing the quill shaft through Tallis's wound and in-between her ribs to allow the air to flow rather than collect in her chest. Once the quill was safely in place, he took another piece of clean gauze and carefully covered the rest of the hole to prevent air from entering the sucking wound in her chest to further put pressure on her lungs.

He tried to ignore her blood on his hands and the squishing sounds coming from Tallis's body as he operated, and, instead, tried to focus on the movements of his hands as he worked. He forced himself to think of the diagrams in his pawned book and not the actual body before him.

This was his one and only chance to save Tallis's life. If he failed now, he would never know if there was even anything left of Tallis to save, and he couldn't honestly say which would be worse to live with afterwards.

Then he was done. Shakily, he moved his hands away from the gauze and quill as it stuck out of Tallis's bare breast and he held his breath.

*Please, Wodan, let her live,* he prayed silently as he waited what felt like an eternity before Tallis managed to take a gurgling and raspy breath.

TOMAS WAS MANY things; he was a brilliant man that was awkward and shy to the point of being almost painful. He was a man so devoted to his faith in Wodan and his own moral convictions that it caused no end of frustration to Rosslyn. But never before would she have considered him to be a savior. But as Tallis began to breathe shallowly, Rosslyn knew that no matter the kind of man she had believed Tomas to be, from now on, she would only ever see him as a hero.

She couldn't stop herself from tackling Tomas with the force of her hug as relief and joy filled her heart where moments ago, there had been nothing but sorrow.

No matter how bleak things had gotten along their journey, Rosslyn had never once truly considered what she would do if they had failed, if she had lost Tallis. Believing that they had, indeed, failed, even for the briefest of moments, had almost completely crushed her.

With a shy smile, Tomas disentangled himself from Rosslyn. Clearing his throat, he turned away, clearly uncomfortable by her sudden show of affection, when before all he had ever gotten from her had been sarcastic eye rolls.

Rather than talk to her about what he had done or the show of fondness, he busied himself with quickly cleaning the blood off his hands and checking the wound in Tallis's hip from where Cullen's arrow had hit her.

"She won't last long without a healer, Rosslyn. We've got to get her to Perth; it's the closest town I can think of that may have someone there to help her."

"Can we carry her all that way? Perth isn't exactly close enough to hit with a stone. It'd take us a few days at best to get there, and that's without stopping and without having to carry Tallis."

Tomas gave her a wide-eyed and dread-stricken look as he wrenched his hands and tried to think as quickly as he could. "We have to." He positioned himself under Tallis's shoulders and tried to lift her without disturbing the gauze and quill that was allowing her to breathe.

Rosslyn carefully grabbed Tallis behind the knees and lifted her up. She couldn't help but marvel at how slight Tallis was. She had always been small and petite, but this journey had taken its toll on her and she seemed even smaller now than she ever had before.

*She's such a tiny little thing. Maybe it won't be so hard to carry her all the way to Perth,* Rosslyn thought as they slowly left the demon tree's smoldering pile of ash behind.

They had only managed to go a few steps when Tomas stopped dead in his tracks. Rosslyn swallowed the lump in her throat, fearful of what trouble they could possibly run into now that would cause Tomas to stop so suddenly. Slowly, she turned her head and gaped, as standing in front of them were the few bull elks that had stayed behind after the demon had been defeated.

They were massive lumbering brown beasts which had yet to lose their enormous cylindrical beam-shaped antlers after the mating season. But their big eyes seemed to possess nothing but a deep and calm patience as they regarded the trio before them.

"Um, are they possessed still or something? What are they doing?"

Tomas was too dumbfounded to respond. Instead, they both watched in crippling shock as the elks slowly lumbered forward to sniff at the limp body of Tallis.

Rosslyn wasn't sure what to do. The last time they had encountered these normally solitary creatures, one had tried to trample Tallis to death. Without Donovan to wield the broadsword that felled the crazed elk from before, Rosslyn wasn't sure either her or Tomas would be able to fend them off if they intended to do them harm.

But murder was apparently not what the elks had in mind as the two hulking beasts kneeled down next to Tallis. It was such a strange and curious sight to see that Rosslyn couldn't help but gawk at the animals like a simpleton.

The day had been so charged with stress, turmoil, fear, and despair that she simply did not know what to make of the latest installment to the long list of strange events to happen that day.

"What … what *are* they doing?" Rosslyn asked as the elks continued to kneel next to Tallis and stare at them with a look of what could only be described as gentle tolerance.

"If this was anywhere else in Selkirk, and if this had happened after anything else except destroying a demonic tree spirit, I would say these animals were sick, and we should get Tallis away from them as quickly as possible. Except, given what the yew tree told Tallis, I'd say they were here to help."

"How, exactly, are a bunch of elks supposed to help us get Tallis to Perth?" Almost as soon as the question left her mouth, her eyes widened with clarity. Breathlessly, she added, "Oh, they want us to ride them."

Neither Tomas nor Rosslyn moved as they glanced nervously between the elks and Tallis as she continued to struggle to breathe. For her part, Rosslyn was struggling to comprehend everything that was happening while trying to force her senses to accept the things she was seeing. She knew if she was having this much difficulty forcing herself to accept such outlandish things, then Tomas with all his logic must have been having an even harder time.

Shifting Tallis as she straightened her shoulders, Rosslyn said with as much conviction as she could muster, "Oi, what are we waiting for? This will surely get us to Perth fast enough to save Tallis, right?"

"Yes, I suppose but … I mean…," Tomas stammered as he stole glances at the seemingly docile animals at his side.

"Fantastic! Then what *are* we waiting for? If this will save her, then it's best not to think about how improbable this would be under normal circumstances. Nothing about Tallis or this entire day, let alone the past month, has been anything even remotely normal. I mean, Tallis should be dead right now. You may be brilliant, but who but Tallis could honestly survive after a wound like that? Come on, the longer we stand here gaping at the elks like a pair of duffers the less time Tallis has."

Reminding Tomas of what was at stake was enough to get his purely logical mind to finally accept what his eyes were seeing. Nodding to Rosslyn, he helped her place Tallis on the bigger of the two elks.

Rosslyn watched Tomas stroke Tallis's cheek as he finished securing her on the elk's back. He was about to climb up alongside her when Rosslyn caught his hand and stopped him.

She knew Tomas loved Tallis and wanted to make sure she was all right, but so did she. She hadn't forgiven herself yet for the agony she had caused Tallis by shooting Donovan, even though it had been the one good thing she had done this entire journey. All she wanted was to be able to do something that could help her save Tallis rather than cause her more pain.

"Let me ride with her," Rosslyn said, voice cracking with emotion. "You've already done everything you can to save her life. Let me … this is the only thing I can do to help her while you cover us with your crossbow. Please, Tomas."

For a moment, she thought that Tomas would deny her request and climb up the elk's back only to lay Tallis across his lap so he could hold her in place. She watched his mouth twitch and his green eyes darken as he seemed to seriously consider her simple request. Just as her heart began to sink, thinking that Tomas had finally found the one cruel bone in his body, he stepped away from Tallis and offered his hand to Rosslyn to help her up.

"Thank you," she murmured as she settled herself on the elk and carefully positioned Tallis so she could hold her in place and keep her from jostling too much as the elk moved.

Tomas nodded as if he were unable, or simply unwilling to speak. Silently, he turned his back on Rosslyn and climbed onto the other kneeling elk. Once they all were settled, the elks clumsily got to their feet and began to trot off into the forest.

It was almost amusing to watch the massive bulls run as they lifted their long legs almost straight up, as if they were stepping out of heavy snow. But no matter how comical it might have appeared to watch these dark brown creatures run with the ragtag trio on their backs, none who saw them would ever doubt how quickly and effectively they moved through the forest. A journey that would have taken Rosslyn and Tomas days to make under the best of circumstances was going to be cut in half, baring no other disasters.

Gently squeezing Tallis's hand, Rosslyn whispered in her ear as the elk gained speed, "Hang in there, Tally. We'll be to Perth in no time; you just have to stay with me."

# TWENTY-THREE

DESPITE ROSSLYN'S BEST efforts to staunch the
seeping blood that oozed its way out of Tallis's hip and
chest, she was still losing way too much. The blood
loss alone was bad enough, but as the day waxed and
waned, the quill that was allowing air into Tallis's
pierced lung was beginning to weaken and collapse in
on itself. At one point, Rosslyn even asked Tomas if
she could fix it, and all he had done was yell at her not
to touch it before trying to urge his tired elk to run
faster.

Tallis had begun to pale, and her breathing was so
labored that Rosslyn questioned whether she was even
getting air at all when the elks finally slowed to a halt.
For the first time since they had started their ride for
Perth, Rosslyn took her eyes off of Tallis.

Rosslyn had never been so glad in her life to detect
the subtle hint of refuse and the clamor of townsfolk
going about their afternoon. It was all she could do not
to bolt from the elk right then and there and drag Tallis
unceremoniously through the last of the forest, so great
was her relief. Tomas must have felt the same, as he

stumbled from his mount and rushed to Rosslyn's side to help her put Tallis down so they could carry her the rest of the way.

Perth had always been an odd little town from what Rosslyn had been told by her parents. It was one of the few towns that had no access to the sea. Its main purpose was to provide a buffer against the tremps for the other towns. It was that fact that tended to make the citizens of Perth a tough bunch with thick skins and a limited fear of the tremps.

It explained why all the citizens of Perth had not fled to the cities of Dumbarton or Hadding when the elf raids had first begun. They had always had the least amount of protection from their woodland neighbors; the elf raids would not scare them the same way it would the other towns. Given that Rosslyn couldn't see any real evidence of destruction, she doubted the elves had ever gotten to Perth before they had their first encounter with the demon.

It took far too long to reach the monastery, as Rosslyn swore Tallis had stopped breathing altogether. They climbed the stately marble steps up to where a group of brothers were quietly talking. One look at their panic-stricken faces and the poor state of Tallis sent the brothers into a flurry of activity as they scattered in every direction. All except one portly little brother.

He was a short, potbellied brother with thinning yellow hair and a bulbous nose. He had small brown eyes that got lost in the many crinkles in his face caused by what Rosslyn could only describe as incessant smiling. He was the first and only kind, if uncomely, face Rosslyn had seen since they fled

Kincardine.

"Oh, my, what have we here?"

"Our friend, she's been badly injured while we tried to escape the tremps," Tomas said, panting. "Please, brother, she needs a healer or she will not last much longer."

"Fleeing the elves, you say? Oh, my, how dreadful! You're lucky more damage was not done, young man. Follow me, yes, yes up this way, if you please. Where was your friend hurt? I'm Brother Clyde, by the by, I don't believe I caught yours, or your poor friend's name?" the brother asked as he huffed and puffed deeper into the monastery.

"She was stabbed in the lung. I managed to create a crude way for her to breathe, but it is failing fast. And it's a pleasure, Brother Clyde. I'm Tomas and this is Rosslyn, and our friend is uh, her name is…," Tomas said, struggling with giving Tallis a fake name.

"Tally! Her name is Tally, Brother Clyde. Thank you again for your help. Yes, as Tomas was saying … he, uh, fashioned this little thing for our friend here and it's kept her alive thus far. Truly amazing it is," Rosslyn said quickly, hoping the distraction would not cause the brother to wonder why Tomas suddenly seemed to forget his friend's name.

"You managed that? My, my, you must have had a monastery or university's teaching! I would love to hear more about it, Tomas. Luckily for you, our resident healer is a very skilled man. I shall pray to Wodan that our man is able to save the young lady." He ushered them into a musty room with a tiny slit of a window high up in the stone walls.

"Sholto? Ah, there you are, Sholto," the ever-jolly

Clyde said to a short man in the back of the room. "This young lady, Tally, has been stabbed in the lung by those nasty elves, and she could desperately use your healer's touch."

Rosslyn was more than a little happy when the jovial brother left the room. Given their situation, his cheerful demeanor was especially aggravating.

Moving further into the musty room, she finally was able to get a clear look at Sholto. Much like the Sipsi woman Tavie, Sholto was barely taller than a child. He had perfect posture, though, as if he refused to let his height keep him from standing tall.

He had a shock of all white hair and deep lines around his bottomless brown eyes from perpetually scowling. Sholto did not look like a kind man, but he did not appear to be cruel, either, as he deftly began examining Tallis without as much as a *hello* to Tomas or Rosslyn.

"You did this, boy?" Sholto asked. His voice was deep and gravely, like a plow going through stones.

"Yes, ser. She was … she was stabbed."

"Aye, I can see that. Put her down there. You may have saved her life for a time, lad, but this is a grievous wound. In fact, she should not even be alive right now." Sholto grumbled to himself before waving Tomas and Rosslyn away as he regained his train of thought. "I'll do all I can for her, but you'd be best praying with the fat brother. It will take more than mere skill to save your friend now."

# THE ROAD TO, AND FROM, RECOVERY

## TWENTY-FOUR

SHE COULD NOT rightfully say how long it had taken her to recover. There had been days where she drifted in and out of consciousness, only aware of an insatiable hunger as her body demanded she eat, her mind unsure if she were alive or entering the Garden that Wodan promised.

But when Tallis finally did wake, it was with sheer terror and panic as she believed the demon must have survived within her. It had taken several long days for Rosslyn and Tomas to fully convince her she was, indeed, herself and that the demon had disintegrated into a pile of ash somewhere deep in the Guldar Forest.

Tallis would have liked those days to have been the longest and hardest of her recovery, but they were not. The healer, Sholto, constantly chastised her for not resting and for aggravating her wounds, but she couldn't help it. She was used to running and climbing without a moment's pause, but as her lung healed, there were days when walking from her recovery room to the brothers' dining hall to sneak more food to quell her hunger left her breathless.

Between Sholto's fastidious—if cantankerous care—Tomas's gentle concern, and Rosslyn's unhampered spirit, Tallis was finally able to relax and rest enough for her wound to slowly heal. Sholto seemed even more fascinated with her wounds and recovery than Tomas was, frequently checking on the wounds whenever he could. Despite her annoyance at how long the recovery process seemed, Sholto swore her lung and her other injuries were healing more rapidly than he had ever seen before. Tallis suspected it had to do with her lineage and the sheer amount of food her body demanded, but she would not tell Sholto that. She would have found the healer's attention and praise endearing, if it wasn't also mildly unsettling. And during that time, no one within the town ever truly questioned or suspected as to who they were or where they had come from.

So many families had been scattered during the elf raids that strangers coming to the otherwise harsh little town didn't arouse the suspicion it otherwise would. So no one ever thought that Tallis and her friends were even remotely responsible for the uprisings or the elves mysterious absence from harrying any caravan or town once the fighting abruptly ended.

Regardless, as soon as Sholto declared her fit to return to normal life, Tallis decided it was time to leave Perth behind. Tallis had not so much as even sent a message to Baird or Nessa to tell them of Donovan's passing and they had been without word for too long.

Tomas and Rosslyn had tried to convince her to

send a letter rather than risk going to Selkirk's capital city. There were still knights and noblemen—all spurned on by Raghnall and Henrik, who had not forgiven her for escaping their clutches—who still actively hunted for the woman the elves had first spoken of. But her Uncle Baird and Nessa deserved better than a letter to explain what had befallen Donovan, and Tallis would at least give them that courtesy, even if it meant she'd risk her life and break her heart all over again.

Tallis had not been in the Telchar Forest outside of Perth for more than a few hours when the now familiar tingle of the antediluvian trees began to encroach upon her mind. She knew that the ancient spirit trees were there, and that they wished to speak with her in one fashion or another, but Tallis could not, and *would* not, stop for them now. She had given the forest enough of her time the past few months, it was time for her to put the sorry remains of her family first.

But the trees persisted. No matter how far they walked or how much Tallis babbled nonsense to Tomas and Rosslyn in order to ignore the nagging, pulsating feeling in her mind, the trees persevered and Tallis continued to ignore them and tear through the forestry. So the old trees finally sent three elves to greet Tallis and her friends as they emerged from a thick cluster of trees and overgrown ferns.

The elves were no longer in rags, but no one would ever look at what they were wearing and consider it elegant. They wore simple robes of plain taupe, forest green, and rich chocolate browns. Instead of wearing leaves and vines to keep their shambles of rags in place, this time they wore them as ways to adorn their plain clothing and to accentuate the gentle curves and dips of their bodies. There was a subtle beauty and lightness to the garments that reminded Tallis of spring as it gave way to summer.

More striking than what the elves were wearing however, were their eyes: They were no longer yellow. They had jade green eyes, sky blue eyes, and even a brown so deep it almost appeared black. If Tallis had not seen them for herself, she would have never known that their eyes had ever been the sickly yellow color, not with how pure and bright they were now.

Despite how enchanting and alluring of a picture the elves presented, Tallis would not be caught off guard. In a flash, she had her daggers in her hands and crouched slightly as she readied herself to spring into action. "Give me one good reason not to cut you down right here and now."

The elves exchanged nervous glances with one another, their hands twitching as if they were unsure what they should be doing. Finally, the female of the group stepped forward and spread her hands in front of Tallis. "Armed … we not armed," she whispered hoarsely.

Tallis looked at her, she may not have been armed, but that had not kept the elves from being any less dangerous in the past. But there was something about this trio of elves that made Tallis believe they would not harm her. It might have been how the female's sky blue eyes quivered as if with tears, or the way the two males could not even look her in the eye, but these were not the ferocious beasts she had killed by the dozens just a short time ago.

That did not mean, however, that Tallis would

sheath her daggers. Standing up straight, she continued to glare at the elves. "State your business, I haven't the time to chat with you."

Still fiddling with her long and elegant hands, the female elf said, "Apologize … we want apologize for … war. For fighting. For monster."

Tallis got the impression her speech was halting and hoarse not because of the regret she had for her and her kinds actions, but mostly because the tremps had not spoken in a natural tongue for over three hundred years. Still, it was a start, if nothing else. Unsure what the elves wanted from her, Tallis said, "Just who are you supposed to be that you can offer your apologies on behalf of all the elves?"

The male elf with dark brown eyes in the taupe colored robes answered for the female. "I … we holy men and women. We … hosts. Were to be hosts for the First. The monster. Names … we don't recall. Too long since knew them."

The female elf only nodded emphatically as she fidgeted with the hem of her simple forest green robes. Eventually, she murmured, "Apologies. Accept, please?"

Tallis glanced at them for a moment in silence. She knew they may want to make amends, and that they could not be held completely responsible, but she wasn't sure how she was supposed to forgive them, either.

Instead of accepting their apology outright, she said, "It's not me you should apologize to. But to all those innocent people you have ripped apart, and not just in this last war, either. But over the hundreds of years you harried our towns and stole our children.

Those are the people you should beg mercy of.

"I … understand why you made a point to capture me. It was your master's bidding and not your choice. I get that, I really do. Even if I didn't agree with it, and even though it cost me dearly, I can understand it. But no one else in Selkirk does. They don't know what happened or why. All they know is that you attacked them hissing my name unprovoked. So go to them, go to King Ailbeart and Queen Morgana and give them your apologies and let me go on my way."

The elves exchanged worried glances between themselves and looked as if they were fighting the urge to devolve back into their creaking, clicking language of before. Twirling her long and curly burgundy red hair, the female elf asked shakily, "Tallis help us?"

"What do you mean? Help you?" Rosslyn scoffed before Tallis had a chance to respond.

"Help us … apologize to humans," the female elf responded, desperation making her hoarse voice shrill. "They not listen. We cannot … go to king and beg. Kill … they kill on sight."

Rosslyn opened her mouth to speak, probably to spout how they would deserve no better for what they had done, but Tomas stopped her with a gentle hand on her shoulder. Shaking his head to silence what she was about to say, Rosslyn firmly shut her mouth and folded her arms over her chest and glared at the trio of tremps in front of her.

"You want me to be your ambassador? To be your envoy to the human king and queen, lords and ladies so they will not retaliate for what your kind has done to them? That's what you're asking of me now, correct?" Tallis asked, waving her dagger about as she tried to make sense of what the elves were really saying.

"Yes," replied the second of the male elves.

He was the least nervous of the three. His jade green eyes did not waver when he did manage to look at her, and he held his bald head high, as if he knew it was an action that would have once been befitting of an elf of his station. He also kept his hands clasped behind his back and hidden in his rich chocolate brown robes so he would not fidget as his brethren did. He had an overall stately air about him, one that Tallis might have respected under different circumstances.

Instead, she was silent for a very long time, conflicted about what she should and should not do. The elves were right; the humans would kill them on sight before they could even attempt to make amends.

Considering they had not wanted to attack them, but were forced to by the demon, it would be a shame for them to die while trying to atone for their deeds. But her heart was still so full of bitterness and sadness that part of her wanted the elves to suffer for their actions.

Sighing heavily, Tallis put her daggers away and rubbed her temples.

"Tallis ... will help?" the female asked.

"I ... I don't know. I need time to think. I ... I must finish what I set out to do. Meet me in Kincardine, the town you sacked first, before the end of spring, and I'll have an answer for you. That's the best I can offer you right now."

The elves exchanged more glances, once again appearing as if they were struggling not to click at one another. The male elf with the deep brown eyes was the one to finally speak as he slowly nodded his head. "Kincardine. We ... be there."

And with that, the trio melted back into the forest without a sound. Tallis watched them go with a deep frown on her face as she kicked at the forest debris around her feet.

She did not speak or move as she took to heart the elves' request. She did not even realize they had not resumed their journey until Tomas brushed her hand with his, still unsure if he was allowed to grasp it or not. "Tallis? Are you all right?"

Chewing her lip for a moment, she shrugged. "No, but that doesn't matter for the moment. Let's just keep going for now."

ROSSLYN HAD TRIED to talk to her about it, tried to discern just why it was Tallis was even considering what the elves said. Tallis had no good answer for her. She just knew it would disappoint her mother, Donovan, and Tomas if she did not consider their request.

Her own feelings aside, she wasn't even sure she would not be captured or killed on sight if anyone knew who she was. No one in Selkirk, save Tomas and Rosslyn, knew the truth of what had occurred, and Tallis's unwilling part in it. Even if she was not killed where she stood, she was not sure how she would even convince anyone her story was true and not the result of some kind of madness. It was these thoughts that plagued her mind night and day as they made the trek from the Telchar Forest and into Isildor.

When she finally found her uncle and Nessa, she was mildly disappointed to learn that her father had not decided to join them in Isildor. Jon had, instead, elected to stay behind in Fordoun before one day returning to Kincardine. For, as Baird explained, he did not want to stay away from the place where his wife was buried for very long.

Outside of the initial pleasantries, the meeting went as she feared it would with tears and curses and threats about what would happen if she ever showed her face in Isildor again. Baird eventually became the only thing that was keeping Nessa from going to the city guards and telling them of Tallis's whereabouts, and Tallis knew it was in her best interest to quickly leave.

# TWENTY-FIVE

FOR THE HUNDREDTH time, Tomas asked, "Why Kincardine? Of all the places we could be meeting this envoy of elves, why would you wish to go back there, Tallis?"

Tallis did not have a good answer. She did not know what would be there when she returned, but she somehow knew that whatever she did—or did not— find, it would be the true deciding factor when she next spoke to the tremps.

She shrugged. "I just need to see it again."

Tallis was in the Brethil Forest around Kincardine when she suddenly longed for more time before her meeting with the elven priests and priestess. The forest was much the same as she remembered it, its prevalent and chilly fog obscuring the majestic firs and oaks. The deep silence that welled around its edges, challenging and beckoning would-be travelers and hunters alike to get lost within its shadows.

It had never been a welcoming visage, and she remembered the fear and excitement felt upon first accompanying her mother into that forest and the crippling heartbreak that had resulted from that visit, for it had been the last time she had seen her mother alive.

Tallis knew she should hate the Brethil Forest, should loathe its silence, the damp smell of the decaying needles littering the ground, and the things that once hid just out of sight.

But she did not.

The forest had not been responsible for killing her mother. Despite its almost spooky appearance, the forest had offered her the most freeing and genuine comfort in the wake of her misery. It had calmed her anxiety on more than one occasion and offered the only explanation as to why she had always felt a little wrong in her own skin. It gave her a home when everything else had been taken from her.

Turning to Rosslyn and Tomas, she said, "Wait here, I need to do something."

"Oi! You shouldn't go tramping about by yourself. Haven't you learned anything?" Rosslyn hissed.

"I'll be fine, Roz, really. Just wait here for me."

"Where are you going, though?" Tomas said, snatching her hand before she could turn away.

"I want … I need to visit my mother's gravesite in case I can't ever come back," Tallis replied softly before sneaking away.

Sticking to the shadows, Tallis crept through overgrown brambles and pungent piles of debris on the way to her family's hut. There were more graves in the fields surrounding the town, and each time she used their cold shadows as cover, a bone chilling shiver ran the length of her body. These graves should not be here, and she felt more than just a little responsible for each fresh mound of dirt she skittered around, the freshly carved stone facades leaving Tallis's hands chalky and dry with a regret she could not brush off.

Standing alone and lonely away from the other houses, still stood her childhood home. It had not survived unscathed, but it did appear as if the tremps had left it largely intact. Her father's shed was burnt to the ground, its charred pieces of wood soggy and no longer smelling of smoke, and the garden her mother had always taken care of was no more than a muddy puddle. But all the same, it had survived the worst of the destruction. It was almost as if the elves had known that this was the place Tallis had called home a lifetime ago, and had left it as a sacred reminder of where their creation had been kept safe for nearly two decades.

Her mother's grave stood in the shadow of the house. Her father had kept it well maintained, even after the destruction the elves had wrought. Its mound was undisturbed, a dew-covered bouquet of roses propped against the stone. It smelled wet, its petals wilting under the weight of the water droplets. A drop of water hit the bouquet, scattering the collected dew water like startled birds. That was when Tallis realized she was crying and dashed the tears away.

A jealous love swelled in her, wishing her father had loved her just a fraction as much as he still loved her mother. So much could have been avoided if he had just protected her the way her mother had. He did not even care enough to dig a grave for her once the riots had started and she was nowhere to be found. Instead, her mother's grave remained alone, away from the other townsfolk who had lost their lives to the elves.

She sat in the mud and stared down at the heavy

stone with her mother's name etched into it, losing herself into the only thing that felt like home anymore, a cold but well maintained grave.

Stroking the stone lightly, she whispered, "Hi, Momma, I'm … I'm home."

Tallis sat in the shadows for a long while, wondering what she would say if she had one last chance to say goodbye. Eventually, she grinned mournfully down at the stone, and said, "I've kept your ring safe. I almost lost it once but … well, the most wonderful man found his way into my life and he brought the ring back to me. He, well, he rescued me, Momma. He's saved my life in more ways than I could have ever imagined. Saved me from things I didn't even know I needed rescuing from. I think you would have liked him."

Tallis was about to say more when a movement in the corner of her eye caught her attention. Blending back into the shadows, she crept to the window of her home and watched as her father went about his business.

Her home was just how she remembered, but colder despite the roaring fire at its hearth. There was a new trail of dust in the house showing the path her father shuffled along day in and out without her. He stayed in the kitchen most of the time, few steps went into the bedroom he had once shared with his wife and not a single step had ever gone into her darkened room.

Tallis did not blame him. So much of their lives had been spent in the kitchen, lingering around the big stew pot that her mother dutifully maintained. The heavy scent of beef and barley permeating through the house and sneaking into every crevice to envelope them in a cozy blanket.

The stew pot was empty now, and the only smell that wafted through the cracks in the window was that of a staleness Tallis did not recognize, not unlike spilled ale that had been left to evaporate weeks ago. It did not smell like her home anymore, just a hut she had once slept in.

For a moment, she was elated to see her father and to know he still lived, but her happiness was short-lived as she saw what he was working on. He had been organizing a stack of parchment on the little kitchen table, and as he stepped away, Tallis saw that Jon had been organizing wanted posters with her likeness sketched onto its center.

These were not posters of a concerned father hoping to gain information as to the whereabouts of his missing child. These were posters of a bitter old man who wanted to turn over the girl he had helped raise to feed his own burning feelings of revenge and injustice.

She knew she shouldn't have been surprised to learn just how far her father had turned against her after what had happened in Fordoun, but his revulsion still hit her like a mace to the chest. There was truly nothing left for her in Kincardine. Turning away, Tallis fled back into the Brethil Forest where Tomas and Rosslyn waited for her with open arms.

Tallis had not been back for more than a few moments when the three elves reappeared once again. They looked much the same; they wore the same colors as before, with the only difference being the placement of the vines and leaves wrapped around their lithe bodies.

She watched them approach impassively and noted

that they all still seemed unsure and nervous about how to act around her. The female elf still fidgeted nervously with her hands, her bald companion still tried to stand tall and stately while avoiding eye contact with Tallis, and the third male elf with his tightly-cropped, black, soft curly hair still hung shyly behind the female elf.

Tallis heard Rosslyn take her little black club off her belt, and even Tomas was readying his crossbow, but Tallis was not worried. The elves had had their chance to kill them and they had not, they would not do so now, no matter what Tallis's answer was.

"You ... decided. You have decided?" the bald elf said as his jade green eyes finally settled on Tallis and held her gaze.

"I have." Tallis folded her arms over her chest as she reclined against a skinny birch tree.

"You ... talk, speak to humans then? Tallis ... will help?" the female elf stammered, her raspy voice only slightly better since the first time they spoke.

"Now, I didn't say that. But hold on before you get upset," Tallis added quickly as the elves began shaking in fear and panic at her words.

"I'm not doing this out of malice. It's the contrary, really. Look, you're right, the people of Selkirk are going to have a very hard time listening to reason, and even beginning to comprehend this business with the demon. I've seen it with my own eyes and I barely understand it. But I'm the last person you want to help you.

"As much as I know it's the right thing to do, that you'll need me to speak to the people of this land and to be an ambassador on your behalf, I simply can't. Not right now, anyway. I can't look at your kind and not see the death and destruction you have wrought.

"I can't help but see my mother's lifeless body and my cousin as the demon took hold of him. What you deserve is someone who'll be passionate about your cause, and who'll try to rally the humans to understand your own victimization in this story, and right now … I just can't do that.

"Even if I could put my feelings aside, there's a great deal of resentment aimed at me, for the part people think I played in this uprising as well. They may not know what my role truly was, but they do know that the elves were hissing a young girl's name as they ravaged their homes. Once they find out that I was … that I am that person … they would just as soon kill me as they would you. And that's all before anyone finds out that I myself am a half-elf. That will surely complicate things even further and only cause more people to actively hunt me down.

"It's for those reasons that I don't think I'm the right candidate to be your champion. Yet. Maybe one day, but right now, I would only hurt your cause rather than help it. You can see what I'm saying, right?"

The group was struck silent by her words. She could not be sure if they were pleased, disappointed, agreed, or disagreed with what she had said, but in her soul, she knew she had made the right choice.

Tallis needed time to heal her heart from the damage that had been done by her loss and anger just as much as the knights and other denizens of Selkirk needed time to forget that she had ever been the catalyst of this war at all. She just could not say definitively how long all of that would take.

"What we do then?" the shyer of the two male elves mumbled. "Hunted ... we already hunted. Killed on sight. Hung as ... example. Hiding ... we hide and wait for return?"

"It'll be difficult to broker a peace, but I don't think it's impossible. There are still Sipsi clans that claim to be friends of your people. I would seek them out first. But trust me, once I have ... healed, I'll do my utmost to aid your people and ensure there is a peace between the elves and the humans. It was ... it *is* what my mother and cousin would have wanted, and I will honor that when I can.

"But you must never *ever* call forth another dark spirit ever again, do you understand? Never again must a demon be unleashed on this land over some silly war."

"What Tallis ... what you do?" the female elf said. "Hide ... where you hide?"

"I'm not going to hide. I'm going to leave Selkirk for a time. At least until I can look back on my memories and not die a little on the inside with each thought."

The silence did not last long, as the bald elf stepped forward and said, "But ... you a child of the forest. Belong ... you belong here."

Tallis shrugged. "I was raised a human. I don't have the same affinity to the forest as you do. Besides, I'll return one day, and then I can discover what being a child of the forest even means. There will be plenty of time for that." The elves exchanged glances and appeared as if they would argue more in order to try and convince Tallis to stay.

Seeing the look of desperation in their eyes, Tallis

held up her hands. "A great deal has been asked of me already by your kind and the ancient trees. I ask you to let me heal my soul for a time and to ensure my own safety by leaving Selkirk. Like I said, this is my home, and despite everything, I don't exactly want to leave, but ... it's the right thing to do. At least for now."

"Wait for ... we wait for return, Tallis," the female elf whispered eventually. "May the Vanir ... guide and bring you home." And with that, the three elves silently trotted off deep into the Brethil Forest, leaving the friends alone before Tallis could ask what a Vanir was.

She could feel the silence thicken around her like molasses as Rosslyn and Tomas stared wide-eyed at the side of her head. She had not told them of her plans to leave Selkirk now that trade with Theda and Andor had been restored.

"You're ... you're leaving us?" Tomas stammered, his heart rattling in his voice as he wrestled with the idea of Tallis leaving his life.

She turned and smiled a little sadly at her friends. "I don't want to leave you, but I felt it was too much to ask you to come with me. I did that once before and look where it got us. I couldn't ask that of you again. Not when I'm leaving everything we have ever known behind."

"I'm not leaving you, Tallis. My home, it's ... well, I've never really had much of a home at the monastery. Since leaving ... I can't say I have a home to return to there. My home is ... it's wherever you are." Tomas blushed as he tucked his chin into his shoulder in a bashful manner.

Tallis could not say how glad that made her to hear his words. She knew she must have been grinning like a fool, as all she could manage was an enthusiastic nod at Tomas before turning her attention back to Rosslyn.

Rosslyn was the most conflicted with Tallis's declaration. She clearly wanted to go with Tallis, but there was also something holding her back.

"I haven't been able to find my family yet, Tally. I can't just up and leave them before I find out if they are all right. If they managed to get Loren through all of this. I just … I can't do that to them if they're alive. I have to let them know I'm all right."

Tallis knew it was a possibility that one or both of them would not come with her across the sea. But somehow, she just never expected it to be Rosslyn who would elect to stay behind when there was adventure to be had.

"I uh … I understand, Roz. I do, really. But, well, are you sure about this? Are you sure you want to stay behind?"

"Wodan's bollocks, why do you want to leave so badly?" Rosslyn snapped, "You could just as easily stay here, you know. Go back to Perth and hide out there. No one would ever know who you really are. Why are *you* so desperate to leave Selkirk?"

"You really think I am just dying to get away from here? Roz, this is my *home*. This is all I've ever known. This is where all my memories of growing up with Donovan are, this is where my mother is buried. This is my life here.

"I'm not leaving because it's easy or because I'm just desperate to wash my hands of this place. I'm leaving because if I stay … if I stay I will be hunted down like a dog at best. Killed at worst, and then all this will just start all over again. There will be more war, and it'll only be a matter of time before another demon is found. I'm leaving so there can be peace one day, not because I want to go."

Rosslyn's eyes had begun to fill with tears as Tallis spoke, and she started kicking at the ground at regular intervals and clenching her jaw in silence. Eventually she gave a ragged breath and said with a great sob, "I have to find my family. Oh, Tally ... I'm going to miss you!"

Tallis was nearly knocked to the ground with the force of Rosslyn's hug. Tallis returned her embrace just as fiercely as they cried on each other's shoulders.

Pulling her away, Tallis said, "Follow us to the docks, find the ship we're on, and every other week or so write to me. I'll come back and check the messages and respond every time, I promise. That way you can tell me the very instant it's safe for me to return. Deal?"

Wiping away the tears rolling down her cheeks, Rosslyn nodded and gave Tallis one last bone-crushing hug. Tallis had never been good at farewells and she never expected them to be easy, but there was something about leaving Rosslyn behind that crushed her soul more than just a little.

TALLIS DID NOT wish to waste any more time lingering in a place that held such bittersweet memories for her. Memories aside, Tallis was not safe in Kincardine, and certainly not with her own father actively aiding the likes of Raghnall and Henrik in hunting her down. So they gathered all the supplies and money they could and made their way to the beach under the cover of darkness.

It was on the beach just out of sight of the large docking area where Rosslyn bid her final farewell to Tallis. It was an emotional affair and they both promised once again to write and keep the other informed, to stay safe, and to tell each other of any juicy gossip that might arise while they were apart. But most of all, they promised they would, indeed, see each other once again, someday soon.

Once Rosslyn had disappeared back into the town, Tomas and Tallis waited patiently for the sleepy bustle of the trade galley workers to begin their morning duties. In the silence, Tomas asked, "Are you going to be all right? I mean, this is your home, and I know … I know it isn't easy, but is there anything I can do to make things better?"

Tallis looked at him and carefully considered his words. She would not have thought of herself as a lucky person, but she was not sure how she had been so blessed that a man like Tomas would be so devoted to her. Giving him a lopsided smile, she said, "You make me better with each passing day, Tomas. I thought I had lost everything, but I didn't because I still have you. You are … you're everything to me now. So I think that yes, with you by my side, that I can be all right."

Tomas didn't answer her; instead, he wrapped one arm around her waist, cupped the back of her head with his free hand, and kissed her deeply. His embrace chased away the majority of her fear and sadness and replaced it with a gentle warmth that bloomed all over her body.

"So, what do we do when we get to Theda?"

Tallis shrugged in the darkness. "Whatever we want. No one knows us there. We can do whatever we want and be whoever we want. Going to Theda, we'll have a chance to be the people we've always wanted to be."

Tomas was silent for a moment as he considered her words. Eventually, he whispered in her ear, making her skin tickle with the thrill of his closeness, "No matter what happens or where we go, remember one thing: that you are amazing *as* Tallis. Don't change. Don't be anyone else but who you are right now."

She did not respond. Instead, she smiled and gave his hand a gentle squeeze before turning her attention to the sunrise. Vaguely, she wondered if the sunrises in Theda would be the same brilliant pink, soft yellow, and coral orange that Selkirk enjoyed. And with Tomas at her side, and Rosslyn, Donovan, and her mother in her heart, she was ready for the next chapter in her life to begin.

Enjoy this sample from the first chapter of:
"The Monster of Selkirk, Book III: The Machines of Theda"

Coming this Winter/2017 from Devil Dog Press

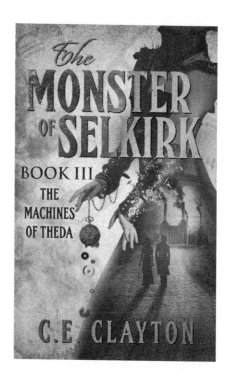

# *ADRIFT ON SEA AND LAND*

## *ONE*

"WE HAVEN'T GOTTEN one of them big crates in a long time, Felix," the young man said, shielding his eyes with his good hand. "What you reckon happened to make them stop?"

It was a hot day, like most days in Theda, with the sun beating relentlessly down upon the port. Otho wondered if Theda, and the port city of Aelius, in particular, would have been a cooler place without the factories and the machinery that always ran hot no matter what you did to try and shield them from the sun. Otho idly glanced down at his mechanical hand at the thought, but decided it was better to have two functioning appendages rather than one; as usual, he would just have to suffer through the heat.

"Now what crates would those be, Otho?" Felix said, handing the ledger he had been reading over to one of the urchins that always hung around the ship. "If you haven't noticed, we ship a lot of cargo for the captain."

Otho fidgeted uncertainly as he glanced over the

various crates littering the dock. The captain shipped a lot of cargo all over Theda, with some crates more innocuous than others, but with all the crates having purposively vague shipping manifests. But the "big crates" never had shipping manifests, not even fabricated ones. Otho had the feeling there was more than just something illicit in those crates, but he never knew what. Weeks, months even, would go by without one of the big crates, and then they would get one without any warning. But it had been over a year since they had moved that kind of cargo.

After a moment longer of shuffling and scratching at his poorly-shaved stubble with his one remaining real hand, he mumbled, "You know ... them crates that came from the monasteries and went to the factories. The ones the captain got paid extra for."

Otho could see Felix's broad shoulders slightly stiffen, but other than that, the big, tattooed boatswain remained silent. Just when Otho believed the comment would be ignored, Felix answered, "You aren't supposed to know about those, Otho. Who's been telling stories about the boss's shipping practices? Used to be only me and the first mate, Wodan guard his rotten soul, knew about *those* crates." Felix didn't even raise his voice, but he made Otho cower against the ship's moorings all the same.

Felix had known the captain almost as long as he had been a captain, and certainly longer than those in Aelius had known him by his current reputation. Only Felix and Emilio, the captain's late first mate, knew how the captain had gotten his reputation. Rumor had it, that after Emilio's suspicious death, the captain had terminated certain aspects of his operation out of reverence for the dead. Otho could understand and respect this, but he missed the coin that the big crates managed to trickle down to him and the other lowly workers.

The captain had so many people in his pocket, from the *Distretto,* some of the masters at the factories, a few of the brothers at the monastery, and he had even been the Seneschal's lover for a brief time before the affair ended, and badly at that. Little concerned the captain, but something serious must have happened to convince a fearless and otherwise ruthless man to change his ways.

"I meant no offense, it's just … them big crates were lucrative, no?" Otho said, avoiding Felix's surly gaze. "I thought what was in them crates wasn't something someone would ever miss. All I meant was why aren't we the ones accommodating the masters in the factories?"

"You think you know the lay of the land, do you now, Otho?" Felix asked slowly. "Think you know what business practices the captain should and shouldn't be undertaking, hmm? Thinking like that is what got Emilio killed. And his death was no accident, either."

"Are you saying the captain killed the first mate?"

Felix balked. "What? No, you berk! The captain's reputation got too big too fast, if you catch my meaning. Made a name for himself shipping the stuff more reputable men wouldn't touch. Emilio had talked him into moving beyond the normal contraband, and into more of the live cargo, if you will. Certain friends of ours in Andor didn't take kindly to it. Reminded them too much of their own trafficking, and they put a stop to it real quick. Namely with a knife in Emilio's thick skull. You remember that next time you think you know what's best.

"Now get back to work inspecting those ships from Selkirk. Captain's looking for *specific* cargo. I won't be subject to his temper if we miss something, understood?"

Otho nodded and Felix turned away, grumbling something about Emilio's death at the hand of Andor pirates who had wanted to send their boss a message. Otho was not sure if all of what Felix said was true; the older man had been known to exaggerate the tales surrounding their employer to keep the younger lads in line from time to time. Regardless of the story's legitimacy, it was enough to end the discussion.

Otho shrugged and went back to inspecting the shipping manifests and cargo ledgers from the ships coming in from Selkirk. It was all rather dull work, but given that Otho's mechanical hand tended to spasm and spark when the sea breeze wafted over the hull of the captain's ship, he was not suited for much else.

He glanced down at his mechanical hand again, more a claw really, as he could not afford the devices with actual fingers. Otho sighed involuntarily, recalling the unsanctioned duel that had cost him the hand in the first place.

He tried to convince himself that he had been lucky; if he had been dueling someone of importance, he would have lost more than just the hand. As it was, his drunken duel with one of the captain's men had impressed him enough to offer Otho a job, even as he lay whimpering on the cobblestone street clutching the bloody stump at the end of his arm.

Otho wanted to believe that losing his hand had opened up more opportunities for him; he was not bright, nor talented enough to go far in a place that valued brilliance and cleverness above all else. At least with the captain he could afford a mechanical appendage; he would not have been so lucky had he stuck to tending the vineyards and olive orchards between Aelius and the city of Cato.

The hand had cost Otho everything he had, plus some. He was paying his debts as best he could, but he could not help thinking that if the captain had not stopped taking the big crates from the monasteries to the factories, that he would be debt free by now. Though, when he thought about it, he hadn't seen any other ships trafficking that kind of cargo lately, either.

He had seen the Dag'ears go to the factories, however.

He wondered if the captain's cargo changes were because of Emilio's death, or if the elves had found a way to cut the captain out of the unspoken agreement between the monasteries and factories on where to take some of the more colorful criminals apprehended around Theda.

"Otho!" Felix barked. "Stop daydreaming! We have a ship from Selkirk due to dock today and we best be ready for it, understood?"

Otho would have dropped his shipping manifests in surprise if he had not been holding it in his mechanical hand. The grip on the artificial hand was impeccable, even if the device did disagree with too much of the sea breeze.

Otho was not entirely sure why the captain cared about what came in from Selkirk. The country sounded abysmal and too much behind modern times to be of any great importance. The rumors coming out of the country were more interesting than any of its cargo, which consisted mainly of timid people, ale, and different kinds of game meat.

Rumor had it that a woman had incited a Dag'ear rebellion, or ended one, or was some sort of demon that had enslaved the Dag'ears to begin with; the stories were never clear on that point. But the one thing they did all have in common was that the person responsible was definitely female, and she was wanted by the king and queen of Selkirk for an absurdly long list of offenses.

If the captain wanted to find a woman like that, Otho could not even begin to imagine why; she sounded like a terror, no matter which way you looked at it. As far as he was concerned, a barbarian woman like that did not belong in a sophisticated place like Theda. But then again, Otho was not paid to think, something Felix reminded him of quite frequently with thumps on the back of the head.

"Yes, Felix … sorry, Felix. Won't happen again," Otho said sheepishly as he went back to scanning the original manifest from Captain Pol and his soon to be arriving ship from Selkirk.

C. E. Clayton was born and raised in Southern California where she worked in the advertising industry for several years on accounts that ranged from fast food, to cars, and video games (her personal favorite). This was before she packed up her life, husband, two displeased cats, and one very confused dog and moved to New Orleans. Now, she is a full time writer, her cats are no longer as displeased, and her dog no longer confused. More about C.E. Clayton, including her blog, book reviews, and poetry, can be found on her website: http://ceclayton.weebly.com/ and https://www.bookbub.com/authors/c-e-clayton

Also by C.E. Clayton

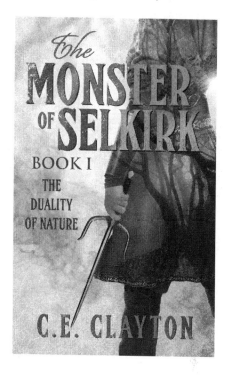

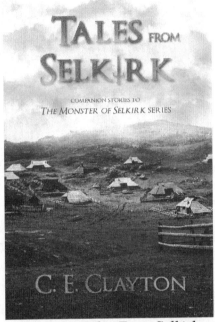

Get the *Tales From Selkirk*:

Companion Stories for The Monster Of

Selkirk free by signing up for the newsletter

now at :

http://www.ceclayton.com/newsletter.html

**Book III Coming Soon!!**

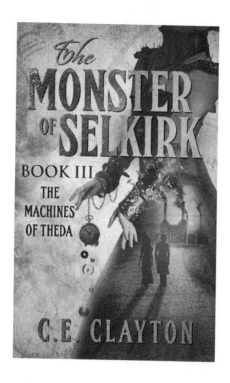

C.E. Clayton

Also From Devil Dog Press

www.devildogpress.com

*Zombie Fallout* By Mark Tufo

The Monster of Selkirk II: The Heart Of The Forest

*Prey by* Tim Majka

C.E. Clayton

*All That Remain* By Travis Tufo

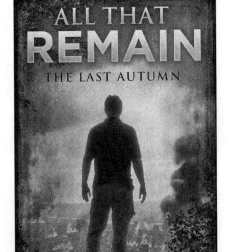

The Monster of Selkirk II: The Heart Of The Forest

*Humanity's Hope* By Greg P. Ferrell

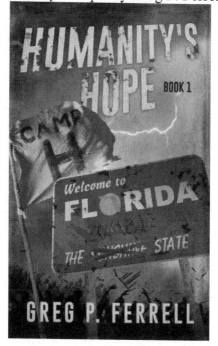

C.E. Clayton

*From The Ash* By Dave Heron

*A Tale Of Two Reapers* By Jack Wallen

Made in the USA
Lexington, KY
16 January 2019